DAWN ANDERSON

Stay Down

This novel is entirely a work of fiction. The names, characters and incidents portrayed in it are the work of the author's imagination. Any resemblance to actual persons, living or dead, events or localities is entirely coincidental.

Calen Martin- Model

K. O'Kelly- Cover Designer

Jenny Steve-James- Personal Assistant/Cover Designer

First edition

Editing by Deborah Peach

This book was professionally typeset on Reedsy. Find out more at reedsy.com

Contents

Prologue

I leaned forward against the kitchen sink, tears welling up in my eyes, blurring the sight of the red truck backing out of the driveway. The hot dishwater stung the fresh cigarette burns on my wrists that Alex caused because I didn't cook his eggs long enough. Wiping my damp hands along the bottoms of my eyes to try to catch any stray tears.

I can't continue to live like this. How much more can I handle? He is out to kill me; I swear it. I have to leave. I had to get out of here. But where will I go? My family had cut ties with me long ago.

I pulled the black plug out of the kitchen sink and barged out of the kitchen. I was determined to get as far away from here as my feet would allow me. Alex believed that a woman shouldn't drive or own a car. Women were meant to be at home, tending to their man's every need.

Grabbing my jacket and purse while I made my way out the front door, my steps were fast-paced. I wanted to get as far as I could in the shortest amount of time. I didn't have cash on me for cab or bus fare, so wherever my feet could take me was where I could go.

I walked further and further through the spread-out, small town. The further I walked, the more my legs and feet began to feel numb. I came upon a small shopping plaza that consisted of three storefronts, one of which was a tattoo parlor.

A tattoo parlor? Hmm, I've always wanted a tattoo. Maybe it could cover up some of the horrendous scarring that Alex has caused.

I pulled open the glass door, hearing the bells chime that were hanging on the door.

"Welcome to Dead Soul Tattoo. How may I help you?"

My eyes landed on this tanned, blonde woman sporting a black tank top that flaunted her set of large breasts. It was no wonder why she was hired. I rubbed my neck, not sure what to say or why I even stepped into this shop. "I would like to browse some samples, please."

"Let me know when you are ready. We have a few openings left." She winked before walking away.

I simply nodded as I took a binder of art samples to the black leather couch. Flipping through the plastic sheets that held the artwork, I realized these artists were really good. Maybe I should get a butterfly? They are beautiful and free with nothing holding them down. I began to think about how it would look, covering the scars. Could they work around it?

"Butterflies? I should have guessed," a male voice said. My head whipped up to see a guy who instantly reminded me of Silent Bob from the movies but with much shorter hair and a more alternative style in wardrobe. "Butterflies are big hits among women."

"Oh." I said, looking back down at the designs, now second-guessing my decision.

"My chair just opened up if you are ready."

I nodded and followed him to the back of the shop. I twirled around, soaking in the atmosphere. I did not think I would ever get a tattoo, but here I am, about to sit and allow a total stranger to permanently mark me. I guess it's no different than Alex marking me up, but at least I have control of the outcome this time. I slid into the black dentist-looking chair and rotated my forearm to where I would want the butterfly design done.

"I'm Kevin. You are?"

"Melanie."

"Beautiful name. What happened here?"

"Uh-" I began to sweat in panic and swallowed a ball of nerves. "History. Could you cover it with the butterflies?"

"I can try. I would have to add more color."

"How much would all of this be?" I asked nervously. I don't even know why I was asking. I had no money with me.

"The extra color should only be an additional $20 for the ink alone. All together, $120."

I certainly didn't have that kind of money on me. I began to think of how to pay for that.

"Something tells me you don't have that kind of money." I shook my head no in response to his statement, "Well...what do you say we make a deal?"

"A deal?" I asked, confusion evident in my voice.

"I need extra help around here, and I'm having a hard time finding the right employees. You want to work for me in exchange for this tattoo?" He asked. I looked from him to my forearm and then back to him.

"I will do whatever it takes." I instantly agreed to the deal he offered me. I wanted all these marks gone, to forget what Alex had done to me. The needle gun pressed to my skin. At first, it was a bit painful, but then I became numb to the sensation. Kevin and I chatted the whole session. Even though I had just met him, he seemed like the brother I never had. Wiping over the design with a paper towel, he applied a layer of Vaseline, followed by a protective covering.

"Turned out perfect." Kevin smiled as he pushed himself to roll backward.

"It looks amazing, thank you, Kevin."

"You can thank me by starting with that bathroom over there. I don't think anyone has given that toilet a good wash in months."

I could have done this at home, but at least I didn't have the dread of knowing Alex would be walking in at any moment. I wiped the sweat off my brow and pulled the cleaning gloves off my hands. I noticed how dark it was outside, gasping that I was here way later than I had intended.

"What's wrong, newbie?" Kevin asked.

"I'm late. Can you give me a ride?"

"Can you wait a little while longer? I'm still with a client."

I nodded. I couldn't give him any inkling as to why I was panicky. I feared what Alex would do to me when I finally walked into the house tonight. Why was I going back? Wasn't I here because I wanted to get away from him? Where was I to go after the shop closed besides back to Alex? I had no choice but to go back. I sat on the leather couch, staring out the window, trying not to cry from fear of what was waiting for me at home.

"There's no crying in my parlor."

"I'm not crying." I sniffed up some tears and got to my feet.

"Are you ready?"

"Yeah, but are you okay? You do know that we are open again tomorrow."

"I know. I won't be late," I said as hopeful as I could. That is, if Alex doesn't kill me tonight.

Kevin drove the distance to my house as I gave him directions, and I forced him to stop a block from my house. I practically tucked and rolled out of the vehicle, not wanting to risk Alex seeing who I was with. Alex was more jealous than anything. My body felt numb for a whole different reason as I pushed the door to his Volkswagen shut. I walked down the sidewalk, which was a darker shade of gray due to nightfall. The soft rumble of the engine of Kevin's car followed me, making me even more on edge. Kevin was a gentleman, so he was probably trying to make sure I got inside my house safely. He was probably confused about why I got out so far from my house. I stood on my front porch, completely frozen, not wanting to go inside. I looked over my shoulder, seeing the Volkswagen parked in the middle of the street, watching me. I swallowed the ball of dread in my throat before pushing the door open and stepping inside.

When I pushed the door shut, I was swung around and thrust hard into the wall behind me. I felt something sharp and cold pressed against my neck, and I tried so hard to breathe slowly and evenly so the blade wouldn't make any marks on my neck.

"Who was that? Your new boyfriend? Where were you? Fucking him? Cooking him dinner? My laundry wasn't done, and I had no clean dishes when I got home. Where the fuck is my dinner?" Alex growled. I couldn't respond, fearing that the knife would slice me open any minute. "You better sleep with one eye open tonight because you do this again, and you won't live another day."

I was sweating, tears leaking out of the corners of my eyes. He backed away, his eyes still dark with fury, glaring at me. "Go make me dinner, bitch."

I scurried off to the kitchen to find something quick to make so he wouldn't have to wait long to eat. The whole time I was cooking, my body was trembling from nerves and being startled.

I filled the plates with chicken breasts covered in a creamy sauce and asparagus on the side. I tip-toed out to the living room, where Alex was drinking his bourbon and having another smoke.

"Dinner is ready," I whispered. He followed me into the dining room and sat across from me at the circular wooden table. I slid into the wooden chair across from him, still on edge from having the knife pressed to my throat.

"Where were you?" He coldly said.

"I, uh, had some errands to run and thought it wouldn't take that long." I lied, poking at the chicken. I couldn't eat due to my body still trembling.

"Who was the dude? He had to be someone if he gave you a ride." He kept glaring up at me.

What lie could I use to explain Kevin?

"What's that?!"

His chair made a screeching sound as it scraped against the floor when he pushed himself back from the table. "What's what?" he repeated.

Play dumb, that's the only option.

Alex walked around the table, grabbed the arm with the fresh ink, and turned it to face him. "This! You got a tattoo?!"

I swallowed, tears filling my eyes out of fear of what would

6

come next. His grip tightened, and I knew there would be bruising in the shape of his hand tomorrow. In a sudden motion, his hands snapped my arm back, and I heard pops, along with cracks, coming from my arm. I screamed in agony when the pain finally radiated from my arm.

****

Tonight was the second time that Kevin had finished late with a client, which in turn caused him to drop me off later than I needed to be home. Fortunately, Alex was so piss-ass drunk when I arrived home the other night that it was a breeze to sneak in. The only thing I had on my side tonight was I didn't see his red truck anywhere. Fortunately, Kevin had already sped off back to the shop to finish closing up for the night.

I did a quick scan of the street and my surroundings before I went up the grass patch that was in complete shadow from the weeping willow tree. I stepped onto the paved driveway, which caused our sensor lights to click on. I hugged the garage doors, trying to be stealthy and not be seen from our front door or window.

An engine revving caught my attention. I turned my head toward the sound to see Alex's truck. Panic caused my body to freeze in place. Alex had caught me in the act. I watched him shift his red Ford Ram truck from park to drive. The truck sped forward, but I was still frozen in place from panic. My mind was screaming to move, but my feet didn't get the memo to move out of the way.

The hot metal of the grill slammed me against the white garage door behind me, pinning me in place, and I was forced to bend over the running vehicle. The hood was hot to the touch. Alex kept the engine running as he climbed out, leaving the door open.

"Look what the cat dragged in. Where were you? Don't answer that." he spoke, getting closer as he leaned over the hood, staring at me. "You think you are hot stuff now, hanging with those freaks? Think that I wouldn't find out? Guess what? I did. I know you snuck in late last night and have been sneaking around for a while now. I'm not stupid. Remember, you are mine. You would be nothing without me. You are supposed to be home, taking care of my every need, not out living some crazy dream. I'm going to the store to grab some beer. Dinner better be on the table by the time I get back, bitch." He snarled his orders and spat onto the cement driveway beside him.

The engine purred below me, still hot from running for a lengthy time. He reversed out of the driveway, turning the vehicle to head toward his go-to liquor store that was across town. I dropped to the pavement below me now that I didn't have the truck holding me up. I landed hard against the pavement, curling into a fetal position, pain radiating throughout my body. My arms wrapped around my midsection, which was still warm to the touch from Alex's truck. Tears began rolling from my eyes. I didn't know when he would be back. Before he returned, I needed to get out of there, so I scrambled to find my cell phone. I was trying to catch my breath when I noticed blood pooling on the cement below me. I dialed the number to the tattoo parlor, begging Kevin to pick it up.

"Dead Soul Tattoo, Kevin speaking."

"Kevin…" A mere whisper escaped me.

"Melanie, is that you? What happened?"

8

"Truck...pinned to the garage...help me." That was all I said before everything faded to black.

My eyes fluttered open to a blue room with bright lighting. I looked around, seeing a curtain that divided the room, and a television hanging on the opposite wall was playing *The Price Is Right*. The other patient must have turned it to this channel because I would never watch daytime game shows.

How'd I get here? I asked myself, trying to remember anything. The last thing I remembered was calling Kevin. Kevin! I began to panic as I started to piece together what had occurred before I blacked out. I began to heave, clenching my fists against the white sheet on the bed below me. Alex. Does Alex know I'm here?

"Melanie, you're fine..." Kevin's voice mumbled out. I saw Kevin's body slouching in a dark blue and brown chair to my right. Kevin's hair was slicked back from the night before, wearing an all-black business casual outfit.

"Does he know?" I asked, hoping he knew who I was referring to.

"Probably. I called 9-1-1 the moment I hung up with you, and the ambulance was there before me. I came straight here after I gave the police a report. They want to speak to you." He moved to a sitting position, rubbing his hands over his face.

"You look like you haven't slept a wink."

"I haven't. I couldn't sleep in this uncomfortable chair or make the drive home. You're stuck here until your burns and bones heal." His voice was weary as he ran his hand over his jet-black hair. "I should call the police station so they can finish processing the paperwork."

Kevin stood up and headed out of the room, and I flopped

back against the firm mattress of the hospital bed. I can't believe he got the police involved, but what else was I to expect? Kevin stepped around the curtain, clicking at his phone. Kevin plopped back down in the same seat and stared at me.

"Will he ever find me?"

"While in the hospital, no. Afterwards, maybe. The nurses and doctors have the room on lockdown. Your roommate is a ninety-year-old veteran with no visitors that come in and out. The only people allowed in are me, Jack, and Anita."

I met his son, Jack, and his wife, Anita, once when they had come to the shop to have dinner with Kevin. His little family was the sweetest and the kindest I have ever met.

"Where am I going to go after this?" I asked. "I have no money, no friends, nor a place to stay." Why was I more worried about that than the condition I was in? Probably because hospital stays have become a routine for me, it was second nature to be the patient.

"Home with me. We have a guest room that Anita can fix up for you. I also need a receptionist, and who else will be a better fit than you?"

"Wouldn't Alex think to look for me there?"

"Well, there will be a restraining order against him after you speak with the officers. If he comes within so many yards or feet of you, then he'll be thrown in jail," Kevin explained as I lay my head back against the pillow, trying to soak this all in.

Did I have any other choice? I could live on the streets for him to find me and kill me, or he could even show up at the tattoo parlor with his handgun. I will eventually die at his hands. If I take Kevin's offer, I get to live my remaining days with a roof over my head, food on the table, and money coming in. Or say no and live on the streets with this hideous gown as the only clothes on my back.

"I'm heading home. I'll send Anita over with Jack to join you for dinner. I've got to open the shop."

"Thank you, Kevin. I owe you."

"You don't owe me anything. I'm happy you called me." he said, patting the cast on my leg. I hadn't even noticed Alex had broken it. "Catch you tomorrow."

I leaned against my pillow to look at the game show that was still playing. "I get to live another day."

Chapter One:

I sat on the bar stool with my elbow resting on the glass case that stored all the aftercare for tattoos. Kevin claims he installed this unit to hold all the body jewelry when we had a body piercer. I'm not sure how long ago that was, but it must have been way before I started here.

My face was pressed against my fist, staring at my latest creation in my sketchbook. I wish that I had brought my colored pencils to finish this, but I just stared at it, trying to think if I needed to add more. I began to correct any lines or flaws I noticed.

I heard the bell on the door chime, as it was the only loud noise I could hear over the subtle buzzing of the tattoo guns in the back room.

"Welcome to Dead Soul Tattoo." I raised my eyes to see who had entered our parlor. Holy shit, this guy was sex on legs. The man was wearing a blue, long-sleeved shirt and black slacks. Tattoos covered the top of his hands, his knuckles, and the sides of his neck. Some even peeked out from under his sleeves. Despite the sun starting to go down, he still had his shades on and a burgundy beanie that showed little wisps of his brown hair. My heart skipped a beat, and my mouth salivated a little.

"How may I help you, sir?" I closed my sketchbook and pushed it aside as I stood up. I stepped up to the register to be closer to the customer that had caught my eye.

"Yeah, hi. I was hoping to get some new work done. Is Kevin in?" the man asked as I nodded.

"He is currently with a customer and should almost be done. What type of work are you looking at getting done? Did he know you were coming in?" I asked curiously. He walked closer while rolling up the sleeve on his left arm, exposing a couple of tattoos. I noticed a word across his knuckles and presumed there was another word on the other hand.

"I wanted to get a set of brass knuckles inked here. I'll add more later, but I want to get that done for now. I've never seen you here before. Are you new?"

"I started working here a few months back, so you must not come in often, sir." I blushed.

"Well, I haven't been here in a while. Since we haven't officially met, I'm Corey, and you are?" he asked as he leaned against the counter across from me.

"I'm Melanie. Are you a friend of Kevin's?" I asked, eyeing him as I rested a hand on the counter's edge.

"I used to work here a few years back."

"Why'd you leave? It looks like you certainly love the tattoo world." I nodded toward his tatted-up arm.

"Other things came up. Bigger and better things, that is."

I nodded, wishing I had bigger and better things coming my way. I was happy with where I was right now because it was better than the situation I had been in.

"What about yourself? You got any tattoos?" Corey asked as I smirked and began to roll up my sleeve, showing the butterfly tattoo on my forearm. Corey leaned forward onto his forearms and rested against the glass case.

"Just that?"

"No, I've got a few others," I answered as he kept glancing at me. His hand inched toward mine, where I felt his fingers outline the blue butterfly. It felt like electricity zapped between us when our skin touched, his fingers leaving a trail of heat.

"Why did you choose a butterfly?"

"I should be asking you the same thing. Why brass knuckles? Or the words 'stay...'" I began to ask as I tried to read the word on his other hand but couldn't.

"Down," he replied with a smile.

"Down? Why any tattoos?" I asked with a smirk and a shrug.

"Because we want to, and it's our body," Corey said with a half-smile. "How did you get a job here? You look so innocent."

"This isn't a sex shop, Mr. Corey. It's a tattoo parlor."

"Okay, true, but you don't look like someone who would be into the whole tattoo and piercing scene."

"I've seen darker shit, so this hasn't begun to show my dark side," I said as I heard him let out a laugh. "What's so funny? You don't know me."

"Nothing, nothing at all. You must be very nice if Kevin trusted you enough to hire you. There's something good about you."

"Obviously. I think I do my job well," I said confidently.

"I wouldn't know," Corey said with a smile.

"I thought I recognized that voice." Kevin walked out from

the back area.

"Kevin, it's been too long. Didn't know you were hiring," Corey said as he walked toward Kevin, meeting him halfway.

"Yeah, the last girl was stealing from me, and Melanie was just there. She was a trusted client, and I figured I might as well hire her. She was here just as much as you were," Kevin added with a chuckle.

Corey glanced back at me with a smile, then turned back to Kevin.

"Well, she seems like she will do way better than that blonde bimbo you had before," Corey said.

I took it as a compliment, but I had no choice but to do better. Messing up wasn't an option.

Kevin's previous customer approached me to pay for their piece while Corey and Kevin talked, allowing me to cash him out. I sat at Kevin's desk, making it easier to continue sketching in my book. Tonight was slower than usual, but it was a weekday. That's when we got little to no business.

My mind was still processing how Kevin knew Corey. Corey was quite good-looking. He had that rough-cut image about him with the tattoos. He was clean-shaven, and his sense of style was alternative-meets-business. I was instantly visually attracted to him, but it seemed too soon to get involved with another man. I kept telling myself that not every man was like Alex. Corey must have been decent if he was friends with Kevin, much like Corey stated about me working here.

I don't know how they knew each other, but Corey had been a customer here before. Corey will always be a customer first, a good-looking customer, but a customer nonetheless. I worked on my sketch without paying attention to anything around me since I had yet to hear any new customers walk through the front door. I heard someone clear their throat, startling me.

"What are you drawing?" Corey asked as I looked up at him. I put my pencil down before I stood up.

"Something stupid. I just like doodling things." I shrugged before I walked around the desk. I met Corey at the cash register.

"So, you provide Kevin with the artwork?"

"No, Kevin does his artwork," I stated. I began to ring up the cost of what Kevin had written on Corey's paperwork.

"Is he bashing my artwork again?" Kevin asked, emerging from the back after cleaning his station.

"What else am I able to bash?" Corey asked with a chuckle.

"If you didn't like my art that much, the majority of those tattoos wouldn't be on your body." Kevin defended his work as I smiled.

"Ooohhh! You got me," Corey said sarcastically.

"You never explained 'stay down,'" I said as I pushed buttons on the register.

"He explained it to me, but that is a story for another time," Kevin said.

"I can answer for myself," Corey said as Kevin smiled.

"I know you can, but I like answering for you," Kevin said. I watched the two interact as Corey handed over the money. I finished ringing him out as Kevin and Corey chatted. I stood listening, hoping to learn more about their relationship and Corey himself.

Corey gave Kevin a one-handed bro hug, saying goodbye before he turned to me with a bright smile. He extended his hand towards me. I rested my hand in his, and he brought the back of my hand to his lips. He glanced up at me as his lips pressed to the back of my hand, and he gave me a subtle wink. Corey broke the kiss from my hand before he began to walk backward. Our eyes stayed locked until he got to the exit. He gave me one last smile before he turned around to push the door open.

"How do you know Corey?" I looked over at Kevin.

"He is one of my best friends from college. He learned how to pierce to help my business."

"But we don't do piercings."

"Not anymore. He was, and will always be, the only piercer I will have in this parlor," Kevin said as I sighed. "You like him, don't you?"

"No," I said in the firmest voice I could manage, but I knew it didn't come across that way. "Alright, he's attractive, but I think it's too soon."

"Too soon? It's been at least six months, Melanie."

"Yes, but that fuckface still shows up looking for me. How many times have we had to call the police on my ex?"

"We called the cops once, and that was because Juan took the liberty of using the bat to turn Alex into a pinata," Kevin said.

Tears welled in my eyes as the memory played in my mind. *I had turned to look at the front door when Juan ran in with the bat in his hand. It had been covered in blood, and Juan was panicky. Juan yelled for us to call 9-1-1, which echoed in my eardrums, and Kevin ran around the counter frantically. I froze in time as the scenes of that night played in front of me.* I wrapped my arms around my midsection, trying to comfort myself. Luckily, Juan had just busted Alex's nose and a rib.

I felt someone's arms wrap around me, causing me to snap back to reality. Juan has refused to work here since that day.

"I didn't mean to bring on any flashbacks."

"I don't want to drag anyone else into this." I wiped my eyes with the back of my hand.

"Corey is a good guy. He will protect you and won't take any of Alex's shit."

"Whatever it may be, I don't want to ruin any relationship because of my past. What if I end up falling in love with Corey, and he notices my sucky, stupid ex trying to ruin my life, amongst other things, and leaves me?" I said.

"He won't be like that, and I'm pretty sure Corey will be back soon."

"Why do you say that?" I asked curiously.

"I asked him if he wanted to come to work for me as the shop's body piercer again when he is off from his other job."

Corey was going to work here? I would have eye candy at work. But did Corey say yes? "Did he say yes?"

Kevin didn't answer right away; just smiled. "Do you care?"

"No, but I'm just curious if I need to update our website or get his station ready." I tried to lie without looking at Kevin.

"He said yes. He'll be here tomorrow to start. You got work to do," Kevin said, patting the glass case before heading to the back area.

I returned to the desk and plopped into the black leather office chair. I swung the chair back and forth, letting the giddy feeling rush through me.

I leaned back in my chair to look further into the tattoo parlor. Kevin was barely in sight but was within hearing range. "Kevin, do you think he will pierce my tragus?"

"I'm sure he would do it willingly and for free," Kevin said, not even looking at me. I returned to work and was happy with the thought of having another person working here. The other tattoo artists only did weekends, so we were mainly a two-person crew.

When it came time for the shop to close, I had all my work done, and whatever was left was for Kevin to do as the shop's owner.

I called out, "I'm ready to head home. Could you walk me out?"

Kevin nodded as he stood from his bar stool and walked me to my car. Kevin always ensured someone escorted me to my car in case Alex lurked outside, ready to pounce. I climbed in my rundown Volkswagen.

Kevin had signed this old car over to me because he and Anita had invested in something newer that fit their family of three. They had decided not to try for more kids after little Jack. From what Anita and I had discussed, they have tried numerous times, but it always resulted in miscarriages. I felt bad for them because they were great parents. I think having a Volkswagen was their dream car for having more children to drive around, but there's no need for it if you only have one child.

Kevin pushed my door shut for me, and I heard him smack the roof like always. He waited for me to pull out before returning to the tattoo parlor.

I drove to the house where I lived with Kevin and his little family. I parked the car along the street before I walked toward the front door. I felt secure living in the gated community, knowing Alex couldn't get in or near where we lived. He had tried; the only time he could ever get in was when he slid in behind another car.

I let myself into the house quietly so I wouldn't wake Jack. Anita sat on the couch reading one of her romance novels for this month's book club.

"How was it tonight?" she asked as I shut the door. I locked it with a sigh.

"Slow like usual during the week, but Kevin is hiring this Corey dude back on. Do you know him?" I asked. If Kevin won't talk to me about Corey, maybe Anita will. That's what us girls do, right? Gossip about boys?

I walked further into the living room and sat on the arm of the loveseat across from her.

"Yeah, he is a good man. He was very close to Kevin, and they were inseparable when Corey was here more often. He was here when I was pregnant with little Jack. When Corey got offered his new position, it was hard for him to do both jobs, so Kevin let him go. Did Corey ask to come back or what?"

"Kevin said he asked Corey to come back to do piercings. I guess it's to bring in more business." I shrugged.

"You like him, don't you? I thought the two of you would be a perfect match when I first met you. He's single. Well, at least when I last saw him, he was," Anita hedged.

"Why did you think that?"

"He just seemed like he would fit your taste in men, and he seems like someone that would do you right. You two would be a great match together. Call it women's intuition."

"I find him attractive..."

"But?" Anita asked with a confused tone.

"But what about Alex?"

"What about Alex? He doesn't control you anymore, sweetie. You have your life back, so do what the fuck you want. You are safe now. We won't ever let him do anything to ruin you or lay a finger on you again."

20

"I just met Corey. I don't want to jump to conclusions, and we didn't talk much tonight. I won't expect much from it besides being co-workers and hoping to be friends. If something more than that happens, then so be it," I said with a shrug.

"Will you tell him about Alex?"

"No, well, not before I have to because I…I don't want it to affect the relationship that may come up between us. That right there is what I'm afraid of. Corey might not want to date me because of Alex. Alex is a psychotic psychopath, and I fear that he is going to be the reason that I won't ever find true love. Maybe it's just me because I also thought Alex was the one."

"We learn from our mistakes," Anita said as I nodded.

"Well, I'm going to make myself something to eat before heading to bed." I stood up from the arm of the couch.

"There are leftovers in the fridge from dinner," Anita responded.

I headed into the kitchen, opened the fridge, and began heating the leftovers from dinner. I plopped down at the breakfast bar and ate in silence.

After clearing the plate, I took it to the sink to rinse off. I slid the plate into an empty slot on the dishwasher's bottom rack. I heard the front door opening and knew it had to be Kevin. I walked out to greet him in time to see him shut the door. He turned the deadbolt to the lock position and then locked the knob.

"When did you meet Corey?" I saw Kevin jump a little when I spoke. "Sorry, I thought you knew I was here."

Kevin turned around to face me. "We met in college. He's a really good friend. He's like a brother to me, honestly."

"Oh, okay. How come I've never met him until now if you two are such good friends?"

Kevin tossed his keys onto the entryway table with a soft sigh. "He has been bouncing between here and Florida a lot lately. We haven't had time to catch up."

"Florida? He travels to Florida a lot?" That piqued my interest. He was someone new, and since I was close to all the employees at the store and Corey was joining the team, I needed to know more about him and what he does when he is in Florida.

Kevin shrugged and shoved his hands in his pockets. "Almost every week, I think. Haven't spoken to him in a month before tonight."

"Well, I'm heading to bed. Good night." I heard the two 'nights' from them before I headed up the stairs. I tried being as quiet as I could, walking past the open door of Jack's room.

I entered my bedroom and made sure my door was closed before flicking the light on. I locked the door behind me to change into a pair of pajamas. I pulled off my shirt, tossing it toward my clothes basket, watching it land on the edge of the basket. I looked over my shoulder at the mirror, seeing the scars that ran horizontally across my back. Four lines were more defined than the others because they had been the deepest cuts.

As I stared longer in the mirror, I began to picture Alex standing behind me in his black jeans and a navy blue long-sleeve that he had worn that day. *Alex had held the brown leather belt tightly in his grip, and I could hear him growling behind me. He was breathing heavily with anger, and his look was dark. The laundry hadn't been fully dried yet, so he couldn't wear his lucky jersey to the game night his colleagues were having. My mind replayed him snapping the belt against the floor in preparation for lashing it against my bare skin. Alex drew back the belt and then flung it toward me, connecting with my bare skin. A sudden, intense burning and stinging sensation radiated from my back. The cracking sounds of the belt connecting with my back echoed in my ear drums. Every crack caused my body to shiver in anticipation. The belt connected twelve times, but only four out of those twelve had cut my skin deep enough to leave scars.*

I closed my eyes, feeling how watery they were from the tears that had filled them. When I re-opened my eyes, I no longer saw Alex in the reflection, just the scars.

I want tattoos to cover the scars, but I haven't decided what designs I want. Even though I will eventually get tattoos to try and cover them, you will still be able to notice them if you touch them. I just hoped that Corey didn't see the small but faint scars along my arms that were self-inflicted. The scarring on my arms are the only ones that are usually exposed.

I sighed, wiped my eyes, and tried to get my head straight after reliving that moment. I looked down at the floor and removed the rest of my clothes to pull on comfy pajamas. I flicked the lights off and slowly tip-toed over to the bed. I slid under the covers, rolled onto my side, and stared out into the star-filled night sky. I let out another deep sigh before I closed my eyes, wanting to get some rest.

Chapter Two:

The next night, I drove to the shop a few minutes after Kevin. I had to start setting up the front of the shop, getting things ready for the night. We weren't open for another hour, so I had time to set everything up. I had the whole process down to thirty minutes.

Upon finishing, I walked to the back room and stood watching Kevin ready his station with new sanitized equipment in preparation for his first customer. Tonight, Corey was going to take one of the unused stations.

We had a couple of other tattoo artists but two empty stations. I had never really wanted to get into the tattooing business. I might think about it if we continue to have an open empty station, but I feel we don't need more artists considering the lack of business.

"Are you ever going to let me teach you how to work this equipment? That is how Corey learned piercing," Kevin said as I sighed. I sat on one of the artists' rolling stools and spun back and forth.

"I don't know if I want to learn."

"What do you want to do then? If you learn how to tattoo, it will help you work elsewhere," Kevin said as I let out a sigh. "I think you are doing great, but with Alex always lurking, I am sure you would want out of this tiny town to get away from him."

"I like where I am right now. I'm content. I like living with you and your family. Alex is the only one that rains on my parade."

"I'm sure you want more." He was right. I wanted and expected more out of my life than this current situation. The ability to tattoo would open more doors and opportunities if I ever left this town. Don't get me wrong, I loved Lancaster, but I wanted to get out of Pennsylvania.

"I think I want to learn." I nodded at my decision. My answer caused Kevin to smile.

"I can teach you the equipment now," Kevin said.

I rolled over to his station to let him show me the equipment. I was familiar with most of the equipment from sitting in on many sessions and getting my tattoos. The black door that separated the guest lobby and the tattoo stations opened. Corey stepped into the door frame, lifting his brown sunglasses onto his brown hair, which was now fully exposed. He shaved his hair on the sides, cutting the top into a shaggy Mohawk. He wore a black wife beater and skin-tight blue jeans with tears.

"So, I see you're going to be a tattoo artist now?" Corey asked, his lips curling up into a smile.

I spun the rest of the way around in my chair to face him. Corey looked hotter than he did the day before, a backpack slung over his shoulder. Why did seeing him fill me with happiness? When he was around, my body became overwhelmed with butterflies. It brought back memories of my puppy love stage with Alex. These were feelings I hadn't experienced in ages.

"He's going to teach me, kind of like how you learned to do piercing." I glanced at Kevin.

"Very clever. Have you told her my whole life story, bud?" Corey asked, patting Kevin on his shoulder.

"No, but Melanie said that she wants her tragus pierced. I told her that you were going to start piercing here again and how you got started." Kevin shrugged at Corey as he answered.

"Your tragus? Really?" Corey asked, now his glare was on me. I sheepishly nodded my head. Corey walked over to a station, dropped his bag, and patted the chair. "Hop on up, and I will get that done in a jiffy."

I stood and eagerly jumped into the seat he indicated. Corey began to pull his equipment out of the special case he carried it in. I waited while he sterilized everything he needed, setting them down on the paper-lined metal tray. He pulled the metal tray with him and plopped onto the rolling stool beside me. I pushed my long hair behind the ear I wanted him to pierce.

"Why the tragus?" He asked.

I could barely see him out of the corner of my eye; he was that close to me. He reached over and adjusted his tray with the equipment, moving it toward him more.

"Why not the tragus?" I retorted.

"Quit being smart," he said. "You aren't afraid of needles?"

"No, did you see how many tattoos I have?"

"This will be different because it's going through your ear…"

"True. I can handle it."

"You want to hold onto my arm?"

"Since you offered," I said with a smile. Corey moved closer if that was possible. Any closer, and he would practically be in my lap. At first, being this close to him felt awkward, but the longer we sat this way, the more comfortable I became.

"Yes, I need to be close," he whispered, his breath tickling the fine hairs at my ear.

I saw him smile out of the corner of my eye. It was like he could read my mind, and I certainly hoped not because then he'd find out that I thought he was hot.

"Blue, okay? I grabbed a blue ring to match your eyes." He spoke quietly so only I would hear him. I felt his fingers gently press the excess skin I was getting pierced. Even though he was supposed to be applying pressure, the moment his skin touched mine, I could feel the electricity between us.

"You remembered my eyes are blue?" I asked, not wanting to move any to look at him. That he noticed and remembered my eye color was sweet.

"How could I not? They are piercing blue, like crystals. I haven't seen a blue like that ever before."

"Thank you?" I asked, not sure if that was a compliment or not. I began to feel pressure and slight pain from him pushing the needle through the skin.

"You're welcome. There, all done. Just need to put the ring in." He asked, "Did you ever think you would be here?"

"No, I never dreamt of being a tattoo artist."

"What did you dream of being?" Corey asked. I heard the clanks of him moving instruments on his equipment tray.

"I wanted to be a lawyer."

"A lawyer? Why didn't you follow through?" Corey asked.

"Do you know how long you need to go to school for that?"

"Not as long as for a doctor."

"True."

"And lawyers are paid very well, so it would have made up for all that schooling. When did you start drawing?" Corey asked curiously as I let out a soft sigh.

"I took a drawing class in high school, and I liked it."

"What about college?"

"No to college. I thought I was in love and never went. Are we done?" I asked. I jumped out of the chair, unsure if he had put the ring in yet. I wanted our conversation to end as I pushed a hand through my hair awkwardly.

Corey pushed himself back and nodded, "Yeah…"

"Thank you." I beelined toward the bathroom.

"You might want to wipe your ear. There might still be some blood," Corey yelled after me.

I went into the bathroom and stared at my reflection. I leaned forward against the sink, embarrassed by my actions. I couldn't go back out there. I had either said too much or too little to him. He was new to me and was probably just trying to get to know his new co-worker.

I sucked up the tears that filled my eyes and aggressively tugged at some paper towels. I was so upset and angry at myself that I didn't want to go back out there. I wiped at the piercing to get the excessive blood off the skin surrounding the freshly made hole.

Kevin stepped into the door threshold. "So, what was that about?"

"Nothing, Kevin. Okay?"

"Well, Corey said you kind of got uncomfortable and stormed off. He said you were talking about college and how you thought you were in love." Kevin stated as I let out a sigh.

"I don't want to tell him about Alex. At least not yet."

"You didn't have to. You could have just left it at what you said. If he had asked you any questions, you could have just told him you didn't want to discuss it." Kevin was right again. I shut the light off in the bathroom and pushed past Kevin. I marched up to Corey while I had the courage and the guts to talk to him.

"Sorry for acting the way I did. It's just that I don't want to talk about my ex."

"I didn't want to talk about your ex. I wanted to know about you," Corey stated as he smiled, "So, now that you are single, you going to go to college?"

"Haven't thought about it." I shrugged as I sat down on one of the rolling stools.

"It's up to you, but having a degree never hurts," Corey stated.

"Do you have a degree?"

"I do." He nodded with a smile.

"But you resorted to this?" I asked.

"I'm doing what I love, but at least I have a degree in something to fall back on."

"That is true. What did you get a degree in?"

"Marketing."

"Really? Are you working in marketing? I can't picture it," I said with a chuckle.

"So now you know why I didn't pursue it after graduation."

"Yeah," I said with a smile. "Why did you go to college and spend all that money if that isn't what you are doing?"

"I wanted to make my parents proud, and I also wanted something to fall back on in case this didn't pan out," Corey explained, which made sense to me. "So, what do you do here?"

"I book appointments, set people up with their tattoos, help prepare the artists with the customers and such. Not much." I shrugged.

"I'm teaching her to use the tattoo guns so she can expand her knowledge. I need new artists back here. Plus, Melanie is such an amazing artist." Kevin jumped in as he walked by on his way to the small break area we had.

"Is that so? I think it'll be great," Corey stated.

"Do you, now?" I asked.

"Yes, I do," Corey said with a smile.

"You don't even know if I will be good at it," I retorted.

"It's just like drawing but with a needle," Corey said, trying to compare the two.

"I'm more afraid of it being permanent. Tattooing is permanent, and drawing in my sketchbook, I can erase and try again," I stated.

"You can draw it up first, then do that stencil trick that most of us do to help so you won't be as nervous," Kevin stated.

"He's got a point. So, now you can't say that it's permanent cause there is a way around it," Corey said as I sighed.

"I think maybe I can try it," I said as they both smiled in victory.

"We'll start tomorrow…but first, I need you to update our website and other things to include that we have piercings available," Kevin said as I nodded.

I stood up, headed to my office area, and got to work on what needed to be finished tonight. At the night's end, I shut the lights off. I headed to the back area where the tattooing and piercing took place.

"Hey, Kevin. I'm ready to head home," I said. I sheepishly gripped my purse strap and felt awkward interrupting him now that Corey was here. Having Corey around made me feel happy, nervous, and giddy. He brought out these feelings within me that I haven't felt in years.

"Give me a few more minutes, and I'll walk you out to the car," Kevin said as I nodded. I looked over, noticing Corey cleaning up his station. At least, that is what I presumed he was doing.

"I'm done and heading out. I can walk her to her car," Corey said. Corey set down whatever he had in hand and pulled his bag on his shoulder.

"Thanks," Kevin said as I smiled. Corey walked over, offering me his arm. I looked at his arm, then up at him with a half-smirk.

"I don't bite. I promise," he said softly with a smile as I rolled my eyes. I slid my arm into the gap between his arm and body, resting my hand on his elbow as I walked beside him out of the shop. "Which car is yours?" he asked as the door shut behind us, and I pointed out my car. "You need to upgrade the ride."

"Right now, my finances aren't great, so this is holding up for the time being," I truthfully answered him.

"I understand. So, what do you have planned for tomorrow?" Corey asked.

"Besides work, nothing much. Why?" I asked as I pushed a strand of hair behind my ear, feeling myself blush.

"Well, I was wondering if you wanted to hang out. Nothing more than going to the mall or a movie or something." He shrugged.

"What about your other job?" I asked curiously.

"It's my day off. I'll bring you here and drive you home after," he said as I nibbled on my bottom lip.

"Sounds like fun. I need some time away for a little while." I was being truthful. Being here in the moment with Corey and when he was piercing my ear, I hadn't thought about my ex, not even once.

"Alright, where should I pick you up?" he asked curiously.

"You know where Kevin lives?"

"Yeah…"

"I live with them." I was ashamed of saying that to him. I looked down between us as I felt his forefinger and thumb gently grasp my chin, lifting my face to look up at him.

"I'll see you tomorrow. Is eleven okay?" He asked.

"That sounds wonderful." I smiled as he reached over, pulled my door open, and watched me climb into the car.

"Drive safe, I'll see you tomorrow."

"Yes, you will," I said with a smile as he smiled back at me. He pushed the door shut and walked back up to the sidewalk, watching me pull out.

I felt like I was a little girl with a crush. Tomorrow would be my first date with someone other than my ex, and I wasn't even sure if it would classify as a date. I headed back to the house, letting myself in and locking up behind me. I headed into the kitchen, where I saw Anita opening the microwave.

"I heard you pull up. How did it go today?" she asked.

"Tonight went well. I have a date tomorrow."

"With who?" she asked curiously, setting the plate of food down in front of where I began to sit.

"Corey. He is picking me up here if that is okay," I said as she smiled.

"Of course, it is. You like him, huh? Your face lights up whenever he's mentioned."

"I find myself attracted to him, but I'm just worried about

32

how he'll handle hearing about my ex," I said truthfully. I bit into the food she had prepared for me.

"Trust me when I say that Corey can take care of himself when it comes to that type of thing," Anita said with a smile. "So, what are you going to do on the date?"

"Not sure. I think he said the mall or the movies." I shrugged as she smiled.

"That should be fun. Did you get a piercing?" She reached out to turn my face so she could see it better. "Corey did that? He does great work."

"You should let him pierce you."

"I'm not that daring," Anita said with a chuckle. Anita had no tattoos or piercings on her, which was funny since she was married to Kevin. Even though she didn't have tattoos like her husband, they loved the same types of music and fashion, so they had plenty in common. Anita and I continued to chat until Kevin got home. Anita was giddier than I was about my date with Corey, and she beat me to spilling the news. "So, Miss Melanie has a date with Corey tomorrow."

"You do, do you? I'm shocked he did it."

"You knew?" I asked as I looked at him, shocked. Kevin chuckled at my reaction.

"Yeah, he was talking about it while you were working. He wasn't sure if you would say yes," Kevin answered as he sat beside me.

"Did you tell him I would?" I asked as I saw him bite into his food. "You did, didn't you?"

"Yes." Kevin smiled and chuckled. I playfully smacked him, and he chuckled some more.

"I'm going to bed so I can rest up nicely for tomorrow," I said. I stood up, taking care of my dishes, before heading to my room to prepare for bed. I lay in my bed, staring out the window, trying to force myself to sleep, but I was so nervous about tomorrow that I couldn't sleep.

Chapter Three:

I woke to the sound of my alarm at seven when Jack usually wakes up to get ready for school. I wasn't sure what time I finally fell asleep. I always make sure I get up to have breakfast with Jack. Today, I stayed in my pajamas because I didn't want to start getting ready for my date until closer to eleven when Corey was supposed to pick me up. I figured he would be here roughly a few minutes before eleven, which gave me a few hours, so I didn't see a need to rush.

I headed down the stairs, pulling my hair into a messy ponytail. I stopped at the bottom step, staring into the living room, and saw Jack sitting on Corey's lap. Fortunately, Corey's back was to me, and he didn't see me. My mouth fell open in shock that he was here early. I looked at Kevin and Anita sitting on the loveseat opposite Corey. They each held a cup of coffee, and I heard Anita laugh while Corey continued to talk. I turned to run up the stairs before Corey saw me in my pajamas.

"Morning, sleepy head," Kevin said right when I put my foot

on the next step. Why did Kevin have to draw attention to me? Is it his job to embarrass me?! I was trying to make a good impression on Corey, and seeing me in my pajamas would not help.

While my back was to the group, I swallowed a big gulp of nerves before slowly turning around, awkwardly embarrassed to be seen dressed this way. By the time I had completely turned around, Corey had shifted on the couch to face me. I pasted a half-smile on my face, trying to swallow the embarrassment that the man I had a date with was seeing me in a spaghetti strap top and shorts that were covered with tears and stains. The pajama set may not be new and had flaws, but they were trusty. I just hoped that the shorts covered enough of the scars that Corey wouldn't notice them.

"Morning," I softly responded. I stepped back down to the main floor and stood behind the couch, trying to avoid Corey's gaze.

"There is still coffee, and breakfast needs to be heated." Anita stood, and I nodded to let her know I had heard. "It's time for me to take little Jack to school."

I walked past them to head into the kitchen. I was still trying to avoid Corey so I wouldn't blush from embarrassment.

I opened the cupboard to pull a mug down. I set the cup on the counter before grabbing the coffee pot, keeping warm on the burner.

"I hope you don't mind me coming over early. I hadn't seen little Jack in months," Corey said as I glanced over at him. He was leaning against the doorframe, wearing skin-tight jeans with rips in various parts of the legs and a muscle shirt with some design. His brown hair was shaggy with curls. Does it always look messy?

"I don't mind. It's just that I wish I had known so I wouldn't have walked down looking like a complete slob," I said softly. I heard him let out a chuckle.

"You aren't a complete slob. I have seen people look worse."

"Oh, that makes me feel so much better." I rolled my eyes. It certainly didn't make me feel better. I went to the fridge to grab the creamer.

"I hope it did. I look worse when I wake up from a bad night's sleep. Why don't you drink your cup of joe, get ready, and we will go do breakfast?"

"Do breakfast and lunch out? Uh, that is a lot of money. I can just reheat some of this food or have a bowl of cereal." I started putting together a plate of food from what Anita had cooked earlier before zapping it in the microwave. I squirted some ketchup on my eggs and poured syrup onto the pancakes. I sat at the dining room table, where Corey was already sitting on a chair that was flipped around. He rested his arms on the back of the chair and watched me as I began eating my food.

"So, what do you want to do today? I was thinking of going to the mall. They have a food court, a movie theater, an arcade, and, of course, stores. I know that all girls love to shop." Corey smiled as he listed everything off.

"I do love to shop, but I can't buy anything. Please, don't let me spend a dime on something I don't need." I warned him as I pointed my fork at him.

"I cross my heart." Corey lazily did the symbol for that with a smile. "It just means I can spend my dime on it or know what I can get you for your birthday." Corey reached across the table and stole a slice of my bacon.

"Hey!" I shouted in a fake offended tone and let out a soft chuckle. Corey gave me a boyish grin before he took a bite of the bacon.

"What?" He faked a confused manner with the bacon still in his mouth.

"You stole my bacon. You can get your own, man."

"But your plate is closer than the bacon plate." I groaned as I walked over to get the other plate and brought it to the table.

"Merry Christmas," I said unenthusiastically as I set the plate before him.

"Thanks. Even though it isn't good for my diet, I can't get enough of this stuff."

"You? On a diet? Aren't you skinny enough? You are also muscular. Why are you even on a diet?"

"How else am I supposed to keep my girlish figure?" Corey asked with a chuckle.

"Good point. Any pointers on losing weight other than stop eating bacon?" I asked as I took a bite of my bacon.

"A lot of determination, dedication, and sweating. I can help you with getting a gym membership." Corey made the offer as he ate another piece of bacon.

"I may like that idea, but I don't have the money to pay a monthly charge, so I have to resort to at-home workouts."

"You want a workout buddy? I can drive over, and we can go for jogs and such. I've got free weights I can bring over, or hell, you can come to my place and do a daily workout routine."

"Why do I feel like you will murder me in a workout?"

"I promise you, I'm not that bad as a workout coach."

"I'll think about it," I said as I poked at my eggs before eating them.

"How did you end up working with Kevin?" Corey asked.

"Well, I was always walking in to see if I could get work done. I never had money to pay for the tattoos, so we made a deal that I would work off the tab at the shop, and I wanted a reason to be out of my current place at that time. Things got worse for me, and I became homeless. Kevin opened his home to me, and I ended up staying here." The whole time I spoke, I looked down at my plate, not wanting to go into more detail than I had to. I was too embarrassed to make eye contact with him.

"Hey, we all have our struggles and do what we must to survive. It's a dog-eat-dog world out there." Corey had no idea how true that statement was and how I was withholding information about my situation. I hoped the truth wouldn't come out until I was comfortable and trusted him enough to tell him.

"Yeah, we do," I said, taking another bite of my eggs.

"So, did you get much ink done since you were always there?"

"Not as much as you have done, I am presuming," I said softly.

"I do have a lot, and I plan on getting more. I can see that you don't have as many as me. How many do you have?"

"I have like six," I said confidently.

"Why are you slacking? Get going, girl. You have to catch up to me," Corey said as I chuckled.

"I doubt I will ever get that many. I would run out of designs I wanted tattooed on my body. How did you come up with all of those things? Do they each have a meaning?"

"They all have a special meaning for me. We will need a longer date for me to go through each one, though. We can save that for a different day."

"If there will be a date after today," I muttered.

"What? You already don't want to go on this date?"

"It's not that. I just meant that you may not want to go out with me again after today."

"Well, I can't make that decision until after today, so don't cross any T's or dot any I's until afterward, okay, Miss Jump Ahead?" He asked as I blushed slightly.

"Okay." I set my fork down. "I'm done here, so I'm going to get ready. Can you give me about a half hour or so?"

"Alright, no rush. I'll be down here chatting with Kevin." Corey stood simultaneously with me. I took my plate to the sink before following him to the living room. I headed upstairs to my room. Now that I knew what Corey was wearing, I had a better idea of what to wear.

I picked out a simple pair of jeans that had rips along the legs purposefully, a black cami top with a white cardigan, and a white knitted hat. I went to shower before returning to my room to finish getting dressed. I dried my hair and did all the daily rituals I would normally do to prepare for the day, but this time, I had done extra prep to make myself extra cute for him.

I turned to get a 180 view in my mirror to ensure my clothing covered all the scars. I didn't want Corey to see them and run to Kevin to ask questions behind my back.

I transitioned my wallet into a wristlet before I headed downstairs to see Anita, Corey, and Kevin on the couches, laughing and chatting. It was nice that he was friends with them, but I felt like the third wheel because I wasn't close to Corey yet.

I stepped off the last step and walked further into the living room to sit on the arm of the couch where Corey sat, looking over at Anita and Kevin.

"You look nice today, Melanie," Anita said as I smirked.

"Thanks," I said as I pushed a strand of hair behind my ear. I glanced over to Corey, feeling his hand settle on the small of my back, gently rubbing it.

"She does. We should get going, huh?" Corey asked as I nodded.

I stood back up. "I'll be back later, before work. I promise."

"Your curfew is 10 PM. Don't worry about work right now. I think I can handle a night without you if need be." Kevin shot us a wink.

What was with the wink? It was strange, but that was Kevin. Kevin was a bit older, but not by much. I looked to Kevin like my older brother, and he always looked out for me.

"I've got work tonight, too, so she would be at work on time, Kevin. Don't you worry about working the front," Corey reassured him as his hand cupped mine, tugging me toward the door. I couldn't help the smile that crept onto my face.

"Well, I'll see you both at the shop then," Kevin said with a smile.

Corey opened the front door, allowing me to step onto the porch first. He stepped out beside me. Kevin pushed the door shut behind us, leaving me alone with Corey on the front porch. Suddenly, the butterflies in my stomach multiplied by a million, if there was even enough room for that many. What should I say? What do you talk about on a date? I hadn't been on a date since high school.

Chapter Four:

Corey took my hand, leading me down the stone path toward the dark green Jaguar with a white roof that I presumed was his. Corey pulled the silver bar to open the car door for me.

"This door tends to stick a little." Corey winked as he pushed the door closed behind me before strolling around the car to climb in on the other side. Corey slid the key into the ignition and turned his wrist to bring the engine growling to life. A smile spread across my face for some odd reason as I finally heard the click that let me know my belt was locked in.

"You have a nice car. How old is it?" I asked curiously.

"She's a 1987 Jaguar. I've put a lot of blood, sweat, and tears into getting it this perfect and running. It was my pet project," Corey explained.

"Do you collect these types of cars?"

"Nah, my dad does, though," he answered, and I just made an 'O' with my lips.

I turned to look out the window as we waited for the cast-iron gate to let us out of the community swing toward us.

Corey pulled through and began to drive the short distance to the mall. After a few moments of awkward silence, Corey asked, "What type of music do you like?"

"I listen to anything, but I like rock the most. My favorites are alternative or old-school rock."

"You sound like my type of girl. That is exactly what I have stored in my radio stations. You ever listen to A Day To Remember?" Corey asked as a fake shock look came over my face.

"Of course! I adore them. I wish I could have gone to the concert they just had out here, but I couldn't make it."

"Man, I went, and if I had known you liked them, I could have given you the spare ticket."

"What?! You had a spare ticket? How did you even have a spare ticket?!" I asked in excitement.

"I was lucky. The next time, I'll make sure to grab two tickets. I got their new CD, too. Do you wanna hear?"

"Absolutely," I said with a smile.

Corey pushed a button on the middle console that caused music to play through the sound system. I began to slightly bob my head to the music while I looked out the window. Corey had parked his car as close as he could to the mall doors, but he also had to find a spot where there wouldn't be a car on either side of his. I guess he wanted to make sure no one would nick or dent his car.

I clicked the button to release my seat belt as I reached for the door handle. I began to pull the handle and push at the door to open it, but it wouldn't budge.

I began to feel penned in. I swallowed a gulp, I looked into my lap, and my hands were tied together. I looked out the passenger window and saw Alex walking away from the car with his back

*to me. I tugged at the door handle but it wouldn't budge. I began
screaming at the top of my lungs for him to come back, hoping for
anyone to hear me. Was that smoke? I swear I can smell smoke. I
began to panic. The car was overheating and was going to ignite
any minute. Banging my best against the window to get anyone's
attention. Why wasn't anyone noticing the smoke?! HELP! I was
screaming.*

The door finally banged open, causing me to gasp, and then
I looked straight up into Corey's eyes. It was Corey! Tears of
happiness filled my eyes.

"Told you that it sticks." His eyebrow perked, "Are you ok?"

Confusion spread over his face as I jumped out of the car
and hugged him tightly. He held me tightly to him, and I felt
warm. Being wrapped up in his arms brought me back to
reality. I stepped back, wiping my eyes with my fingertips.

"Sorry. I'm fine," I said, trying to brush it off. Corey seemed
very confused about what happened, but he nodded. He didn't
pester me for any more information, just slipped his arm
around my waist, letting his hand slip into the pocket on my
ass. I bit my bottom lip, trying to fight back the smile that
came to my face. We walked a short distance to the entrance.

"So, what store do you always hit first when going to the
mall? Is it the shoe store? The arcade? The lingerie store?"
Corey asked with a boyish smile.

"Why would I have to shop there? I don't wear panties." I
replied. I could hear him choke back a moan at my answer.

"Well, I guess we aren't going there." I could see him trying
to adjust himself a little as he walked. I bit at my bottom lip,
trying not to let out a giggle.

"I haven't been to the mall to go shopping in what seems
like months. I only come when it's time to take Jack shopping

for school clothes or Anita needs something." I shrugged with a little pep in my step.

"Even then, you must have a favorite store. Maybe Hot Topic? That tends to be where people our age tend to shop," Corey said as I smiled.

"I do like that store but haven't gone there since Jack is too young."

"Well," Corey said as he spun around, pretending to look around us, "Little Jack isn't here now, is he? Only the grown-ups have come out to play today."

I rolled my eyes and let out a soft laugh. He was ridiculous but super cute. The doors to the mall automatically opened for us, and we walked into a blast of A/C.

"We will hit stores along the way. When does a girl not like shopping?"

"I never said I didn't like it. I just said I don't go often," I corrected him as he nodded.

"You're right, so explain. Why don't you go often?"

"Money. If you couldn't tell, I'm at rock bottom right now and slowly trying to crawl out of the deep end. With that said, I can't go to the mall and spend my money buying a new pair of shoes like that." I nodded toward a pair of shoes on display in the window front.

"What caused you to hit rock bottom, if you don't mind me asking? You probably tried your hardest not to let it get to this point. I don't think anyone wants to hit absolute bottom, but I was just wondering," Corey asked as I shrugged.

"Everything. Honestly, my life was a joke before this, and fortunately, Kevin was there when I needed someone the most. He was there to rescue me at my lowest and to help me get to where I am now. I am forever in debt to him for getting me this far. Can we change the subject? I don't feel comfortable going into any more details." I answered. Corey simply nodded his head in understanding.

We walked past various storefronts as the conversations seemed to move along smoothly. We eventually found Hot Topic and stopped in front of the entrance to look at each other. A smile spread across Corey's face, making him look super cute. He slid his hand out of my butt pocket, only to grab my hand, and he tugged me inside the darkly-lit store. I was quite nervous to be in this store because I knew I would find something I desperately wanted and would have to leave it behind. I think that is why I hated window shopping. Because I knew I would find something I fell in love with but couldn't afford.

I swear we spent over an hour in that store. Corey and I looked at every item we came across. I think I just needed to make up for lost time since I couldn't come in here. We discussed pop culture. I discovered he wasn't a big fan of The Big Bang Theory but loved the Simpsons and DC movies. As for musical taste, he's a bit more into heavy rock, which differs from what I listened to. I think I could eventually come to love the music he was into, but today was the first time I had ever heard that particular kind of music. Corey wasn't into the fashionable style they had. I couldn't see Corey in the leather jackets or the black pants they sold. He wasn't that type of person, and that was okay because I wasn't either.

"Hey! It's A Day To Remember shirt," Corey said while staring at the plastic squares on the wall above us that displayed various band shirts. My eyes browsed over ones for the Ramones, Green Day, Red Hot Chili Peppers, and the Rolling Stones. My mind was getting lost in the various band shirts until my eyes landed on the four versions of shirts they had to offer for A Day to Remember.

"Which one do you like?" Corey asked as he glanced at me.

I bit my bottom lip as I looked over the options before telling him, "The one with the wolf and orange lettering."

"That's the one I liked too," he said with a smile. I smiled, too, as I saw Corey rummaging through the stacks of folded shirts. "What size are you? Medium?"

"I'm not getting it," I said, shaking my head no.

"Yes, you are. I hope you fit a medium because that is the size I grabbed you." He tucked the shirt under his arm.

"Put it back, Corey. I'm being serious."

"I'm getting it for you," Corey said as he unfolded a shirt and held it to his chest. "You think this will fit, or should I go a size up?"

"I think it'll fit but might be a bit on the tight side."

"Oh, well, I like my clothes a bit form-fitting to show off my muscles." He shrugged, "Medium for the lady?"

I sighed, giving in. "I prefer a large. I like my clothes on the looser side."

Corey simply nodded, placed the medium shirt back on the neatly folded pile of shirts, and grabbed a large for me, too. We continued to browse the rest of the store. I spent most of my time at the clearance rack since, at the moment, that was all I could afford. I stood next to Corey at the register in disbelief that he was buying me a shirt.

"Thank you for the shirt," I said as I stepped out of the store, holding the black plastic bag with the red gothic writing on it. I was smiling wide and brightly. Alex wouldn't have bought me this shirt, so I appreciated such a sweet gesture.

"You're welcome," he said. "Do you want to play a few

games?" He nodded toward the arcade that was across the way from us.

"I don't have any cash on me."

"Did I ask if you had cash?" Corey asked sarcastically as I shook my head no. "I asked if you wanted to play a few games. Come on."

He led me into the storefront filled with arcade games. We were the only two people in the whole arcade. I looked around at the different games, all blaring music or sounds. I heard the coins clunking into the metal bowl, which, somehow, was louder than the games. I looked at Corey, who scooped up the numerous quarters from the bowl and approached me.

"What's first, beautiful?" I blushed and bit my bottom lip after being called beautiful.

"Air hockey." I couldn't pull my eyes off the air hockey table. I led him to the table, and Corey deposited the required quarters to turn the machine on. The ugly yellow puck fell into the slot on my side.

"There isn't any crying in video games."

"I won't be the one crying," I stated seriously. Corey smirked as I put the puck on the machine and hit it hard enough for it to shoot down to his side. It was an intense game, and it was nice not having to take it easy. When I played against Jack, I had to go slow and easy on him since he was only seven years old. Corey eventually won by one point; the outcome was 4-3.

"What's the next game, loser?"

"Don't get too cocky." I stood, glaring at him. I looked around as I pointed at the motorcycle racing game. "You're on," I said as he began to laugh. I glared at him harder, grabbed his arm, and pulled him over to the connected machines.

I climbed onto the green and black motorcycle while he dropped the quarters into the two machines. Corey straddled the machine next to me while we discussed the game's race options. When we had crossed the finish line, I was in third, and he was fifth, so I had beat him that round. The rest of the games were single players, so we spent the remaining coins playing and trying to earn tickets.

"We won one hundred and thirty tickets. Now, what can we get with that?" he asked.

I looked at the wall of prizes in front of us, where everything displayed on the wall was at least five hundred tickets. I looked down into the display case below us.

"Is it okay if I surprise you?" he asked, causing me to look at him.

I simply nodded before walking out of the arcade to wait for him to decide what to buy with the tickets. I checked my phone to see if I had missed any texts from Kevin and logged onto my social media to see the latest updates while I waited. I felt his hand wrap around me, covering my eyes.

"What are you doing, Corey?" I asked with a soft laugh. When Corey finally uncovered my eyes, I saw a tiny stuffed gorilla holding a pink heart.

"I thought you would like it." He stepped up to stand beside me.

"Like it? I love it." I gave him a big smile. I grabbed it from his grip and held it with both hands, smiling wide. "What now?"

"We still have time and a lot more mall to cover." He began to lead the way through a part of the mall we hadn't been to yet.

As we continued walking, I saw the one thing I did not

want to see: my ex-boyfriend walking toward us. My heart began to beat faster when I saw him. I slammed on the brakes, staring at the dark-haired, six-foot-tall man wearing a Magic basketball jersey and dark brown cargo shorts. My breathing was sharper, and I felt numbness and tingling. Panic was overtaking my body. My mind started to shut down about where I was, and any thoughts of Corey disappeared.

I needed to hide. I couldn't let Alex see me. Not here. I would be a goner if he saw me. Where to hide? I began thinking more about where to go so he couldn't follow me. I turned to look at the storefront beside me and saw Victoria's Secret. It wasn't ideal, but they had to have a fitting room.

I bolted into the store without wondering what Corey was thinking or doing. He may have even tried to talk to me, but I zoned out and couldn't respond. Pushing my way through the crowds of women looking over the tables covered in lingerie, I found a long row of black doors for their fitting rooms.

One has to be open! Come on, come on! I began to try every door until another female came out, and she held the door open for me. I rushed into the room, shut the door behind me, and clicked the lock. My breathing began to slow as I turned around, pressing my back against the door, and slowly slid to a sitting position. My arms wrapped around my legs, holding them tightly to my chest.

I was trying to hold back the tears that were threatening to escape. After a few moments passed, I heard a knock on the door. I gasped softly. I didn't know who was on the other side, so I didn't do anything besides hold my breath.

"Melanie? Are you in there?" I heard Corey's deep, raspy voice ask from the other side.

"Is...is that you, Corey?" I asked, trying not to let my voice crack.

"Yeah, who else would it be?" he asked.

"Anyone with you?"

"A store associate by the name of Heather," he answered.

I moved to lie on the floor to look under the door. I saw the black boots that Corey opted to wear along with a pair of Nike's that I knew Alex wouldn't be caught dead wearing. I slowly stood up and pulled the door open enough to peek out to see Corey and the store associate.

"What's wrong, Melanie?" Corey's expression contorted with concern. He reached out to grasp my hand, his thumb rubbing the back of my hand soothingly.

I nervously slid out of the room and pressed against him for a tight hug. My face buried into his chest. I wanted to feel secure and comforted at that moment. Being pressed against Corey's solid frame made me feel that. I cried into his shirt, a wet stain forming from my tears.

"I want to go home," I whispered. Corey wrapped his arm around me and gripped my hip. He pulled me close to him, and I molded to his frame perfectly. My head pressed against his shoulder, and our hips pressed against each other.

Corey led me out of the store, and I stopped him at the entrance as I began to look both ways, making sure the coast was clear. When I didn't see Alex in the surrounding areas, I nervously stepped out, cuddling against Corey's side, hoping he could protect me. We headed straight back to his car, and I didn't say a word the whole time. Even on the ride home, I didn't utter a word. I didn't know what to say to him right then, and I wasn't sure how to explain this without going into too much detail.

Corey parked in front of Kevin's house, leaving the car

purring lowly before he finally turned the engine off. I stared at the two-story house and let out a sigh. I didn't want to go in there. I was still emotional after seeing Alex in the mall. I hadn't seen him in person recently other than at the parlor, and the last time he dropped in was before Corey showed up. Alex had instilled this fear in me that caused a certain reaction. I think being in public makes it worse because I am so fragile, and I would probably go back to him rather than create a scene. I have no one there to protect me.

"Look, I don't know what happened at the mall and whatever caused you to react like that. I want you to know that I will listen to whatever you want to talk about. I won't judge you either. I'm an open book. I'm just like Kevin, and whatever you can tell him, you can tell me, okay? I won't let anyone or anything hurt you, nor would I want you to be hurt physically or emotionally. It hurt me to see you in tears and to watch you respond in fear to whatever you saw. I don't know you as well as I wish I did. I like you, Melanie, and I hope we can become more than friends," Corey said as I listened. I turned to look deep into his brown eyes, seeing how serious he was.

"I'm sorry for today. I will tell you sometime soon, but our friendship and relationship are too fragile. I'm too fragile right now for it." I managed to get it all out as he patiently listened and nodded.

"Okay, it will take time, and I understand that. Whenever you are ready, I'm here for you, beautiful." He gave me a reassuring smile, and I nodded. I turned to look back at the house behind us as we went back to silence, each waiting for the other to make the next move.

We sat quietly in his car for a long time. I appreciated him not bombarding me with questions right now and supporting me in letting me take my time. I also felt guilty that I had ruined this date. First, with my flashback, then ending it abruptly by reacting the way I did. I thought I should apologize to him, but my lips weren't moving. The awkward silence was broken before I could even force my mouth to open, but it wasn't by me.

"You hungry? You want to go get some food?" Corey asked, and I couldn't help the smile that came to my lips. Of course, my lips will respond to the mention of food but won't listen to my demands to apologize. I glanced at him and pushed a strand of hair behind my ear.

"I would love to if you want to. I feel bad because we are already at my place and–"

"We can still get some food. There is a McDonald's on every block, and it's not a problem." Corey's suggestion reassured me, making me smile wider. "I take that as a yes. Food it is." He turned the key in the ignition, bringing the engine back to life. Corey pulled away from the curb and made his way out of the gated community. "What sounds good to you? Tacos, hamburgers, pancakes?"

"Tacos."

"Good choice. Now, Taco Bell or Del Taco?"

"Whichever one you prefer, I'm not that picky." I shrugged. Corey turned the vehicle to head toward whatever restaurant he had decided on. Corey pulled into a Del Taco lot and claimed a parking spot in front of the restaurant.

It felt comforting that he still wanted to spend time with me. Whether he knew why I had freaked out or not, it meant a lot to me because he still liked me without knowing all of me. We ordered our food and claimed a booth until the server called our order.

"I do want to apologize for earlier. I promise that doesn't happen often. Sometimes, flashbacks happen when I see a certain someone, and unfortunately, I spotted them. "

"Too much? Someone you're afraid of, I presume, if they scared you that much." He filled in the blanks as I nodded.

"Big time, but it's all about moving on and just trying to cut myself off from this person. I don't want to let my new life get involved with my old life."

"Gotcha. Hey, it's hard, especially in a small town like this. Maybe you should come and stay at my place. I've got a place outside the city limits. The possibility is slimmer that you'll run into them, and you can ride with me to work." Corey offered as I smiled, and I liked that offer. "That smile is beautiful. It's telling me you would like to do it."

"I do…"

"I hear a but in there," he interrupted as I sighed.

"I don't think me moving in with you is best for whatever level our relationship is at right now," I answered him as I bit my bottom lip, and he let out a chuckle.

"Okay, but let me know if you ever change your mind or want a night away from Kevin and his family to have personal time. I travel to Florida often for work, so I'm rarely home."

"I'll keep that in mind. So, any weird or scary exes on your behalf?" I asked, my curiosity coming out as I sipped at my drink.

"I had one scary one with a scar that went across her eye." He showed me where on his face with his finger as I made this grossed-out face.

"Why'd you date her?"

"I met her through an online dating site, and in my defense, she used a picture of someone else, so I didn't know."

"You got catfished?"

"Is that what it's called?" he asked as I smiled and chuckled. The server called our number, and Corey went to get our food from the counter. He returned with a tray full of food and set it between us. I grabbed my burrito and fries, placing the two items in front of me as Corey grabbed his food.

"I don't understand why a guy like you is on dating sites anyway. You seem chill, laid back, and friendly. I don't know why you would have a hard time picking up a girl."

"Well, I spend most of my free time working or hitting the gym. I'm not the social butterfly type where I go out to bars and strike up conversations with every girl I see."

"You didn't seem to have a problem talking with me."

"But I met you at work, so we are coworkers. It would be rude of me to ignore you."

"True," I said with a chuckle as I ate one of the fries.

"Are you on any dating sites?" Corey asked as I let out a sigh.

"No, I'm not looking at getting into a serious relationship. I'd rather meet someone face-to-face than through a computer screen," I said truthfully.

"Where were you when I needed that advice?"

"Working?" I sarcastically answered with a chuckle as he smiled.

"Right," he said. "So why Kevin's tattoo shop?"

"Why not? I had to leave the house, and that was the farthest away I could walk. I wanted to dull the pain somehow, so I got tattoos to take me away from it all. One day, Kevin saw more than I wanted him to see, but I'm thankful he did because he saved me from a horrible situation."

"You never say how bad it was or what your situation you were in."

"It's not anything you should be concerned about right now. When the time is right, I will let you know." I hoped that I could hold off on telling him when I was more emotionally stable and before my ex decided to make himself known. Alex hasn't shown his face at the shop recently.

"When is the time going to be right?"

"Don't you worry about that. I'll know when the time is right, and then I will tell you," I said honestly, taking a sip from my drink.

"My ears are always available for listening and are there for that purpose."

"I know, but not now. My ears are always open, too," I said with a smirk.

"I'm glad. But speaking of ears, how's that piercing?" he asked as I turned for him to see.

"Not infected, I've been cleaning it."

"Like you are supposed to," he said with a smile. We made small talk over the rest of the meal. Even after we finished eating, we sat there chatting about anything and everything. Something about Corey just clicked with me. He truly made me happy.

"Well, look at the time. I should be getting you home," Corey said as he adjusted his watch. A feeling of sadness came over me that our date was at an end.

I helped collect our trash and put it on the brown tray. I stood up from the booth, following Corey to the trash can before we exited the restaurant. Corey cupped my hand and led me to the passenger side of his car. He pulled the door open and allowed me to climb into the vehicle. He was the only one who seemed to know how to open this door.

Corey gripped my hand, pulling it into his lap while he drove the short distance back to my house. The subtle sound of some Foreigner song playing on the radio filling the car. I was full of smiles. Even though we weren't conversing anymore, the silence was still comforting.

Corey parked his car behind my Volkswagon, and I patiently waited for him to come around the tail end of the car and open my door for me. He opened the door, offering his hand to help me out, and slammed the door shut behind me. His arm snuck around my waist and firmly gripped my hip, pulling me close to walk side by side. Corey walked me to the front porch, where I stepped in front of him and turned to face him, knowing this would be our goodbye. Corey gripped my hips, tugging me to be held against his solid frame, his hands snaking around my body and cupping my ass.

"I enjoyed the date, and I want another," he said. A smile crept onto my face. I was relieved I hadn't fuck it up. Before I could respond, his lips were on mine. My arms acted on their own and instinctively wrapped around his neck, my fingers tangling into his hair as the kiss deepened.

Corey pulled his lips off mine, and I panted, trying to catch my breath, feeling my cheeks burn from embarrassment. Corey had this boyish smile on his face. "Now that's a good night kiss."

I chuckled as he leaned in for another intense kiss. His hands began to roam my body, and I began moaning softly into his lips at the sensation of his hands all over me. I began to feel a bulge pressing against my stomach. It was good to know that Corey was getting as turned on as I was. I broke the kiss and swung away from his embrace.

I told myself that I wasn't ready; I couldn't be ready. Yes, I wanted him. I wanted all of it with him because he made it feel good and right, but now was not the right time or place.

"Everything okay?" He asked, clueless.

I scratched at the back of my head, nodding. "Yeah, I'll talk to you later."

Before Corey could respond, I dove into the house without saying another word. I bolted up to my room, pacing in the small space. Why did I keep freaking out so much? There's nothing wrong with Corey getting turned on by me. Fuck, I don't even know if I could be sexually active after Alex had fucked me up. I looked out the window in time to see Corey drive off. Poor guy was probably just as confused as I was. Now, I would have to call and explain myself somehow to him. He's probably angry, too. I just gave him blue balls. He's probably going to drive home to take care of himself.

I flopped back on my bed. Images of Corey sprawled out on his bed naked, his cock fully erect, popped into my head. Just from what I had felt, Corey was bigger than Alex. I began to feel myself getting turned on by the visual image of an unclothed Corey. I could imagine him stroking his cock slowly, his moans would be raspy and deep. His moans came more often as his hand began to jerk his cock harder and faster. Hearing him moan my name as he jerked his hand faster was making me wetter and wetter. I was about to orgasm without even touching myself because the images were turning me on so much. He would growl my name between his gritted teeth as he began to cum over his chest. My legs bent inwards, my thighs pressing hard together, as I almost orgasmed myself. The images in my head of Corey masturbating will forever haunt me.

I needed to get my mind off Corey. I jumped up and began to pace my room again, but the activity wasn't helping. I reached for my phone, calling Corey up. I had to get this over and done with. The phone clicked, and I gasped as he answered.

"Hey, babes."

"Hey…are you busy?" I asked, hoping he was so my little imaginary scene of him masturbating was true.

"Not too busy for my beautiful, what's up?"

"Um, look. I'm sorry I freaked out on you. I enjoyed the kiss and the make-out session. Could I make it up to you? How about another date tomorrow?" I asked, biting my bottom lip, hoping he would agree and that I could now stop thinking of him playing with his cock.

"I'll be there at eight and take you out on my boat."

"Your boat?" I asked, shocked.

"Yes, my boat. Bring a swimsuit and a bag packed with what you need to stay for the night. You owe me a sleepover for dashing on me like that."

I smirked. Maybe by staying the night, I could get more intimate with him.

"Sounds good, see you at eight."

Chapter Five:

I woke up to my phone blaring through my room and smacked at the nightstand to turn it off before it woke everyone else. I rubbed a hand over my face, trying to wake up enough to get out of bed. I decided to shower, hoping the hot water would bring me to life.

After my shower, I returned to my room with a towel wrapped around my body and my hair in a second one. I stood in front of my closet, which had five outfits hanging in it. I sighed as I quickly pulled on my swimsuit. Well, it was a bikini bottom and a faded Motley Crue shirt that Kevin gave me when it no longer fit him. I pulled a pair of ripped jeans over my swim bottoms.

I pulled my hair into a tight bun so it wouldn't become a tangled mess from the water. I didn't even consider applying makeup because it would just get ruined. The only thing I bothered to do was to grab the bottle of sunblock I had for occasions like this. I looked at the two bags I had resting on my bed. Were two bags too much? One for today on the boat and one for the stay at his place.

I zipped up the bags before hitching them onto my shoulder and carried them downstairs. I set them down beside the front door. I entered the kitchen, sliding onto a bar stool to join the rest of the family.

"When is Corey going to be here?" Anita asked.

"Eight o'clock. We're planning to have breakfast before he takes me on his boat," I said as I looked at Kevin and Anita. "You guys never mentioned he has a boat and that you have been on it," I said as they looked at each other before Kevin looked at me.

"You never asked," he said as he casually drank his coffee.

"When are we going on Uncle Corey's boat again?" Jack asked as he put another spoonful of cereal in his mouth.

"Little Jack knows, so I can ask him all my questions. Jack, you won't lie to me, will you?" I asked as Jack shook his head no.

"Or you can ask Corey himself. You aren't going to bribe the information out of my son," Anita said.

"I won't bribe him. It's easy to get information from him when he has a bowl of ice cream." I smiled as I answered Anita.

"Would you get mad if Corey did the same thing?" Anita asked.

I glared at her because she had a point. I wouldn't want Corey to find out about Alex through Jack. Corey needed to learn about that from me and not from a seven-year-old.

"You do know that you guys are worse than my guilty conscience. I've got an angel and a devil, gah," I said, glaring equally between Kevin and Anita.

"Well, this angel of conscience needs to get Jack to school and get to my cycling class. Kevin, will you be home when I get here?" Anita asked.

"Probably not. I need to go into the office and finish the paperwork I didn't get to last night," Kevin answered as he took another big gulp of his coffee.

"Well, I guess the last one out needs to lock up." Anita stated. I patted my pockets, realizing I hadn't grabbed my house keys. I jogged upstairs, retrieving my keys from my dresser before I headed back downstairs.

"How long are you staying at Corey's?" Kevin asked, coffee in his hand when I approached the bottom floor.

"I honestly have no idea. However long he lets me stay."

"He may keep you there forever, so you may be moving in."

"I wouldn't hold your breath. You can't get rid of me that easily," I said with a chuckle.

"Aunt Melanie, I don't want you to move out," Jack said as he walked down the stairs, pulling the strap of his backpack over his shoulder.

"I won't, Jack, at least not right now," I said as I ruffled his hair. Sometimes, Jack melts my heart. The things he does make me wish that I would have kids one day, but then I bring myself to the reality that I may not ever bear children.

I think of my current situation and know I am barely scraping by. I want to get my life back on track before I have any kids, but I also know that kids sometimes happen before you are ready.

Corey is the first guy that I have even considered dating since Alex. I still fear that Corey could turn into Alex. When I first met and started to date Alex, Alex was similar to Corey. It was when I moved into the dorms with him that everything changed. I should be more worried about spending these next couple of nights at Corey's. What if he becomes exactly like

Alex behind closed doors? What if he locks me in his house? What if he is worse than Alex? How much do I know about this Corey guy?

I didn't think Alex would abuse me until that one drunken night. *He wanted to celebrate something, so I made him a steak dinner upon his request. I saw the steak sizzling in the pan and brought a knife to the steak, trying to cut it slightly to see if it was done cooking. It looked medium well to me, just how Alex likes it. Pulling it from the pan, I plopped it onto his plate, already topped with mashed potatoes and green beans. I grabbed the A1 sauce from the fridge and took that with me to the table.*

"Dinner is ready," I called to Alex, who was lying drunk on the couch. Alex stumbled over to the table with a half-drunk bottle of beer in hand. I grabbed my plate to join him and enjoy the meal. Once I slid into my seat, the clatter of his silverware dropping caught my attention.

"What's this?" He snarled.

"Steak, like you requested," I whispered as he pushed back, the chair scraping against the floor. Fear overcame my body as Alex stomped to my side of the table with his beer and plate in hand.

"Does that look well done to you?" He growled right outside my ear.

"I thought you liked it medium well," I whispered, not wanting to look at him. It was then that I felt pressure and then pain with the sounds of glass shattering. Liquid began to douse my hair and roll down my face. I was in mere shock as my lip began to quiver.

"Fuck, that felt good. Now, clean up the mess and remake my dinner. I got to go get more beer," he snarled as I saw him take his keys off the hook. The door slammed behind him, leaving me sitting there covered in glass and beer. I began to pat my head, unsure if the glass broke the skin or if I was bleeding anywhere.

"Melanie! Earth to Melanie!" Kevin called, finally snapping me out of my flashback. I scratched at the back of my head, ensuring it was just a flashback, not real life.

"Huh?" I asked.

"Flashback?" Kevin asked as I nodded, not wanting to go into more detail with Kevin. Kevin already knew too much of what had happened in my past. " Everything okay? Nothing to be nervous about going to Corey's."

"How'd you know?" I asked.

"Lucky guess. He is nothing like Alex. He was raised right, and I know he would never lay a hand on a female or start a fight. He's a big cuddly bear." Kevin's words reassured me as I let out a sigh. I needed to trust Kevin because he had known Corey much longer than I had.

"Alright, but if you are wrong, I have the right to rub it in your face," I said as Kevin rolled his eyes.

"Alright, deal." He agreed as I stuck my pinky out for a pinky promise with him. Kevin hooked his pinky with mine to make it official. I heard the doorbell, looked at the front door, and then back to Kevin.

"Your man awaits."

I rolled my eyes and chuckled at his playfulness. I got up to answer the door. I didn't know why Kevin was still waiting, but it was probably to make sure I didn't back out at the last minute due to my insecurities.

When I opened the door to see Corey on the other side, I tried not to let my mouth drop open. Damn, he was looking finer than wine. Not everyone can rock a pair of swim trunks, but Corey certainly could. His swim trunks were black with blue at the top around his waist. He was wearing this gray, skin-tight wife beater to expose his fully tattooed arm sleeves along with the tattoos on his neck. He was rocking a pair of light brown shaded sunglasses and a fedora that was an off-shade of white that somehow matched his attire.

"Good morning, beautiful. Are you ready to go?" Corey asked. A smile spread across his lips, and I couldn't help but smile too.

"Yeah, I just have to tell Kevin I'm heading out and grab my bags." I turned around to find Kevin leaning against the back of the couch, watching the whole interaction. He took a big gulp of his coffee. I could tell he was fighting a smile.

"You guys have fun, but not too much fun because I don't have bail money." He laughed at himself.

"What are you implying? If anything, I'll get away because I have the car for it," Corey said as I gasped.

"You'll leave me?" I was shocked. Corey let out a chuckle and had a bright smile crossed his face.

"Never!" Corey said while shaking his head no. Corey reached out to grab my bags, resting beside the door. "Would Batman ever leave Robin and vice versa?" Corey asked as I thought about it. "No answer? Good." Corey said with a wink, but he was right. No superhero duo would leave the other behind. I stepped out onto the front porch with Corey, and my smile must have gotten bigger and wider. "See you later, Kev."

"Have fun, and just relax," Kevin tried to say, but his glare was directed at me.

I nodded. Oddly, my nerves had returned but were amplified from before. I pulled the door shut behind me. I walked along the paved sidewalk toward Corey's muscle car. Corey set my bag down to pull the passenger door open for me. I climbed into the vehicle, watching him as he pushed the door shut, and I watched him through the side window.

I couldn't believe that I was doing this. I was sitting in Corey's muscle car, about to go on his boat for the whole afternoon. I hadn't thought about dating since leaving Alex. I may have gone out to do a few things with Kevin's family, but I was never alone with a man I was interested in. I was beginning to really like Corey. I had all these butterflies when I was with him. He was the sweetest guy ever. I don't know what he saw in me, and I was so scared of entering into whatever this was. I was scared that he might suddenly snap or leave me broken-hearted. I had dated Alex for years. We were high school sweethearts, and he had turned my world upside down. Corey was doing the same thing but in a completely different way. Do I even know what love is? Alex certainly never made the butterflies dance around in my stomach.

I was snapped out of my thoughts when I heard the driver's door being pulled open. My head twisted to look at Corey sliding into his seat and pulling the door shut. With a flick of his wrist, the engine purred to life. A smile crept across my face. Why did I love this car of his? Was it because it was a classic car or because I was happy about who I was with?

"You did bring your bathing suit, right?" Corey asked.

"I'm wearing it underneath this," I answered, looking at the outfit I had pulled on.

Corey nodded as he shifted the car to drive before pulling away from the curb.

"Alright, where should we go to have breakfast?"

"Isn't there a rule not to eat an hour before getting into the water?"

"Well, we aren't going to get into the water for another hour," Corey said.

"Denny's?" I suggested.

"What about IHOP? I am in love with their Strawberry-Banana French Toast."

"That does sound delicious. Let's do that," I said as he smiled.

"IHOP it is," he said as he turned toward the closed gate to leave the neighborhood. We sat there awkwardly, watching the black iron gate begin to swing out.

"Thanks for taking me out on your boat today, for allowing me to crash at your place for a couple of days, and for opening doors for me," I said awkwardly. I looked into my lap, where my hands played nervously.

"Please don't say thank you for everything. I was raised to treat a woman properly," Corey stated as I nodded. Kevin had been trying to tell me all about how Corey was great and such a sweet guy.

"How long have you had a boat and a place in Florida?" I asked out of curiosity.

"My boat, for a year and a half, and my place in Florida, I'd say three or more years. I got a boat because I live near the beach and boat pier in Florida. My friends always liked going out into the ocean or being on the lake, so I figured it was smart to invest in a boat."

"If you can afford those items with your other job, why are you still with Kevin or come back to Kevin's shop?" I asked as Corey let out a sigh.

"I don't need the pay from Kevin, but is it wrong that I offered to come back to help his publicity and get closer to his secretary?" He asked all this with a boyish smile on his face. I rolled my eyes at him, not believing he had said that.

"Nothing wrong with that," I said, blushing a tad. I pushed a strand of hair behind my ear as I looked out the window. "But what place do you like more, here or in Florida?"

"Florida. Florida is so much nicer, with the weather and everything…"

"Still, I don't understand why you came back here." I shook my head in disbelief with a chuckle.

"I chose to come back because I've got friends living here, and I just happened to meet this beautiful girl who's won my heart. I can't just let her go. I'm stuck coming back for her."

Corey had a bright smile on his face. His eyes glanced at me briefly before they darted back to the road. Corey always said the right things. He made me feel wanted and special.

When the light became green, he turned left, and we continued. It wasn't much further until he pulled into the IHOP parking lot.

I tried the door, and surprisingly, it opened for me this time. Maybe today was going to be my lucky day. I climbed out and met Corey in front of the car. Walking beside him toward the front door, I felt his hand slowly slide into mine. It felt nice to hold hands with someone again, but the sensation felt awkward at first, as it does with all new relationships. His fingers folded between mine to interlock our fingers. There was this static between our hands, and I could feel his pulse pounding against the palm of my hand. Corey reached out to open the restaurant door, letting me walk in first. Then, he quickly grabbed the second door so I wouldn't have to pull it open.

"Thank-" I began to say as he glared at me.

"Don't you dare finish that," he said.

I bit at my bottom lip, holding back some giggles as I sheepishly stepped through the second door. I moved aside, allowing him to step into the restaurant beside me.

"A table for two?" the hostess asked.

We both nodded. Corey let me walk before him to follow the hostess to a two-person booth. I slid into one side of the booth to face Corey, who was now sitting down on his side of the booth. The hostess set the menus in front of us to look over until the waitress came to greet us.

"Where is this Strawberry-Banana French toast you were raving about?" I glanced up at him from the plastic menu I had flipped open. Corey opened his menu, his gaze staring down at it as well. I browsed over the pages before me when my eyes landed on the meal he talked highly of. "I think I'll copy you and get that as well."

"You aren't copying me. It just means you have good taste when it comes to food. I'm positive that you will love it, too." Corey flipped his menu closed and rested his hands over it.

"Does that give me a plus in your book?" I asked curiously.

"Most definitely. A girl with good taste buds is number three, right after a good personality, and loves tattoos."

"If they didn't like tattoos, they wouldn't like these tattooed-sleeved arms of yours." I reached out, tracing my finger over one of the tattoos that had drawn my attention. I looked up at Corey, locking eyes with him, and the moment became even more intimate than I had expected. The static between his skin and mine amplified. I wanted to touch more of him, all of him. I wanted to feel every part of his body against mine. I looked at Corey again as I continued tracing the designs, and he watched intently, his tongue swiping over his bottom lip.

"I can buy those things that cover them up."

"Wouldn't you get annoyed having to wear those 24/7? What about intimate moments? The girl you're with would notice it doesn't match your skin tone." I said truthfully. Corey had an even tan, and the sleeves he was discussing to cover his beautiful tattoos wouldn't match the rest of his body. Corey let out a manly laugh at my comment.

"If that is her biggest concern during an intimate moment, then she may have issues." Corey and I burst into laughter. I felt myself blush, and the thought of him naked and masturbating shot back into my head momentarily. I had to shake my head to erase those images to continue this meal.

"You're probably right…"

"Plus, the sleeves cannot hide the tattoo on my belly button, back, or neck."

"That is what make-up is for."

"But that would just rub off from the sweat on our bodies."

"Why are we even discussing this?" I asked when I began to get images of Corey naked in certain sexual positions. I had to shake my head to try to push the images out of my head so I wouldn't get awkward sitting here, thinking about sex with him.

"You started it. I am just trying to finish it."

"Well, you win," I said. Corey gave me the brightest smile when the waitress approached our table.

I watched Corey's actions. He didn't even give the tall blonde with double D breasts a second look after she left the table. Alex would have been drooling over her, and his eyes wouldn't have left our waitress the whole time we were here. I was shocked that Corey wasn't even giving her a second look. I guess not all men are pigs like Alex, then. Corey was winning my heart over in every way possible.

"So, tell me more about this job in Florida?" I asked.

Corey sighed, and he seemed a bit hesitant to respond to me. What was he hiding? What kind of job would you be ashamed of? Stripper? Him, a stripper? Doubtful. Trashman? Not down in Florida. Disney costume character? I was trying to think of any possible job he would be so hesitant to answer with. He finally responded with, "I'm an entertainer."

"An entertainer? So, you act? Or a magician? Circus act? Do you blow fire?"

"You can say that I act," he clarified. He was an actor, so he was famous? Why was I giddy that I was dating an actor?

"Do you act in theater shows or movies? Acting is a wide range of careers."

"Uh, I act on a local television show."

"How would you get cast on a local show in Florida if you lived in Pennsylvania?"

"They saw the work I had done up here and liked what they saw. They contacted my casting agent and flew me to Florida for an audition. I flew down, did the audition, and got cast for the role."

"So, you are signed strictly with that one show? Can't you work on other shows?"

"Not due to my contract with them."

"Oh, they give out contracts?"

"Yep. It was a four-year contract, and I still have one more year with the show. If they want me to continue, they will try negotiating to keep me, or I will return to being a free agent."

"Why wouldn't they still want you if you are prominent in the show? If you are good, wouldn't they want to keep you on? Are you a lead character on the show?"

"How do you know I am good if you haven't seen me act?" he asked. That was what he heard? Not the other questions I had asked?

"I just presumed you were." As I bit my bottom lip, I asked,

"Would I ever be able to go on set with you?"

"One day. I'm pretty sure Kevin, Anita, and Jack would love to return."

"They've been?"

"A couple of times. Jack loved it more than his parents."

"Well, Jack is amused by the simplest things." I laughed when the server placed our food on the table. We thanked her before we dove into the food. Our conversations dwindled since we spent more time indulging in breakfast than talking.

I guess we were both hungry. I was happy I wasn't the only one eating at hyper-speed. Corey seemed to be eating just as fast or faster than I was. Why is it that when you are starving, you can't seem to slow down eating?

I wondered what type of show he was acting in. Soap operas? Comedy? Action? Oddly, a part of me didn't want to investigate more. He would have given me all the details if he wanted me to know more. Considering he didn't go into further details about this television show, I just figured maybe he wanted to keep his acting life in Florida separate from the badass piercing career he had in Pennsylvania. If it were a local show, no one here would know he was an actor or famous. Maybe it was a relief not being recognized, and he didn't want to mix the two. So, he is living two lives. Would he ever take me to Florida, or what if he only wants me in his life here in Pennsylvania? What if he has a girlfriend or wife in Florida that I don't know about? Why must I think of anything and everything that makes me want to push myself far away from him? I was getting upset and wanting to push myself away from Corey, thinking these negative things.

"Are you ready to go?" he asked.

My head snapped up to see him wiping his mouth with a

napkin. I nodded yes before I tossed the used napkin onto my empty plate and slid out of the booth. Corey reached for the check on the table, carrying the black bifold in hand while his free hand slid into mine. I dug into my purse to find my wallet to grab some cash.

"What are you doing?" he asked, noticing the wallet I was holding in my hand.

"I was going to pay for my half of the bill."

"Why do you think you need to pay for half?"

"Because it was my food, too."

"I understand that, but I have the means to spoil my girl, so you never have to worry about helping pay."

His girl? I was his girl? What does he mean by that? Are we in a relationship now? I pushed my wallet back into my purse as I stood beside him. I wrapped my arms around a muscled, tattooed arm, hugging it as I watched him pay for our meals. Corey glanced at me during the process, and his lips curled up in a smile each time. He signed the receipt, returned it to the hostess, and led me back to his car. I continued to hug his arm while we walked out of the building. He led me to the passenger side, and I turned to lean back against his car. Corey stood in front of me with his hands gripping my hips firmly. He spread his legs to be the same height as me, and I smiled as I stared into his brown eyes.

"Was I or was I not right about that French toast?"

"You were right, and it was quite delicious."

"Told you."

I smiled as he pulled open the passenger's door, and I climbed in. I began to buckle up as he shut the door and went to the driver's side.

"Now, off to the boat."

I nodded with a big smile, hearing the engine softly come to life. He pulled out of the parking lot. I let him drive to wherever he docked his boat. He was in charge for the day. Hearing him say that I was his girl was playing repeatedly in my head. What did he mean? I know we had gone out yesterday, and today was a make-up date for me freaking out on him yesterday. It's been so long for me that I may have lost my understanding of the logistics of dating.

"Corey?" I softly asked, seeing him glance at me.

"Yeah, babe," he answered. Did he just call me babe?

"Back there, at IHOP....What did you mean by me being your girl? I know we have gone out twice, but I didn't know these were considered dates. Were they dates?" I asked sheepishly. I looked down in my lap, knowing I was blushing for even bringing it up.

I heard him let out a soft chuckle. "Do you know how cute you are when you are blushing?"

I gasped and looked at him. "Corey! I'm being serious."

He chuckled. "I thought they were dates. I couldn't pass up an opportunity to take out such a beautiful girl. And if you don't mind, considering you are an equal part of this, I would love for you to be my girlfriend."

Corey kept glancing at me as he drove, and his eyes always returned to the road that took us out of the city limits. I liked Corey. The way he had made me feel was like nothing I had ever felt before. My palms were always sweaty, butterflies had taken up permanent residence in my stomach when he was around, and my smile never left my face. I keep hearing Kevin's voice echoing in my head about giving Corey a shot. I may not know Corey as well as Kevin does, but Kevin trusts him implicitly. Oddly, I find myself trusting Corey more day by day, with what he calls these dates we have been on. Hell, I am placing my trust in him by allowing him to take me on a boat and stay at his place.

"So, what do you say, babe?"

His voice snapped me out of my thoughts. I looked at Corey, who was now staring at me while we sat at a stop sign. We were the only car at the four-way stop, so he had time to kill. I instantly became nervous and a tad withdrawn.

"I-I, uh, say yes, but…"

"But?" Corey asked, a little in shock. He then proceeded to drive through the intersection.

"It's nothing, never mind," I said. I didn't want to ruin today by bringing up Alex.

"I know you had a bad ex, but I promise, whatever he did, I am not like him. I will hopefully prove that to you over time," he said as I nodded. I tucked some loose strands of hair behind my ear before letting my hand fall back into my lap.

"You're doing okay so far," I said with a slight smirk. I saw that he smiled.

"I am glad to hear that," he said.

"And he didn't have a boat."

"He didn't even have a boat. What a tragedy," Corey said, his sarcasm getting me to chuckle. The drive was longer than I thought, but it seemed to pass by fast because we chatted the whole time.

Chapter Six:

Corey parked the car in his assigned parking spot in the pier parking garage. I thought seeing his name on the parking spot was awesome, but I didn't want him to think I was weird for being amused by that.

"Will my bag be okay in your trunk?"

"Yeah. No one will break in or know it is there."

I nodded as I grabbed the smaller bag meant for the boat. Corey grabbed a bag for himself.

"Lead the way," I said as he smirked.

Corey reached for my hand, interlacing his fingers with mine again as he led the way. We approached a boat that was a lot nicer than I had imagined it would be.

Corey handed me his bag when we had stopped at the edge of the wooden pier, staring at the white boat with beige trim. I held the bag for him as he reached up, pulled the ladder down, and locked it so we could climb up. My jaw dropped as I watched him toss our bags onto the ship.

"I hope you didn't have anything fragile in there." He looked slightly uncomfortable as he explained, "It's easier to climb up without a bag weighing you down."

I began climbing the ladder and felt the boat gently rocking with the water's current. It was subtle, not strong enough to throw me from the ladder. I just hoped I wouldn't get seasick.

As I approached the top of the ladder, I swung my foot over to step onto the boat. I took a moment to take in my new surroundings. I'd never been on a boat before. I turned to look back down to the pier just in time to see Corey had begun to climb the ladder. Soon enough, he stepped onto the boat beside me and began pulling the ladder onto the ship.

"I'll go pull the anchor up and get this baby started. If you want to take our bags below deck, the steps are over there." He nodded in the general direction, and I followed where he had nodded, seeing a set of stairs that led downwards. I picked up the two bags he tossed aboard and walked below the deck. I set the bags down at the bottom of the stairs and stared around the room.

It wasn't a large area, but I saw a kitchen with a sink, fridge, and microwave, plus one of those stove tops you would put on the counter. A few cabinets and a table that could seat at least four people sat directly across from his kitchen area. I walked further in, finding the bathroom. It was small, but it would do for the time being. I noticed a door that was closed. I bit my bottom lip, wanting to open the door to see what was on the other side. I was curious about what this boat had to offer. Would I be too nosey if I opened this door? Maybe it's just a closet. I slightly panicked as my hand grasped the gold doorknob and twisted. My heart beat faster as I opened the dark wooden door to reveal a king-sized bed and dresser. It was a freaking bedroom!

I turned around, shutting the door behind me. I sighed in relief that Corey hadn't caught me snooping. I headed back up to the upper deck. While making my way up the stairs, I scrambled to grab the railing when the boat jerked into motion. After finding my balance, I moved up the last few steps.

I tried not to get lost on the boat, somehow finding my way to Corey. He stood behind the captain's wheel with his back to me. I noticed he was now shirtless, exposing a dragon tattoo between his shoulder blades. I bit my bottom lip as I slowly approached the extremely attractive man I was with. I stepped up beside him, trying to keep my eyes ahead, but I couldn't control my eyes from roaming over his exposed body. My eyes dropped to his pelvic area, and I bit at my bottom lip, trying to imagine how big of a package he had. I shook my head, trying to stop those thoughts so I wouldn't turn red as a tomato from embarrassment.

"This is a nice boat you have." I broke the silence. Corey's lips curled up into a smile. I couldn't tell whether or not he was looking at me from behind the dark lenses of his sunglasses.

"Thanks," he said. I walked past the captain's wheel to claim a beach chair and watched the greenery pass us by as he steered the boat down the river.

"Do you ever sleep on here?" I asked curiously.

"I have once or twice. Usually, if I decide to make the boat trip down to Florida or back instead of flying." He answered as we sailed along.

"I bet it is a beautiful sail from here to there."

"Very much so, but it's a long trip. If you want it just over and done with, I would suggest flying."

"Why have you done the sailing thing?"

"I've done it to get some peace and quiet. I find sailing clears my head."

I nodded, noticing that the river was getting wider and wider. Were we entering the ocean? I jumped to my feet, running to the railing for a better view. "Are we in the ocean now?!?!" I asked excitedly, only to hear him laugh at my excitement. I looked at him over my shoulder, and he was nothing but smiles.

"Yep, but not for long. I promise it'll be a few hours tour, and we won't get lost like on *Gilligan's Island*," he joked.

I rolled my eyes as I stood there, staring out at the pure blue ocean. With the breeze blowing in my hair, I felt free. Oddly, I wanted to copy the scene from *Titanic* but felt that was too cliché.

"Do you have any favorite spots out here? How do you even remember where the spots are?" I asked as he chuckled.

"I do have a couple of favorite spots. But as to finding where they are or remembering, there's a GPS in the boat that will tell you the latitude and longitude. If you jot those down, you will never get lost or forget those particular spots."

"That must come in handy for sure. Are you taking me to one of those today?" I asked.

"Nowhere else would compare," he said with a smirk. I smiled and went back to the lawn chair and stretched out. I was trying to relax while letting him do the sailing. I couldn't help but glance over at him.

He was extremely attractive, rocking nothing but his swim-suit, flip-flops, and sunglasses. I had left him in charge of planning this trip and trusted that he wouldn't risk our lives. Why was I so confident and comfortable with him being in charge of our lives right now? I hated being in any type of vehicle with Alex. I feared the worst-case scenario in any moving vehicle with him. Yet, here I was with Corey, sailing on the ocean where he could throw me overboard and leave me for dead. Something about Corey made me feel secure and safe. He had this masculinity about him that made me feel safe and comfortable. He oozed this confidence that made him even more attractive.

My eyes roamed over Corey's half-naked body, and I nibbled at my bottom lip. I hadn't found myself attracted to a man sexually or found myself wanting to experience sex in ages. My sex life with Alex was complicated. I never wanted anything from him. How could I want that from him with the way he treated me? My mind began to think of the times I was with Alex. I momentarily closed my eyes and reopened them to see Alex above me.

I heard him moan with pleasure, but it wasn't him between my legs, feeling something cold, slender, and nothing human-like pumping hard and fast into me.

"You know what this is?" he growled. I shook my head no, wanting it all to end. If it wasn't Alex, I wasn't sure what his sick mind was using or doing to me.

"This is my Smith and Wesson." I gulped and swallowed a big ball of air as he began to thrust the blunt object into me roughly. "Remember this forever. If you ever think that this tight little pussy of yours can be fucked by anyone but me, then Mr. Smith and Wesson is going to become reacquainted with you. He is going to blow a bullet right through your pussy, killing you from the inside out, and then he's gonna kill the man who even tried to take this from me."

My body tensed up as I began to remember when this happened. Tears began welling up in my eyes, and I completely forgot I was on Corey's boat. I feared ever being intimate again, but Corey had that spunk I liked and was sexually attracted to. I felt that if we eased slowly into it, then I might be open to sexual relations. This whole relationship with Corey needs to be slowly eased into. I hoped we could build trust by spending time together here and at his house. We had already made ourselves exclusive, and that was a big step toward wanting to get more comfortable with him.

"Hey, beautiful. Could you come help?" Corey called out. I got up from where I lay and crossed to the captain's wheel. "Can you hold onto this as still as you possibly can?"

I grasped the wheel and held on tightly. I tried to watch what he was doing from where I was, but it was hard to determine what he was doing. Based on the large splash I had just heard, I realized he was tossing the anchor overboard. Was this the spot he was taking me to? It was a nice spot, and I could see why he had picked here.

"Alright, we are anchored. You don't have to hold onto the wheel anymore. Are you ready to go in?" he asked.

I let out an 'uh' before I followed him to the back of the boat. Nerves and butterflies filled my stomach, hoping he wouldn't question my swimsuit choice. I slid my shoes off and began to pull the shorts off to show the bottom half of my bikini. I kept the Motley Crue shirt over my bikini top, as I always swam in it.

"You're not taking off the shirt?" he asked, rubbing some sunblock onto his skin. I looked down, noticing all the marks on my legs. He hadn't said anything about them, but I knew that my upper body was far worse than that. I wasn't ready to bare the rest of my body to him yet.

"Umm, no. I'm more comfortable with it on," I answered. I bit my bottom lip, and he shrugged.

"Whatever you are comfortable with, sweetie." He handed me the sunblock he had just been using, and I rubbed the white cream onto my bare legs. I walked over to the boat's edge.

"Have you ever gone diving?"

"No, you?" I asked as he smiled. Corey jumped off the boat, doing a backflip and landing feet first in the water. I rolled my eyes, waiting for him to resurface. Guys are such show-offs.

"You show off!" I yelled down at him. Corey chuckled and pushed the wet hair out of his face. I began climbing down the ladder and jumped when I reached the end. I swam to the surface, gasping for air as he smiled.

"You trust me?" he asked as I looked at him questionably.

"Why?" I asked with uncertainty.

"Come on." He began to swim behind me, and I followed wherever he led.

He reached over, grabbing my hand and his other hand pointing in a general direction. "Watch over there," he instructed.

My eyes followed where his finger pointed in time to dolphins jumping in the distance, and I couldn't help but smile.

"Sometimes, I like going to that spot and getting into the water to swim with them, but not today. There's a cave that I can take you into if you want."

"Sounds great," I said with a grin. feeling adventurous. I felt like I hadn't lived until I met Corey. With Alex, I had been trapped, his slave in every aspect. Even after escaping that relationship, I still felt I was in a prison of his making. I live at Kevin's house freely but don't get paid. If I do, it's just enough to buy necessities. My paycheck isn't worth it, and Kevin deserves to keep it to cover my rent and food. I still felt like a captive in a way. All I do is go to work and come home.

What kind of life is that?

At work, I'm always fearful of Alex rolling in and that he will drag me away to my death sentence. Maybe that's why I'm being so daring today. Because, after being with Alex, I was at death's door. He had no mercy. He can still easily take my life. Kevin has tried his damnedest to stop that day from coming.

Corey and I entered the cave, and the walls were sparkling from the sun's reflection off the water. We swam to a plateau at the edge of the cave we could sit on. I kicked my feet to keep afloat, watching as Corey used his arm strength to pull himself out of the water. It was one of the sexiest moves I had ever seen. His muscles were tense and stood out, the water droplets rolling down his skin, making everything more defined.

I planted my hands beside him, trying to be as graceful as he was in pulling myself up. I knew I wasn't as strong as him and that it wouldn't look as sexy. I felt him wrap his strong arms around me and help lift my body the rest of the way. I turned to sit beside him on the plateau. The cave seemed magical.

"What's with the sparkles?" I was mesmerized by them.

"Crystals that no one has dared to dig out and risk being killed while doing it," Corey explained while looking up at the cave ceiling. We sat there in silence for a lengthy period.

"This is nice, Corey. Thank you for bringing me here." I broke the silence. A smile came to both of our faces. It was oddly romantic, staring at the cave ceiling as the crystals sparkled from the little daylight shining in.

"I think we should get back to the boat." Corey broke the silence. We both jumped back into the water, swimming easily to the boat. Corey grabbed the ladder, pulling himself up far enough before reaching down and helping me hook onto the ladder. We got to the top, and he assisted me onto the ship, where our bodies pressed against each other awkwardly.

"I'll get the towels and some drinks. You can stay out here if you want." He scratched at the back of his head in the uncomfortable silence.

I nodded as I walked to where my shorts were and claimed one of the lawn chairs.

Corey returned with our towels, along with two bottles of water. "A towel and water," he said, handing me just that. I wrapped the towel around my lower half, removed the tie from my hair to shake it out, and sat down.

I opened the water to take a big drink from it because I was dying of thirst.

"You want to change, or are you fine in these clothes until we get to my place?" Corey asked as he squinted at me due to the sun's position.

"I'll be fine like this until we get to your place." I scooted my chair closer to him. "Now, you don't have to squint so hard to see me."

"I like this." He stretched his arm out, and it was the right distance between us to lay across my chair and under my neck. I rolled onto my side to face him better and scooted closer, resting my head on his shoulder. My hand rested flat on his chest, feeling how solid it was. My finger began to trace slowly along his defined six-pack. My fingers got to the hem of his shorts, and I rolled my bottom lip between my teeth. My blood was starting to flow to all the right areas, and I had to stop what I was doing before I got myself too worked up.

"Are we going to leave now?" I asked.

"Nah, I was planning on making a quick lunch on board before starting the journey back to the dock."

I nodded.

"Chef Corey. I think that would be a nice side job."

"Don't get used to it, and it isn't going to be much."

"I am sure it will be great whatever you make, and I don't expect much. I am used to peanut butter and jelly sandwiches because that is practically all that Jack eats," I said, and we both got a good laugh out of it.

"It may not be much better than that, but I think I can make more than just peanut butter and jelly sandwiches, so you're lucky."

"Well, aren't you Mister Betty Crocker?"

"Far from it. I would love to be Guy Fieri, where I can just go places and eat rather than cook the food." I laughed even harder as he said, "I'm just saying, when was the last time you saw him cook something?"

"I'm laughing because you've got a good point there," I said with a smile. Corey brushed his fingers through my hair, gripped a handful firmly, and I felt him pull my head back slightly. I had to hold back a groan as he pressed his lips roughly against mine. Corey's hand roamed up my body. I could feel his hand cup my breast, and his finger began to rub over my nipple.

I followed his lead, my hand roaming over his upper body, sliding lower to the hem of his swim trunks before I became unsure. I worked up the courage to go further, running my hand over the front of his swim trunks, being greeted by his thickening hard-on. Moans escaped my mouth from surprise. My hand began to stroke him through the shorts.

I felt his hand caress my pussy through my bikini bottom. I instinctively opened my legs wider so he had better access. I wanted to feel his fingers on my pussy. He must have read my mind because I felt his fingers slip underneath the fabric. I jumped a little at the sensation, and suddenly, I wasn't sure if I was ready.

"Too much?" he asked. I nodded and ran a hand through my hair. Corey quickly removed his hand, and I scooted back some. "Sorry," he leaned forward and gave me a soft kiss.

"Don't be, it's not you." I felt horrible that he felt he had to apologize for the sexual connection we had. "It's just my ex…"

"No need to explain. I can wait," he said with a reassuring smile and gave me a wink. "Now, I need to see about that food. You want to come keep me company?" he asked. I smiled slightly and nodded as I followed him down to the kitchen. I slid into the little booth table and watched him cook. Corey began to slide on some gloves, glancing over his shoulder at me momentarily to ask me, "Are you allergic to anything?"

"No. What are you cooking?"

"Do you mind getting messy?"

"No, now I'm officially afraid."

"Don't be. Trust me, you'll like it," he said confidently.

I watched him cut up some onions and green peppers before he put some meat into a pan.

"You didn't have to cook a fancy meal for me."

"It's not going to be all that fancy because this is going to be sandwiches," he said. I began to wonder what it was that he was cooking.

"Do you cook big meals like this for yourself?" I asked curiously.

"Eh, sometimes if I feel like it and have time. Other times, I don't like making big meals since it is just me. I know I will have leftovers, but it's something for us to eat for dinner or tomorrow." He shrugged.

"Where'd you learn this recipe?"

"My mother," he said as I smiled.

"Are you close to your parents?"

"You can say that."

"Where do they live? Around here or in Florida?"

"Neither." He said as he glanced over with a smile. I looked at him with a question in my eyes. "They live in Cincinnati."

"Any siblings?"

"One, and it's a brother..."

"Poor parents, having two boys."

"What about you?"

"I have one of each. I was the middle child but the rebel."

"What was the worst thing you did to your parents?" he asked me as he leaned against the tiny counter. I presumed he was waiting for the meat to brown.

"I kind of ran away for a month or two while I was in high school, and because of it, I almost didn't graduate," I stated as I bit my bottom lip.

"Why in the world did you do that?"

"Because of my ex. I thought I was in love and my parents hated him. They thought he was bad for me, but I didn't see it that way, so I ran away."

"Were you at his house?"

"Yes and no. I would come over for dinner some nights. The nights I didn't have dinner with them, I would sneak in through his bedroom window when his parents went to bed. He would zap leftovers for me and tell his parents he was staying up late to do homework, and the leftovers were a midnight snack. I would leave before they would come to check on him in the morning," I explained, staring blankly at the grayish-blue table in front of me.

"How long ago did you two break up? I am assuming he was your only ex. You were together a long time if you were high school sweethearts."

"We broke up about six months ago, but sometimes it seems less due to other circumstances. It's still very fresh in my mind."

"I figured that out from what happened at the mall. Why did you two break up?"

"That is a story for a different time," I responded as it fell silent. "Whatever you are cooking smells good."

"Thanks. Do you know how to cook anything?"

"A few things. Do you want me to cook you something tonight?"

"Yeah, I'll even take you to the store to pick up whatever you need."

"You're on. So, are you allergic to anything?"

"Nope, besides bullshit."

"Of course. We're all allergic to that." I chuckled. "Do you need help with anything?" I asked.

He shook his head no while he reached into a different cupboard. I recognized the Hawaiian roll packaging.

"I've never had the buns of those."

"Do you like their rolls?"

"Yes."

"It's just like their rolls but in a gigantic form."

"Rolls on steroids?"

"Yep. A way better analogy than what I had," he laughed. Corey pulled down two paper plates and put a bun on each one before adding the last ingredients. I saw him stir for a few minutes.

"I could get used to a man that can cook."

"But you shouldn't. I'm not home every night to do it. What do you think of a man that isn't home every night?"

"Well, I understand. You have work in Florida, so it would be ridiculous to expect you to come home every night if you work for a couple of days there," I said truthfully. "Would you expect me to go with you?"

"I might occasionally because I would need to bring a plus one with that job."

"Really?" I was curious about what he would need a plus one for.

"Yeah, but it's nothing anytime soon, so you can relax."

"I just hope I can live up to the standards of your job."

"Trust me, you are beyond the standards because there are some girls…" He broke off as he shook his head, and I couldn't help but chuckle because that was all he had to do.

"Note taken," I said with a chuckle.

Corey turned off the stove and began scooping the contents from the pan onto the buns. He carried the plates to the table, sliding my plate in front of me.

"I don't have much to drink besides water, and I think I may have milk."

"Water is fine." Corey grabbed us new water bottles before he sat down across from where I sat.

"This looks delicious," I said as I looked at my plate. "What do you call this?"

"It's a Philly cheesesteak sloppy Joe," he answered.

"Hmm, interesting." I picked it up to take a bite, only for some of the contents to fall out of the sandwich. "Well, I hope I still have some on my sandwich, and I'm sorry if I become a disgusting eater."

"No worries, I'm going to be just as messy and disgusting."

"Why even make this if you knew that would happen?" I asked with a chuckle.

"To make sure you aren't some prude that won't eat this type of food." He took a bite as I grinned.

It was quite good, and I covered my mouth as I slowly chewed and swallowed it.

"Prude? For not eating this? You had previous relationships that won't eat this?"

"Well, not this per se, but they were afraid to get a little messy with their food. There was one girl who wouldn't eat anything with her hands. She HAD to have silverware and even ate pizza with a fork."

"Yeah, no. I don't mind using my hands, especially for pizza and sandwiches. How would she eat ribs?"

"You eat ribs? Girl, I like you even more." He smiled as he spoke. He took another bite as he continued with, "Speaking of ribs, does Kevin still do that annual BBQ thing?"

"Yeah, it's next week, I believe. Are you coming?" I asked as I crossed my legs.

"Am I invited?"

"I'm officially inviting you as my plus one. It is the only time I will ever be able to do a whole plus one thing," I said with a shrug.

"Consider me your plus one, then," he said as we continued eating. We were able to chat about things as we sat and ate. I found myself liking him even more the longer we talked. I felt that we had so much in common.

Chapter Seven:

Our sailing adventure ended, and Corey docked the boat back at the pier. I climbed into the car's passenger seat and pulled the door shut to buckle up while Corey finished loading the last of our belongings into the trunk. The trunk slammed shut before he climbed into the driver's seat. The engine purred with the flick of his wrist.

"I had a great time," I told him. He grasped my hand and pulled it into his lap. He let go of it momentarily to shift the car's gear. "Do you live nearby, or do you live closer to where I live?"

"Somewhere in between." He responded, but it wasn't a straight answer. His hand gripped mine in his lap, his thumb rubbing at the back of my hand. A comfortable silence filled the car the whole drive to his house.

Corey's house was huge, and that was just looking at it from the outside. All I could do was stand there staring at the house in awe. 'What does he see in me? A rich man like him, with a broken, homeless girl like me?' I thought to myself, the slam of the trunk stealing my attention. I slid out of the way of the car door enough to push it shut. I followed him up to the house's front door and stood awkwardly behind him, patiently waiting for him to unlock the front door to gain entry.

"Is your Florida home just as big?" I asked.

"Nah, I only have a condo in Florida. I had a house for a while but began renting it out."

"And now you are a renter. Why not just keep the house for yourself?"

"Why do I need a four-bedroom house in Florida when I'm the only one there for three days a week?" Corey asked. He had a point.

Corey pushed the front door open, and I followed him into the house. I firmly shut the door and locked it behind me out of habit. I followed Corey like a lost puppy as I looked over every detail in the house. Corey certainly had a unique taste in his art and how he decorated.

"True, but why not sell the house?" I asked.

"I can, but my renters didn't have the money to buy me out, and they are just happy with renting at present. I figured I would just let it play out." Corey shrugged as he led me upstairs to a bedroom. "This will be your room for the time being."

I stepped into the room furnished in a maroon and purple scheme, which wasn't too bad.

"I'm not staying with you in your room?"

"I am okay with you staying with me, and I don't mind the cuddles. But I have also noticed how skittish you are and the anxiety you have. I didn't want to feel you had to sleep with me." It saddened me that he felt I didn't want to share a bed with him, but I also thought it was a sweet gesture. I nervously twirled on my foot to look the room over again.

"Where is your room?" I curiously asked as I hooked my thumbs in my pockets.

"Right at the end of the hall, so I won't be too far away if you need anything in the middle of the night. Let me show you where your bathroom is," he said. Corey barely put my two bags inside my room before I followed him to the bathroom. It seemed like it should be a master bathroom due to the size, but I wasn't complaining. After the tour upstairs, I followed Corey back downstairs.

"I meant to ask, is that a record player?" I asked, pointing at the item that had caught my eye when we first walked in earlier today.

"Yes, it is. Do you have any records?"

"Nah, but I love that classic vinyl stuff. I wish I had a player so I could buy some, but it's kind of pointless to spend money on something I can't use." I shrugged as I ran my finger over the edge of the player.

"They're collectibles, so you can be a collector."

"True, but I'm saving up for some big-ticket items, so the collection will have to wait for now," I said, sighing.

"What might that be?" he asked.

"Just some things…" I shrugged, 'A car, an apartment to myself, maybe a one-way flight out of this god-forsaken town.' I listed them off in my head as he smirked.

"Well, you don't have to tell me if you don't want to. Do you want to see my collection?" he asked.

I nodded as he led me to the bookshelf filled with VHSs, DVDs, vinyls, and books. It was nice to bond with someone over this type of thing. From what I could judge by his vinyl collection, we both have similar musical tastes.

After he showed me his vinyl record collection, he gave me

a tour of the rest of his house. There was only one room that he didn't show me. I didn't question why, but I figured he had a reason why he didn't. Who was I to question him or make a stink over it?

"Out here is my pool. I should be the one doing BBQs since I have a bigger pool than Kevin."

"Yes, yes, you should," I said with a smile.

"Do you want a snack? I'm getting kind of hungry." We returned to the house, and I watched him in the kitchen. "So, I was thinking, I'm gone for my other job three or four days a week, and you have that living arrangement with Kevin. What do you think about house-sitting for me?"

"Uh, great, sure," I said, running a hand through my hair.

"For now, I promise I will take you to Florida when you are ready," he said as I nodded.

"I don't have the money to go right now, so it would have to wait," I said as I bit at my bottom lip as he glanced up at me. 'Yeah, that is why he won't take me.' I thought to myself as I was mentally smacking myself in the forehead.

"We'll find the perfect time to go then." I nodded. I began to think about how a trip to Florida would be great for me mentally. A trip there would be worry-free time about Alex popping up unexpectedly. I would be thousands of miles away, and he wouldn't be able to show up when he saw fit.

"You want to listen to the record player?" Corey's voice broke into my musings.

"Well, duh. But who first?" I asked, looking at his endless collection. Corey chose for us, and I bit my lip nervously, waiting to see who he picked. Mayday Parade sounded from the machine, and he turned to look at me.

"Figured you may like them too," he explained. He plopped

on the couch and patted the seat beside him. I sat beside him, his arm snaked around my shoulders, pulling me closer to his warm body. "I have some bad news."

"What's that?" Panic arose, and I tried not to let what he was about to say consume my body.

"I have to leave for work tomorrow. I won't be back until the BBQ next week. Will you want to stay here, or should I take you home?"

"Um, I think maybe I should go home. I won't have my car and can't drive yours."

"I can take you home, and you can always come back if you want. I would love for you to be here more often so I can get to know you better."

"I don't know if I'd feel comfortable in a house alone." Corey had no idea the number of anxiety and panic attacks I had suffered ever since Alex or that he was the cause of them. I wasn't even sure how tonight would go if I had to stay in the room he had shown me.

"Understood, but it's an open invitation for you to stay here while I'm gone," Corey said as I felt his fingers twirling the tips of my hair. I curled up closer to him, enjoying the music playing. The sounds were crisp, and I loved how vinyl played better than any other form.

"We never picked up groceries for me to cook you dinner." I waited and spoke when the record ended, and my stomach began to grumble.

"I could order from Grubhub. What's your poison?"

"How about pizza?"

"Little Caesars okay with you? The half pizza and half cheesy bread?"

"Sounds delicious. May I take a shower while we wait?" I

asked nervously. I rose from the couch at his nod.

"I want to do the same," Corey said, following me up the stairs.

I stopped at the guest room, watching him enter his bedroom leaving the door open. I could see his California king bed with the black oak bed frame and red comforter. It looked a bit gothic, just like him.

I opened the guest room, rummaging through my bag to find my pajamas, and went to the bathroom. I locked the nickel doorknob before I stripped my clothing and showered the salt water off.

After freshening up, I headed down the stairs, arriving in time to see Corey pushing the door shut and holding a brown and orange box.

"Dinner is served."

I followed him into the dining room, with a dark oak circular table with four chairs placed evenly around it. I slid into a chair while Corey filled our plates and brought them over. I crossed my legs at my ankle before diving into the fresh, hot, delicious pizza.

"Thank you, Corey," I said after the first bite. He glared at me. "Sorry, I can't help but say thank you."

"Old habits die hard."

"I guess so." I shrugged, "When do you leave tomorrow? And are you flying or taking the boat?"

"Flying this time. I need to get back quickly because I'll have a sexy girl here waiting on me."

"You have another girlfriend I don't know about? I'm not into the polygamy lifestyle," I stated before taking another bite, and he burst into laughter.

"No other girl, just you. I'm hoping I'll be home soon. I just don't know how much I'm needed."

"Do you need a ride?"

"Nah, you've got to help Kevin with the BBQ. I should be back just in the nick of time."

"I can't wait," I said with a bright smile. "When do I get to go on set?"

"I'll let you know soon. I have to show off my girlfriend."

"Any girls down there I need to worry about?"

"Nah. I don't dig coworkers."

"What am I?" I asked offensively.

"Well, my secretary." He laughed.

"You said your parents are in Cincinnati. How'd you end up in Pennsylvania? Why begin acting?" I asked, stalling to take a bite to hear his answers.

He leaned back in his chair as he finished chewing his food. I wanted to know more about him. Maybe this dinner would let us get to know more about each other.

"My parents live in Cincinnati. That is where I am originally from, born and raised. My mom was a librarian, and my dad was a mechanic."

"And they ended up with a child who is a tattooed bad boy who does piercings and acts?" I asked, trying not to laugh.

Corey let out a chuckle, too. "Yep, the two of the most wholesome careers, and they got me."

"So, how'd you get here?"

"I transferred to the University here from my local community college and switched majors a shit ton. My parents weren't happy that I ended up sticking with marketing. They wanted me to be a doctor to make them proud. While at the University, I met Kevin at a local jazz night, and we hit it off."

"Jazz night?" I chuckled.

"Don't judge. Jazz is very nice music. Anyway, he told me about his idea of wanting to open a tattoo shop, and I was his test subject. I learned how to pierce and was with him through the whole process. I even co-signed for the parlor. I was there when he met Anita."

"Why did he choose here?"

"This is where Kevin grew up."

"You did that for him? Why?"

"He is like another brother to me. You would do anything for those you love and care about," he said as he stared blankly at the table, then glanced up at me. "Like you, I would do anything for you."

I blushed a little, breaking eye contact with him. "I bet your parents weren't that happy about it."

"My parents? Ha! They certainly didn't understand but supported me in whatever I decided."

"Must be nice." I didn't mean for it to sound so harsh as it came out. "No offense."

I realized that what I said could come off wrong. He stood up and went to grab two beers. He returned, handing one to me. "Thought you would need one of these."

I smirked, "Thanks."

"Your parents weren't that supportive, it seems?"

"Yeah, they were supportive right up until I met my ex. I should have listened to them. My parents wanted so much more out of me. I was set up for a good life. I had so much going for me, but I chose my ex over my future, thinking he was my future. I gave up everything for him." I fought back tears and drank some of the beer. "Excuse me."

I stood up, walked out of the room, and up to the guest room. I sat on the edge of the bed, wiping my eyes, trying to collect myself before I went to find Corey. A soft knock sounded at the door, and I looked over to see Corey leaning against the door frame. "Hey."

"Sorry about that."

"Don't be." He pushed himself off the frame and came to sit beside me on the bed. "You haven't talked with them since you broke up?"

"No, they cut me off when I ran away with the guy. I got accepted into all the universities I wanted and had dreams. I was so head over heels for him, and when I realized we wouldn't work, look where I ended up." I glanced over at Corey. "I mean, I met you, which I am happy about. I just feel that I am trapped. I was trapped with my ex, and now I am trapped here."

Corey simply nodded as I went silent, "Can I go home? I feel like I've ruined this whole night."

"If you want to, but I wish you would stay. I thought we were getting to know each other better. We can stop discussing this subject and watch a movie or something." I nodded as he got up from the bed. He held his hand out to help me up, and I obliged. I followed him down the stairs and sat on his black leather couch while he popped in a movie. He went to the kitchen and returned with the dinner we had never finished.

"Corey?"

"Mmhmm?" He said as he was trying to get things situated.

"I appreciate you. You are such a breath of fresh air compared to my ex. I was nervous about being in another relationship so soon because my thoughts always bring back horrid memories of him. You continue to prove to me that you are nothing like him. It's refreshing. Our relationship reminds me why I first fell in love with my ex. You are completely different from him, and I thank you for that."

"How bad was he?" Corey asked. I didn't know what to say or how to answer that. I am sure Corey could sense that as he let it be quiet. "You don't have to answer that if you don't want to. I can sense that you'd rather we just dropped it. I'm here for you, babe." He winked to let me know it was okay. He sat back, his arm snaking around my body, and pulled me into his embrace. As much as I wanted to tell him everything, I had already had one freak-out tonight and didn't want to have another that would force me to go home.

I found myself falling asleep by the end of the movie. The credits had begun to roll, and I sat up, rubbing my eyes. I stretched a little before I stood to clean up the mess while Corey shut down the electronics in the living room. I walked out of the kitchen to find Corey at the bottom of the stairs with his arm outstretched for me to grab. I blushed a little, grabbed his hand, and walked with him up the stairs, hand in hand.

"Good night, beautiful. If you need anything, feel free to come get me," Corey said as we stood toe to toe. I stared up into his eyes. A smile curled up on his lips, and I snuggled closer to him. Corey's arms snaked around my body, hugging me tightly to his solid frame. I felt him kiss the top of my head, and it felt like time stood still.

"Can I sleep in your room?" I mumbled. I don't know why I had asked, and I surprised myself that I had even managed to get the words out. "If that's okay."

"Absolutely, beautiful," Corey answered. I finally looked up at him, seeing a confident smile.

"Thank you. I'm just feeling emotional and having a lot of anxiety when it comes to staying in new places."

"No need to explain. I'll warm up the bed while you do your bedtime routine." He winked as I smiled. I hurried to the guest bathroom, quickly brushing my hair and teeth before sheepishly walking to his room. I stopped in the doorway, staring into the room. Corey was already sprawled out in the bed with the red comforter pulled over his legs and ending at his belly button. "You can come in, I won't bite."

I chuckled as I timidly walked around the bed and climbed in. Slipping under the comforter and scooting up to him, his arm snaked under my neck. Corey pulled me closer to his body. My head pressed against his chest, and I could hear the subtle beat of his heart, which was soothing. I closed my eyes, trying to ease my anxiety so I could get some sleep. Corey's grip on me tightened. Remembering that I was in a safe place put my fears to rest.

"Good night, beautiful," Corey whispered, kissing my head.

I scooted even closer, and our bodies pressed firmly against each other. I finally took note of the tattoo he had mentioned on his belly button. Did he get a sun? I rolled my eyes and chuckled to myself softly. He had defined abs, and his chest was hard as a rock. When did he ever find time to work out?

"Good night," I whispered back, my lips placed a kiss on his bare chest where I had buried my head. I closed my eyes again, focusing on the soft sounds of his light breaths and the echoes of his heart thumping in his chest. His grip was tight, holding me snugly against his body, which was providing a lot of heat. I was comfortable and drifted off to sleep.

Chapter Eight:

I woke up still pressed against Corey's chest, his arms locked behind me. I inched closer to him just to feel his body heat. My hand began to trace his pecs and outlined his defined abs. I bit my bottom lip as my fingers approached where the waistband of his pajamas rested. Images flooded my mind of waking up next to him naked, his warm, sweat-covered body lying beside me. Both of us exhausted from a night of him fucking me senseless.

"Good morning, beautiful." Corey's morning voice was raspy, and I wonder if that's how he sounded during sex.

"Good morning. Did I wake you?" I asked, embarrassed that he woke up while dirty thoughts of him flooded my imagination, and I felt guilty that I may have woken him.

"Nah, I had to get up anyway. Before taking this pretty little thing in my bed home, I have my bags to pack," he said, brushing his fingers through my hair.

"When's your flight?"

"Noon."

"You're going to be late." I laughed as I sat up to stare down at him.

"I don't want this to end." His hand rubbed circles on my lower back, his eyes locked with mine. He was telling the truth; I could just tell. "Promise you'll come back and stay with me when I get home?"

"Promise. But Corey..."

"That's not good when you say that way." His hand did not stop the rubbing motion.

"I can't help but wonder about things. I can't put my life on hold."

"What are you saying?" He sat up while holding my gaze.

"Let's talk over breakfast?"

He nodded, and we headed downstairs after getting dressed. I sat at the table with my hands holding the freshly brewed coffee from his Keurig machine. He was pouring milk over two different-sized bowls of Cheerios. I couldn't have a part-time relationship with him. What was I going to do when he was gone? When he leaves, will I be dropped off at Kevin's like a sack of potatoes, only to be picked up again when he's home? I don't feel comfortable staying here by myself yet. This relationship is fresh and new, but I need to know where we are going. I can't sit here waiting for him to come home, thinking he was living some other life in Florida. Once he slid into the seat across from me, he sat back against his chair, staring at me.

"Corey, am I going to be in a part-time relationship with you?"

"Huh?" His face was a mask of confusion with a raised brow.

"You leave in a few hours for a few days, and I'm being dumped back into my reality. Or my horrible life as I think of it. I'm not perfect, and I don't want to continue this relationship if I am going to be only a part-time girlfriend to you."

"You aren't going to be a part-time girlfriend to me. I have to go to work in a different state. That is the only reason I am leaving. I don't want to lose my job. I wish you could come with me, but our relationship is still fragile, and I feel we need to strengthen it before I can take you with me. I would love this relationship to work, and when I get home, I want to spend every minute of every day with you. I can't get enough of you, Melanie."

"I just don't want to put my life or your life on hold if this isn't going to work."

"It's going to work, sweetie, and I'm sorry I have to go. What did your ex do to you?"

"I thought he was my everything, and he was until it all turned horrible. Corey, you are my glimmer of hope. I had reservations about entering this relationship and knowing you are leaving caused my doubts to flare up. I'm worried you won't come back. Or believing that you only want me in your life when it's convenient for you."

Corey burst into laughter. "Oh, sweetheart. I want you in every aspect of my life, beautiful. You can move in while I am gone for all I care. You said you didn't feel comfortable in this house by yourself yet. That is the only reason I am taking you home. You've got your car, and I will give you my spare key. You can come and stay here. That bed upstairs reeks of me if you insist on sleeping in there."

"So, you are serious about me?"

"As serious as white on rice." He gave me a genuine smile meant to allay my fears. "Now, I know that your ex was a nut job of sorts, but I am different. I am here to help you through whatever trauma he put you through. I'm not him. I like you, Melanie. I want this to work, and I'm willing to take it at your pace. Let's eat our breakfast, and you can listen to some of my vinyl collection while I pack my bag. We'll head to Kevin's and then say our goodbyes there."

I nodded in agreement. I was still worried there wouldn't be an us when he returned. I would miss him so much while he was in Florida. I felt myself getting attached to him and hated that he had to leave for so many days. I went into the living room to look over his vinyl collection. I got super excited over a Blondie LP and popped it onto the record player. I danced around the living room and sang along. When I heard him clear his throat, I stopped and slowly turned to look at him, watching me from the bottom of the stairs. I could tell he was trying so hard not to laugh at me, and I instantly blushed.

"Sorry, I love this album."

"I couldn't tell," he chuckled. "Come on, beautiful."

I followed him out to his car. I couldn't get the door handle to work for me this time, so I waited for him to toss his luggage into the trunk before assisting me. Corey held my hand in his lap the whole half-hour drive to Kevin's house, pulling up behind my run-down Volkswagen and placing the car into park.

"Are you going to be okay?" Corey asked, his hand still firmly gripped mine. I looked straight into his eyes, trying to be strong.

"I'm going to miss you. It's hard letting you go when we just started getting to know each other."

"I know, sweetie, but it's only for a few days. I'll video chat with you tonight when I land. We have technology to help these days fly by," he said with a half-smile.

"Thank God for that." I chuckled.

"Come on, babes. I got to make my flight." He winked as we headed up to the front porch.

"You want to come in?"

"I can't. I'm already running late."

"Okay. I guess I'll see you next week?"

"Or sooner."

"I'm hoping for sooner," I said, my hands nervously twisting together. Corey gripped my chin, lifting my face to look into his eyes. I couldn't help the smile that came to my face. He made me happy. His hand gripped the back of my head, pulling me in. His lips pressed roughly against mine, and his hand held me there. His tongue begged for entrance, opening my mouth slightly to allow our tongues to tangle in passion. Corey's other hand gripped my waist, tugging me to press against his frame. I could feel his length hardening beneath his pants, pressing against my stomach, and I moaned into his mouth. I was relieved I wasn't the only one getting turned on. His hand slipped around my waist, cupping my ass, moaning for a whole different reason now. I broke the kiss to catch my breath, staring into Corey's eyes, glazed with lust. I felt myself begin to blush. He pried himself off me, giving me a smile and a wink before he turned on his heels to head back to his muscle car. I watched him get back into the car and speed off.

I was reeling from the kiss that Corey and I had just shared. I let myself into the house and snuck up to my room. I didn't want my presence to be known. I knew that Kevin and Anita would ask 50 questions about our date. I locked the door and turned to face my bed. I leaned back against the door, staring at my queen-sized bed. I walked across the room and lay down, staring up at the ceiling. That kiss had my blood pumping in all the right areas, but I wasn't sure if I could even experience sexual pleasure anymore, much less get to the big "O" after all that Alex had put me through. I slowly slid my hand into my panties while biting my bottom lip. I can't believe I am about to do this, but I have to try. After spending the night lying next to Corey, I felt wrought out, and just that kiss was enough to send me over the edge.

My fingers slide to my wet, throbbing center, and I gently caressed circles around my clit, making me feel so good. I let out a soft moan. I began to rub faster, increasing the pleasure, holding back my moans, not wanting anyone to hear.

I stroked lower, slipping a finger into my pussy, my back arching off the bed. With a simple curve of my finger, I squirmed with pleasure, knowing I had found my g-spot. I pulled my finger out and plunged it back in. My eyes clenched shut, images of Corey flooding my mind. I pictured him between my legs and how sexy his moans would be. Fuck, he'd be huge, judging by the quick feel I'd had of him, and I longed to feel my tight pussy around his cock, clenching it tightly. His cock was so big it would stretch me so wide it would almost break me in half. I imagined him hovering over me, his dark, lustful eyes staring down at me. I slipped a second finger into my pussy and pumped harder and faster.

I wanted him to fuck me hard and deep. Corey would have me calling out his name, and my juices were flowing with every thrust of my fingers. My body began to throb with pleasure, my pussy convulsing and contracting around my fingers. My toes curled as I held back cries of pleasure, making me want to scream Corey's name. My back arched further off the bed, my legs clamping themselves closed due to the pleasure I had achieved. I slid my fingers out of my pussy as I tried to catch my breath. I couldn't believe I just did that. Alex hadn't broken me after all. I still enjoyed sex. I couldn't wait to see Corey again. Maybe I would be ready to let him fulfill my sexual needs and desires.

Chapter Nine:

❧

One Week Later (The BBQ)
Corey's Point of View-

My flight was delayed by two hours, and my headache worsened, making me even more agitated. I knew Melanie was anxiously awaiting my arrival, and I hadn't made it on time. My phone is dead, so I can't text to tell her that I'm okay. My nose is still swollen from being broken during my fight two days ago. Some of the swelling went down, and the doctors splinted it up the best they could.

I have no idea how I am going to explain this to her. I grab my bag off the carousel, wheeling it behind me as I beelined to the parking structure across the street. I toss the silver luggage into the trunk and climb in, flipping the ignition to get the engine to rev to life.

I drive to Kevin's house, and I may have had a lead foot, speeding the whole way there. I missed Melanie and couldn't stand being away from her any longer. Maybe that's why I broke my nose. I was so focused on her that my mind wasn't in the game. Thoughts of her clouded my mind often, and being away from her for that long was hard.

I pulled up to Kevin's house, and the street was already crowded with cars. I was the last to arrive, finding a spot on a different street around the corner, and hurried to his front door. Melanie banged the door open, and she jumped into my embrace.

I caught her and spun her around. My hands gripped her thighs, staring deep into her blue eyes, smiling. She pressed her lips against mine roughly, holding back moans of pain and pleasure.

"I missed you." She barely stopped kissing me long enough to get the words out.

"I missed you too, beautiful." My lips curled into a smile as she slid down my body to stand.

"What happened to your nose?"

I chuckled. "I was distracted. I was trying to text my sexy girlfriend, and someone opened the door. I walked right into it. Smashed my face. The writers now have to find a way to incorporate the broken nose into the show."

"More time off then?"

"I wish, but I'm starving."

"Food is almost ready, I think." Melanie grabbed my hand to lead the way into the backyard filled with a bunch of other people, some of whom I recognized and others I didn't.

Melanie led me over to Kevin, who was at the grill.

"Hey, Corey. How was your trip?"

Kevin put his fist out to give me a fist bump. I bumped my fist with him as I looked at the food he was grilling: hamburgers and hot dogs. I was starving, so I would gladly eat anything they put in front of me.

"And what happened to that nose of yours?"

"I was walking while texting, wasn't paying attention, someone flung a door open, and I walked right into it." Kevin glared at me. He rolled his eyes in disbelief that I had gone with that lie. He flipped a burger on the grill.

"Did Corey tell you what his job is down in Florida?" Kevin asked nonchalantly. Melanie's arms snaked around my arm, giving it a tight squeeze.

"He just said he was an entertainer. Now the writers have to change up the script to include his broken nose." Melanie gave Kevin my explanation, then turned to ask me. "Do you need an ice pack?"

"Yeah, that would help the swelling. Why don't you go get one for him?" Kevin answered for me. Melanie headed inside to retrieve the ice pack. "Look, you need to tell her what you do, or I will. She needs to know, Corey."

"Please, don't tell her. I promise to tell her when the time is right, but right now isn't that time." I sighed heavily. "She still seems fragile about her last relationship. I feel she is finally opening up to me and getting comfortable with this relationship. I don't want to tell her and ruin everything we've worked so hard on."

Melanie seemed to be so fragile and on edge from her ex. I don't want to drop the bomb that I am an MMA fighter and instructor, only for her to leave me high and dry. These last few days without her have killed me, and I can't imagine my life without her. I feared losing her.

"I know she hasn't told you about her ex. I just...you need to tell her and tell her gently. Tell her that it's a form of entertaining and acting," Kevin explained. I gave him a weird look. Unsure what he was trying to get at.

"Kevin, trust me when I say I have told many people about my career as an MMA fighter. Telling Melanie won't be any different," I said, unsure why Kevin was being so weird about this. I know Kevin always means well, and he looks at Melanie like a sister. From what Melanie has told me, Kevin has helped her out with her ex. Kevin was there for her, so he knows more about her situation than I do. I'm the new guy trying to slide into her life. I've got work to do. "So, her ex, what's his name?"

"That's all you want to know? His name?"

"Yes, that's all I want to know. I want to know more, but you won't tell me anything else."

"True. The guy's name is Alex," Kevin answered.

"You got any beer?"

"Yeah, in the blue cooler. Can you grab me one?" Kevin asked. I went to grab us both a beer when Melanie returned with a Ziploc baggie filled with ice cubes.

"We didn't have any ice packs, so I had to improvise," Melanie said, handing me the small baggie of ice cubes. I grabbed her hand, leading her to an empty lawn chair. I planted my butt in the chair and pulled her to sit in my lap.

Melanie turned her body to look at me better and pulled her legs up to lay across my other leg. I pressed the ice to my nose. "I've missed you, baby. Do you want to come with me next time? I don't know if I can go that long without you again."

"I don't know if I can, Corey. I don't have the money."

"I got you covered, beautiful. I will always take care of you," I said, rubbing her back. She sighed at my suggestion. "Think about it. I don't leave for another week. Maybe we can go out tomorrow, and you can stay at my place?" I asked, and she blushed a little. "I would love to wake up next to you. I love having you wrapped up in my arms at night and just having you around. Maybe you can show me more of those dance moves."

She playfully smacked at me again. "Shut up!"

She scooted onto my lap and leaned with her back against my chest. My free arm wrapped around her body, holding her close. I kissed her neck, scraping my teeth against her skin, and my hand slipped under her shirt, rubbing her stomach. I want a handful of her breast, but she's wiggling in my lap, causing her ass to rub against my cock. She's turned me on so many times and continues teasing me. I tried to fight down an erection, but that wasn't happening. My cock had a mind of its own. I heard her slight moan, knowing that she must have felt my hard-on. I continued to leave a mark on her neck, and her soft moans went straight to my cock.

She went to stand up, and I tugged her back down, "Not yet, baby," I growled in her ear. I didn't want everyone to know I was rocking a boner.

Melanie looked at me with her smile, and she was just so damn beautiful. I was trying to think of anything to kill my mood. I was finally able to calm my dick down enough to let her loose. She returned with another beer and took her place in my lap.

We had drunk numerous beers, and I was too drunk to drive home at this point. "Can I sleep with you tonight, beautiful?"

"Of course. You ready to sneak out of here?" She looked around the dwindling party.

"All I need is you. You're the only person that had my attention all night." I push my fingers through her hair and firmly grip a handful of her wavy auburn curls. I tug her head back and slam my lips against hers for a rough kiss. I can feel vibrations from her lips as she moans from pleasure. Shit, it's going to be a long night battling these boners.

"Let's go to my room," she whispers. She stands, takes my hand, and leads me upstairs to her room. A queen-sized bed? Melanie will be pressing her ass against my dick all night.

I pushed the door shut and made sure to lock it. We don't want little Jack to walk in on anything he shouldn't. I pulled my shirt over my head, tossing it aside. Melanie walked backward to the bed, and when her legs hit the edge, she fell back on it. Her eyes locked on me as I stripped out of my clothes.

I undid my belt and jeans, pushing them down over my hips, and they fell the rest of the way to cloud around my ankles. I stepped out of the jeans, leaving me in my boxers. I walked up to her, planting my hands on either side of her, and planted a rough kiss on her lips.

"Your turn, babes," I said with a wink. I slid into the bed, resting my head on my hands and watching her intently. She seemed too sheepish to strip down in front of me, and I fully understood why. My cock was already perking at the chance to catch the slightest sight of any skin.

Melanie stood, walking to her closet, leaving her back turned to me as she pulled her shirt over her head, tossing it aside. Her arms wrapped around her back, strategically unhooking the clasps of her bra. *Fuck, she was releasing those babies. Her perky nipples would be poking through her shirt and will drive me crazy.*

Melanie dropped the bra to the floor. She bashfully looked over her shoulder at me, and my eyes locked with hers. I winked as I watched her change, even if she wasn't showing me what I wanted to see most. She reached into the closet to find a new shirt and pulled it over her head. She turned around to show me the A Day To Remember design on the front, and I realized how long it was on her.

Melanie faced me as she began to push the fabric of her leggings down her long legs. Tucking her legs beneath the tee, she tried to step out of the stretchy legging material. The shirt was long enough to cover her that I couldn't tell if she was or wasn't wearing underwear. My mind hoped for the latter of the two. Melanie turned around to bend over, and the shirt rode up to expose enough skin that I saw she was rocking a thong.

Melanie tossed the black fabric into the laundry basket before she quickly walked over to the bed, and I peeled the blanket back for her to slide in. Melanie climbed into the bed beside me and rolled to her side. She scooted back until her ass was rubbing against my pelvis, and I let out a groan. "Shit, baby, you are going to wake him up even more. He's already stirring from watching you change."

She looked over her shoulder at me with the brightest smile as my arms locked around her. "Good night."

"Good night, sexy," I whispered back to her.

Chapter Ten

Corey's Point of View-

I woke up to Melanie shifting on the bed, her ass practically grinding against my pelvis and making it hard not to get morning wood. I rubbed my hand over my face. I can't believe I got so trashed last night, but I'm more than happy that I could wake up to the woman I love wrapped in my arms. She was also daring enough after a couple of beers to change into her pajamas in front of me.

"Good morning, beautiful," I mumbled.

"Good morning, handsome." She rolled over to face me, a smile creeping onto my face. I would love to wake up to her staring back at me every day. "Do you think Kevin and Anita are up?"

"Yes, Jack probably woke them an hour ago."

"Coffee?"

"Please, anything to help this hangover," I said as she chuckled. I loved her laugh. In fact, I loved everything about her. I broke the distance, giving her a soft kiss. I was afraid if

I tried for a deep, passionate kiss, I'd wake my dick from its slumber.

"I need to put my pants on first."

"Do you have to?" I pouted as she giggled. She rolled on top of me, her slender hands resting against my bare chest, her pussy too close for comfort. The only things separating me from feeling my cock engulfed in her tight pussy were my boxers and that thin, black thong of hers. I couldn't fight the hard-on anymore. My fingers dug into her thighs, holding her in place, and I moaned. "Shit, Melanie, you can't be doing this to me."

I shifted a little below her, and she let out a soft moan when she felt my girth press against her core. She looked down at me with dark, lustful eyes. Fuck, she was so sexy. I had to wait for her to be ready, but she was unwittingly taunting me until then. Her eyes clenched shut. I was confused about what was happening when I suddenly realized she had acted the same way at the mall and in the car. *FUCK! She's having a flashback.*

I reached up, grabbed a handful of her hair, and pulled her down, pressing a rough kiss to her lips. I hoped that the kiss would bring her back to reality. Melanie's eyes fluttered open, and she let out a soft moan against my lips.

"You're not my ex." Her eyes cleared as she became aware of her surroundings once more.

I chuckled a little as I smiled up at her. "Not your ex."

She sat back on her legs, rolled her hips, and smiled. "Definitely not my ex."

I took that as a compliment as my hands soothingly rubbed her thighs, letting her just sit in my lap for however long she needed, even if it was causing my dick more pain from not getting its pleasure. Melanie's finger traced down the middle of my chest to the hem of my boxers. I held my breath, anticipating what she was going to do next.

Melanie scooted down my legs, tugging my boxers with her to allow my cock to spring free. She gasped, and I let out a sigh of relief that I wasn't confined anymore. I locked eyes with her as she leaned forward, wrapping her lips tightly around the tip. Shit, she was going to give me a blow job. Her mouth lowered on my dick until I could feel her gagging over my size.

"Sit on my face," I demanded.

She slid my dick out of her tight-lipped hold with a loud pop. "Excuse me, what?"

I held back a chuckle as she seemed confused about what I had asked her to do. "Sit on my face. I have to muffle these moans somehow, and I know of no better way than delving into that sweet pussy of yours."

She seemed hesitant initially, but she crawled up the bed to kneel beside me. I helped her straddle my face, nudging her legs further apart, and my hand gripped her thigh to hold her exactly where I wanted her. If I were to die right now, I would die happy. I pushed the thin piece of fabric aside to see the glistening wetness of her pussy. A moan escaped for a whole different reason.

Melanie wrapped my dick in the warmth of her mouth, letting me dive into my reward. My tongue slid along her exposed clit, and her juices tasted so sweet. I felt the vibrations of her moaning along the length of my cock. In turn, I moaned into her pussy. I could eat her pussy every minute of every day, for every meal. Melanie began to wiggle above me, and my hand fought to hold her still, but her legs clenched, trying to shut.

"I'm going to cum." She whimpered while she sat up to her full height. My fingers dug into her thighs, continuing to lick up the flow of juices. "Corey!"

Moaning into her pussy as she rode out her orgasm, I wanted to lick up all that she had to offer. She climbed off my face, repositioning herself to begin sucking me off again. My fingers tangled in her hair, guiding her. I loved watching her head bob along my length, her ass in the air. "Melanie, shit. I'm going to nut."

She looked up at me with wide blue eyes, not stopping. *Fuck, was she going to swallow?* I thrust up into her mouth and firmly held her head there as she swallowed every drop that leaked out of my cock. Melanie sat back on her legs, wiping at her mouth with the back of her hand.

"Gah, baby, that was so hot," I said, rubbing her arm soothingly. Melanie blushed a little and smiled.

"I should get us some coffee. You may want to wait a few minutes after me to come down. I just hope no one heard anything." Melanie crawled down the bed, giving me the most excellent view of her exposed ass, causing me to growl under my breath. Fucking her from behind would feel so good. That ass pressed against my pelvis and my balls slapping against her clit? She had just sucked me off, and here I was, getting hard again. I got a taste of her sweet core, and I wanted more.

Watching her slide on a pair of jean shorts, I noted the clothes in the closet and how little there was. How many clothes does she own? She slipped out the door, stopped, and turned to look at me. I locked eyes with her and smiled. Melanie gave me her trademark smile before she stepped the rest of the way into the hallway and disappeared downstairs. I got up from the bed, gathered my clothes, and began to take my time pulling my clothes on. I ran a hand through my hair, giving it all a good shake.

I should have taken a shower because I reeked of sex. Kevin and Anita will know we did something. Hmm, I wonder if she has anything to mask this smell? I began to look over her room, coming up short. I jogged down the stairs and walked around the corner, seeing everyone sitting at the dining room table.

Melanie's beauty stopped me in my tracks and took my breath away. I loved this girl. I couldn't imagine a life without her. I was positive I wanted her with me every second of the day. I know that at some point, I wanted to marry her, but was I ready for marriage? I wouldn't want to spend forever with anyone but her.

"Hungry?" Anita called out from the kitchen.

"Yes, please, I am starving." I walked over, claiming the chair next to Melanie. Melanie looked at me with a shy grin. My hand grasped hers, bringing it to my lips for a soft kiss.

"We got a long day at the shop today, man." Kevin chimed in.

"Melanie coming?" I asked, glancing over to her.

"Nope, she has her work cut out for her today. She's helping Anita clean up that backyard," Kevin said.

"I can only imagine, but you'll be there later?" I asked, looking at Melanie directly.

"I wouldn't miss it, especially since my boyfriend is there." She said with a smile.

"Just remember, no flirting on the clock," Kevin said, pointing between us. Melanie's hand rested in my lap while we ate breakfast with the family, all of us making small talk.

"Come on, Corey, we have to get to work." Kevin was raring

to get the shop open.

"Okay, I'm coming." Standing up from the table, I looked over at Melanie, "Don't forget to bring your bags so you can follow me home after our shift." I said with a wink, and she smiled widely. I bent down, giving her a gentle kiss. "I'll see you later, beautiful."

"Let's go, lovebird," Kevin said, shoving me toward the front door.

I drove the short distance to the tattoo shop and arrived not long after Kevin. I followed Kevin inside the parlor, where I began to help him by setting up the different workstations in the back. Once we had finished set up, I returned to the front of the parlor with my jewelry container to fill the now-free display case. Kevin sat at Melanie's desk typing away at the computer.

"Kevin, do you think Melanie would want to get married?" I asked, not even looking up at him. I heard him drop the pen he had in hand, causing me to glance up at him. He had leaned back in the chair and stared at me intently. "I was just asking a general question, Kevin."

"You thinking of asking her?"

"Kevin, I can't imagine a life without her. I want to spend every second of every day with her. I want her to be the last thing I see before I go to bed and the first thing I see when I wake up. She consumes all my thoughts. Even right now, I'm thinking of her. I love her, Kevin."

Kevin ran his hand along his face. "I felt the same about Anita when I began to think of asking her to marry me. I don't think Melanie would say no, but I don't know if she will say yes. I don't know what mindset she is in right now. I know I've never seen her happier than she is with you. You have brought her a lot of happiness and brightened up her life."

I was happy to hear that she felt something about me and was happier since I had entered her life. "I just like the sound of Melanie Mathison."

We had been so involved in our conversation that we didn't hear anyone enter the parlor. "That's not her name."

The male's voice startled me, and I turned to look at the customer who stood in the parlor with us. "Oh, hi. I didn't realize we had a customer. How may I help you?"

"Who the fuck are you? The new hire? Mr. Mathison, maybe? Thinking of stealing my girl?" the man stated. My brow rose, confused as to what that even meant.

"Get the fuck out of here! How many times do I have to tell you that you aren't welcome here?" Kevin asked. I looked at him as he began to approach the counter.

"You know him?" I asked Kevin cautiously, then looked back at the man. He wore a light gray blazer matching his pants with a white button-up shirt underneath. His jet-black hair was slicked back. He seemed too clean-cut for this lifestyle, but who was I to judge?

"You didn't tell him about me? I'm surprised Melanie didn't tell you either if you are inclined to change her name, Mr. Mathison, or should I call you something else?" the guy asked.

"You need to leave, Alex," Kevin said. I watched as he was reaching for a bat under the counter.

"Alex?" I asked Kevin with a raised brow. I glanced at the six-foot-tall man with jet-black hair, then looked back at Kevin. Kevin simply nodded when I began to put two and two together. This was Melanie's ex.

"Your usual weapon? I brought my weapon too, big boy," Alex said, flicking open the blade in his hand. I began to size

Alex up. He was on the skinny side and a couple of inches shorter than Kevin and me.

"Alex, you know that the police are on the way."

"No, they aren't. You didn't bother to press the silent alarm. If you had pressed the alarm, that would mean Melanie was here. Does that mean she's at home with that wife and kid of yours?" Alex asked, and I turned to look at Kevin.

"He knows where you live?" It pissed me off that this guy knew that much about her. Kevin just glared at me.

"I see you two are having a moment. I'm going to go get my bitch," Alex said, closing the blade.

"She's not your bitch!" I yelled, slamming my fist down on the glass counter.

"Yes, she is, and who are you to tell me she isn't? You don't know shit."

"I know that she isn't yours and that you need to leave her the fuck alone," I said, getting toe to toe with him. I didn't care if he had a blade.

"You don't know shit. You'll never own her like I do, so get out of that delusional mindset that you are going to change her name. She is mine and always will be mine."

"She isn't yours. She's mine," I said through gritted teeth, and he burst into laughter.

"Keep dreaming. She will never be with anyone but me. I made sure of it. Do you know what I did to her?" he asked, stepping closer to me.

My breathing got heavier, and I saw red. I was getting fuming mad with this guy.

"I made her understand very clearly what would happen if she was with any other man. A very nice Smith and Wesson got very intimate with her and made her understand that if she were ever with another man, Mr. Smith and Wesson would kill her from the inside out before I would use it to kill the other man. If I were you, I'd think twice about being with her."

I tackled him to the ground, straddling him, and pinned him to the ground with my knees. My arms kept swinging, and I felt my hands connect with his face on every swing. I couldn't stop myself. Why would you hurt the woman you loved? I was so angry that he hurt her, and I wasn't there to protect her. I felt Kevin trying to pull at me and stop me. I kept pulling against Kevin, and I couldn't stop. Kevin finally managed to pull me off Alex, shoving me toward the back of the parlor.

"Walk it off, Corey!" he yelled, pointing to the back of the parlor. I wiped my mouth, staring down at Alex. He lay there, dumbfounded, unsure of what had hit him. Blood was covering his face, and I didn't know if it was from his nose or mouth. I walked toward the back of the shop.

"You didn't finish the job, you crazy fuck!" Alex yelled. I turned to charge him, and Kevin locked his arms around my waist, holding me back.

"Go!" Kevin said, pushing me to the back. I headed to the back of the parlor, pacing and shaking out my hands that were now throbbing from punching the guy so hard. Kevin opened the door and stood there in the doorway. "Cigarette?"

I looked at him, rubbed the back of my neck, and nodded. I headed outside with Kevin to lean against my car, popping the cigarette he gave me between my lips.

"I'm leaving. I need to go check on Melanie, especially with that sonofabitch walking around and knowing where you live," I said as he lit his cigarette before handing me the lighter. I flicked the lighter on and lit the cigarette in my mouth. I took a deep inhale of the nicotine.

"She's fine. I called my house. Anita is taking her and Jack to her parents' house."

I nodded. I was still fuming or still on a high from beating the shit out of the guy.

"How bad was he?" I asked, staring at the cigarette between my fingers and flicking the ash off the tip. I couldn't look at Kevin right now.

"He was pretty bad to her. She called me one night. He had pinned her against the garage door with his truck. I will never forget that call. I called 9-1-1 immediately, locked up shop, and rushed over to their house. When I arrived, the EMTs were already loading her into the back of the ambulance. She was unresponsive, and the driveway was stained with blood. She had third-degree burns from the metal grill and had to have a blood transfusion. I moved her into my house. I thought her being in a gated community would help, but he sneaks in with other cars. His favorite narcissistic game is to come here looking for her, and she has been here a couple of times when he did. It's always dramatic. Melanie wants out of this. She needs better and someone to protect her. She needs to know what love is. She doesn't deserve to be here and to keep being harassed by him," Kevin explained. He exhaled some of the smoke, and I took another hit of the cigarette.

"Does she have scars and stuff?"

"Yep, on her legs, all over her back, some on her arms. A couple of the ones on her arms she did herself. She was in a dark place when she was with him. She wanted to die before she found my family." Kevin carefully answered before he took a drag. Flashbacks of her undressing began to play in front of my eyes, and the scars on her back began to be noticeable this time around. I guess I was so horny at the time that I hadn't even noticed or cared.

"How did she find you guys anyway?"

"She found herself wandering into my shop when he was at work, the only time she was able to leave the house. I asked her to work for me to pay off her tattoos, not realizing it was her attempt to escape. On her first day here after she got her butterfly tattoo, she walked in with her arm in a cast. I asked her what happened, and she said she tripped and broke her wrist from trying to catch herself from the fall. I shrugged it off. I began to notice that she was always too scared to stay late. She HAD to be home before he got home, and I never understood why. She occasionally came in with bruises. I never thought about it until, eventually, I put two and two together. I didn't want to impose or intrude on her life. I finally approached her about it and told her she couldn't live like that. Anita talked to her, and everyone tried to put some sense into her head. Then, when she got pinned by his truck, it clicked," Kevin explained.

I hated having him tell me this. It wasn't his place, but after Alex came in, I had to know. Melanie is probably freaking out right now at the house.

"Do you have it here?" I said, taking another long hit from the cigarette before tossing it on the ground and stomping it out.

"Yeah, Joseph and I can handle it here."

"Thanks. How often does he come by?"

"Uh, I've lost count. No one knows when he'll show up."

"You think she wants to move? Get out of here, move away from him?"

"She might. Thinking of taking her to Florida?" Kevin asked.

126

I wanted to take her down there for a vacation first and was already madly in love with her. After tonight, I want to protect her from him. She had to get out of there.

"Yeah, I love Melanie. She and I were meant for each other. Tonight, I just-I couldn't stop myself from wanting to beat the shit out of him for what he did to her."

"But Corey, knowing this, you need to be careful with how you tell her about your fighting," Kevin stated.

"I know, but right now isn't good. I'll tell her, I'll find a way," I said. I had to tell her eventually before she showed up for a fight. But knowing how her ex was, I had to find the time to tell her when she wasn't fragile and a way not to get her too spooked. If he had abused her, she wasn't going to be too thrilled with my other career.

"I'm out," I said. I fist-bumped Kevin before I jumped into my car, zooming over to Kevin's house. I just hoped I could make it there before they left for Anita's parent's house, or even worse, if Alex did decide to show up. What if he came to the house and I wasn't there to protect her? I pulled up to the cast iron gate, watching as it slowly swung open.

Why is it that when you are in a rush, everything is in slow motion? I pulled up to Kevin's house and saw Melanie sitting on the front porch. Good, they hadn't left yet. I sighed, relieved that I had made it in time. I parked the car, flicking the engine off before I jumped out of the vehicle and jogged up to Melanie.

Chapter Eleven:

Melanie's Point of View-

Kevin called Anita not too long ago and told us that Alex had shown up. When I heard him say that, my body flooded with panic. Corey now knew the truth. Anita said we were all going to her parents' house, as was our routine when this happened. I threw what little clothes I owned into a gym bag and tossed it aside.

I went out onto the front porch, sat on the porch swing, and pulled my knees to my chest. I hugged my legs to hold them close to me. Jack and Anita were still in the house, grabbing things for the last-minute trip. I always hated going there because I was the third wheel. I wasn't family. They had to leave their safe place because I brought danger into their home.

I was beyond upset and angry right now, knowing that Corey was at the tattoo parlor. He knew everything now. He was NOT supposed to find out this way. I was supposed to tell him when the time was right. I could only imagine how mad he would be at me for this. This wasn't a secret to keep from somebody you wanted a relationship with. I pushed a hand through my hair to get the loose strands out of my face. I could hear the rumble of an engine coming down the street, getting my attention. I looked up, making sure it wasn't Alex's car. To my surprise, it was Corey.

I stood up from the swing, stepping beside a wooden post as he pulled up to the curb. I was confused. What was he doing here? Corey jogged up the lawn, cupped my face, and pulled me in for a rough, passionate kiss. His arms snaked around my body, pulling me into his muscular frame. Tears threatened to escape. I was trying to hold them back when Corey stepped back, and I stared into his eyes.

"I'm so glad you are here and okay. I had to come see you after that." He pulled me in for another hug, and I let the tears fall this time.

"I guess now is the best time to talk to you about this, huh? Unless Kevin already spilled the beans." I stepped back, breaking the hug this time. I glanced up at him, and the look on his face told me that Kevin had already told him the majority of it.

"Kevin told me what he knows," he started, and I nodded.

"Well, there isn't much more to tell. All you need to know is that Alex was a fuck tool who abused the hell out of me," I truthfully answered as I ran a shaky hand through my hair.

"The scars, how many are there?" he asked as I sighed.

"I'll show you one day, but not now." He nodded, seeming to understand. He hugged me again, this time even tighter if possible.

"I know that he sexually assaulted you at least once." Corey whispered the words in my ear, and I began to ugly cry. Tears flowed like a river, causing a huge wet stain on his shirt. I had bottled up so much hurt Alex had caused that I forgot what it felt like to have these feelings. "Alex told me in explicit terms what he did. Unfortunately, Kevin heard, too. Why don't you come and stay at my house tonight? That way, I can protect you."

I didn't immediately respond because I couldn't think straight. Going to Corey's house would be more beneficial than Anita's parents. I looked up at Corey, my eyes still filled with tears. I nodded yes. I didn't even bother grabbing my bag from inside the house, and I let Corey drive me to his house. I shot Kevin and Anita a text that I was going to Corey's house tonight and would be back.

I felt numb. Corey knew I wasn't myself. His hand held mine tightly in his lap, not letting go to make turns. He pulled into the driveway, and the rumbling engine went quiet when he turned the ignition off.

We hadn't spoken for the whole drive. He hopped out, coming around to open the door for me, and his arm snaked around my waist, pulling me closer to him. Once we got inside the house, he led me up to his room, where I stood awkwardly in the doorway, watching as he rummaged through drawers in his dresser.

"I think this will suffice for pajamas tonight." He tossed something onto the bed. I walked to the edge of the bed, seeing a men's XL shirt with Tupac on the front.

"Shorts?" I whispered.

"You don't need any. It'll be in the seventies all night, and the shirt will be super long on you," he confidently stated.

I carried the black shirt into the connected bathroom to change. I looked down to see it stopped right above where the scars started on my legs. I closed my eyes.

I stared at the top of the staircase where Alex leaned over the banister, giving an evil laugh before slowly strutting down the steps and squatting beside me. Both of my legs were bent the opposite way they were supposed to be from him, shoving me down the staircase.

"Aww, it looks like you took a nasty tumble. This little accident better not get in the way of you providing for my every need. Remember, I'll want a hot shower next time, so you better not use all the hot water again." He growled at me before standing, walking away, leaving me there to fend for myself.

I shook my head to get rid of the images and stared at my reflection. I took a deep breath before I gripped the knob of the bathroom door and hoped that I wouldn't have to relive it again with Corey.

I cautiously walked into the room while Corey was plugging his phone in. He wore a pair of jersey shorts that hugged his hips and exposed the right amount of his hip dents. "I turned on my alarm system and the security cameras."

I had no idea his house had all that, but I felt even more secure. I slowly took another step closer toward him. I felt overwhelmed with sadness again, and tears threatened to come again. It was like he could read my mind as Corey enveloped me in a hug and held me for what felt like an eternity.

"Are you hungry?" he mumbled against the side of my head. I shook my head no. "Are you tired?"

I didn't know what I was. I wasn't sure if I could sleep, but I knew I couldn't eat. He led me to the bed, where I curled up against his side, his grip firm. I feel safe and secure being held tight to him.

I must have dozed off because I was woken out of my

slumber by a banging coming from downstairs. I shot up, and the sound cut off. I looked to my left; Corey was still asleep. I told myself I was imagining things and laid down, hoping to go back to sleep.

Bang, bang, bang.

I shot back up and heard Corey groan beside me this time.

"I'll go investigate." Corey rubbed his hand along his face, trying to wake himself up. I quickly jumped out of the bed, hot on Corey's tail, to see what was causing that ruckus.

Bang, bang, bang.

It was coming from the front door. Who could it be at this time of night? I tightly gripped Corey's bicep as he pulled the door open to reveal two police officers standing on his front porch. Why were the police here?

"Corey Mathison?" the one officer said sternly.

"That's me. What is the problem, officers?" Corey asked, confused.

"You are under arrest for aggravated assault on Alexander Stevenson," the other officer said.

Did he assault Alex? I stepped back from Corey.

Corey turned to look at me, guilt written on his face along with sincerity. "I'm sorry, sweetie," he said before turning back to face the officers. "I'll come willingly, but can I at least change out of my pajamas?"

The officers nodded. "One of us will stand guard to make sure there's no funny business."

One of the officers followed Corey and me back upstairs, stopping at the bedroom door where he could still see us.

I went into the room with Corey, sitting on the edge of the bed to stare up at him. I was upset that Corey had chosen violence. This was exactly what Alex would want. Would

Corey ever hit me if he got that angry with me?

Corey walked into the bathroom while I sat there, deep in thought, so many questions flying through my head. How much did I really know about Corey? Was he capable of hitting me? What did Alex do to cause him to snap? Was Corey a ticking time bomb? Would he become just like Alex? The bathroom door banging open snapped me out of my thoughts. Corey stepped between me and the dresser.

"Why?" Was all I could manage to stutter.

"Why did I beat his ass?"

"Yes."

"Why not? He deserved it. He was an arrogant asshole who beat the shit out of a woman for no reason but for pleasure and raped her with a gun. Then you want to question me? Why are you even defending him after all the shit he did to you? You should be thanking me because I will NOT, I repeat, WILL NOT, let him disrespect the woman I love. If you want to sit here and shame me for defending you, for teaching him that he messed with the wrong guy, then you better think again. I am protective over what's mine, and as far as you've led me to understand, you are mine. I don't think that you're on that crazy guy's side. If you want to stay on his side, then you better be gone by the time I get released from jail." He snarled as he pushed past me to go downstairs.

The officer separated us as we took every step down. "Wait, can I talk to him?"

Corey looked at me, confused, then at the officers. The officers stood there with their arms crossed over their chests. "Thank you, Corey. Yes, he deserved it. I wasn't trying to defend him. But can you understand how scared I am of you now? Alex would relentlessly beat me. And now you go ahead and beat him?"

Corey stepped closer to me until our bodies pressed against each other, and still, I didn't fear him hurting me in any way. If Alex even stepped toward me, I would quiver or flinch. I never knew what Alex had up his sleeve. With Corey, I did not react to his quick movements. He was gentle, and I had no reason to fear him. Even after giving Alex the beating of his life, I didn't worry that Corey would hurt me.

"I would never abuse you, mentally or physically. I do not regret what I did to Alex. I love you, Melanie." He closed the distance between us, giving me a passionate kiss. Our foreheads pressed together, and I was left staring deep into his eyes, trying to determine if there were any lies in what he said.

"Corey, that's all the time we can allow," the one officer said. I watched as he led Corey down to the other police officer, and they began to pat him down while reading him his Miranda rights, then placing him in cuffs. I stood there in disbelief that this was happening.

Corey said he loved me. Alex never said those words the whole time we were together. I didn't say it back to Corey. Did I love him in return?

I stood there staring as the police car drove off. I was trying to wrap my head around the fact that Alex had gone ahead and pressed assault charges on Corey. I shouldn't have expected less of him because Alex was vindictive as hell. I was angry that Corey hadn't controlled his anger, though. I went back inside, beelining up the stairs to find my phone to dial Kevin's number.

"Melanie?" Kevin asked groggily.

"Corey was just arrested. Alex is pressing charges against

him for assault," I blurted out. Through his phone, I could hear him shoot up in his bed.

"Melanie, are you sitting down?"

"Yes, why?"

"We need to be very diligent in what we do."

"We need to bail him out, Kevin. What the fuck are you saying?"

Kevin sighed, "No one can find out about this. It'll ruin his career."

"His acting? Actors get arrested all the time."

"Melanie, he isn't an actor."

"He's not?"

"He's an MMA fighter."

I gasped and dropped my phone. I could hear Kevin yelling for me before he eventually hung up. I sat there in a state of total shock.

I quickly found his car keys and sped to where they had booked him. I was hot under the collar, and I barged through until I got the police to let me visit Corey.

I sat there facing a pane of glass, waiting for them to escort Corey to the window. He slid into the seat across from me, his face lit up, and we both grabbed a phone receiver.

"You're a fucking MMA fighter?!" I yelled and slammed my hand on the counter. "And you're not violent?"

"Melanie, please listen."

"No, you listen. I'm not stupid anymore. I'm not going to continue living with lies. I'm lucky it was him and not me. You fucking fight for a living, Corey! I can't do this, Corey," I said, shaking my head from side to side. I slammed the receiver down, letting the tears roll down my face.

"I'm sorry," he said, putting his hand against the glass. I

stood up, shaking my head no. I beelined it out of the visiting area and drove back to his place.

I paced the driveway, calling Kevin to come and get me. He said he couldn't since he was trying to figure out the bail money. I went into Corey's house, waiting for someone to pick me up. While I waited, I decided to use my phone to research Corey's MMA career.

I watched video after video of him fighting, and he was good at it. But, given my past, would I be safe with him? He hasn't shown any reason not to trust him or violent tendencies until now. He was right, Alex had every reason to get his ass beat.

My phone began to ring in the middle of a video, so I paused Corey's match. I immediately answered when I read Kevin's name on the caller ID.

"Corey is being released. The police have determined they aren't charging him because he was defending us and my parlor. We need to be stealthy when picking him up. How are you holding up?"

I swallowed a ball of nerves. I didn't know how I felt right now.

"Right now, I don't know how I feel, Kevin. What do you need me to do?" I asked. Regardless of how I felt toward Corey, his career shouldn't be at risk because of my stupid ex. I think he and I needed to have a long conversation.

"I need you to bring his car to the jail and on the down low. Anyone who realizes what has happened can release it to the tabloids. Stay put there," Kevin explained.

Chapter Twelve:

Last night, I analyzed this MMA fighting he did. But the light of day made me realize I was nervous about picking up Corey. I got into the oversized Tupac shirt he gave me, tied the bottom to make it shorter, and put on a pair of his basketball shorts. I was too nervous to even think about eating breakfast.

I drove to the jail parking lot and circled until I found Kevin, Anita, and Jack standing at the back of Kevin's car. I parked next to them, climbed out, and met them by the trunk of their vehicle. Giving them each a hug, we stood there, watching the doors patiently.

The double doors pushed open, and Corey strolled down the sidewalk toward us. I leaned against his Jaguar while he hugged and talked with them. He turned to look at me, his anxious gaze meeting mine.

Corey slowly stepped toward me, and I pushed myself to stand up straight. We stood mere inches apart in awkward silence. Quietly, I asked, "Drive me home?"

His lips curled up to a smile as I handed his keys over.

"Certainly. Where do we stand?"

I bit my bottom lip, not quite sure of myself. "We will see how the day goes."

Corey began to drive us home when he turned down a different road. "We're being followed. What kind of car does Alex drive?"

I glanced at him, then peeked in the side mirror to see the trademark red Ram truck Alex had used to pin me to his garage. My breathing became shallow. My nails dug into the leather seat. I tried to calm myself before I went into a full-blown anxiety attack. Clenching my eyes shut, I focused on what I could feel.

I feel the leather seat under my hands, the fabric seat belt across my body. My breathing was shallow, but I was breathing. I heard the Motley Crue song playing in the background on the radio. I could hear the tires screeching. Wait! Why are the tires screeching?

My eyes flung open as Corey slammed on the brakes, causing the car to spin around the cement median. My fingers dug deeper into the leather seat, scared of the sudden movement. The red truck swirled around in a not-so-sharp manner.

I trusted Corey. I had to believe in him. Corey did some evasive but fancy maneuvers, doing his best to get Alex off our tail. I repeated mantras and tightly squeezed my eyes shut for most of the ride.

"Lost him," Corey finally said. I was so relieved when I opened my eyes to find him pulling into the familiar parking lot of the lake where he docked his boat.

Corey slammed his car into park, flipped the ignition off, and jumped out of his side. He ran around the car, opened my tricky door, and hustled us down the dock. He led the way up the ladder to board the ship, and I went to the front deck. I let him do what was necessary so we could set sail.

I stood there staring out at the lake, leaning against the railing, when the boat jerked alive. I walked over to the captain's wheel where Corey was standing.

"Why are you with me, Corey?"

"Why am I with you?" He repeated, and I glared at him. "Because I love you, Melanie. I thought I told you that before I got booked."

"Why me? You just had to lose Alex on a high-speed chase like in Dukes of Hazard. Is that something you want to deal with daily? And I don't need to keep bailing you out every time you decide to go assault happy on his ass."

Corey burst into laughter. "Maybe if you move to Florida with me, we won't have to worry about Alex."

"Not until we discuss you and the whole MMA thing. I need the truth. How'd you get into that?"

"The whole story?" he asked with a glance at me.

"Yes."

"It started in college, my junior year. I was in the cafeteria with my friends when I overheard them discussing some fight club."

"I thought the first rule of Fight Club was not to talk about Fight Club?" I interrupted. Corey burst into laughter. "So, I was right?"

"Yes, but they didn't hear that rule. My parents cut me off financially because I wasn't pursuing a doctor's career. I had no job and no money to cover expenses. I went to a fight club, dropped $20 in a betting pool, and walked out with $300 that night. I kept going back. One night, a fighter didn't show, and I volunteered to help get some of my aggression out. I knocked the other guy out in less than five minutes. I got paid $1,250 for winning. I kept coming back for more. My name grew in popularity, and then I was offered a job in Florida. I now do taped matches, get bigger payments, and even teach classes to younger kids. I think I have a couple more years left in my MMA career. I want to continue teaching the kids, whether it be in MMA or anger management training. I also want to take time to be a family man. I would love to be a dad by then and spend quality time with my kids. I want to open up my own MMA clothing business eventually. The shorts, the gloves, the mouth guards, the whole nine yards."

A smile came to my face upon hearing his plans for the future and about how he wanted to be a dad. You could tell that he loved kids. All of his plans involved kids. He had such a big heart and was involved in the youth. "You teach younger kids?"

"Yes, I do, and I love it. I teach them to control their anger and to fight safely."

"That sounds rich coming from you," I chuckled. "I'm still wary, though, Corey. Can you understand why I'm so torn?"

"How are you torn?"

"I haven't ever felt this way toward anyone before. I want this. I want to love you. The way you make me feel is new to me. It's just that I don't understand why you allow yourself to get beat up or beat others for a living. I lived in hell for years with Alex, being consistently beaten and torn down. I meet you, and you get paid to beat someone else up."

Corey nodded as he waved me over. I nervously walked over to him, and I didn't have this fear of him. He whispered, "Are you scared now?"

I looked up into his brown eyes, staring at me intensely, but there was no fear inside of me. "No."

Corey smiled. His hand pushed through my hair, gripping the length, and I didn't flinch at the movement. Even after he beat the shit out of Alex, learning that he beats people up and everything, I still didn't fear him. "That's because you know that I would never lay a finger on you. I haven't given you any reason to think I would. Now, as for Alex, what do we do about him? He won't let you go without a fight, and I won't be able to control my temper with him."

"What do you suggest?"

"Florida. He can't track either of us there."

"Yes, he can. Your MMA." I said, and he burst into laughter. "What's so funny, Corey?"

"You can't find me unless you know where to look. How bad was he to you? I want to hear it from you."

I sighed, turning to look out into the water with the breeze blowing through my hair.

"I met him when we were in high school. I loved him. We were homecoming king and queen. He promised we would have this big cottage with kids and dogs. He had earned a full ride to Harvard. I dreamed of being that stay-at-home mom. Somehow, my parents saw through his crap. I guess he was disrespectful to my parents on more than one occasion when I wasn't around. I ran away multiple times to be with him. I didn't listen to them and thought they were trying to ruin my life."

"Typical teenager, thinking their parents are out for them," Corey teased. I glared at him, then chuckled when I realized he wasn't being derogatory towards me. Corey stepped away, and I watched him toss the anchor overboard.

I walked over to claim a lawn chair while Corey sat on the one next to me. "I crashed in his dorm at the university, which was harder than I thought it would be. He was kicked out of the dorm when the university discovered I was crashing in his room. With no money to afford an apartment on his own and neither of us working, we were homeless. That's when it began. The degrading comments, the resentment that it was all my fault. As we began to get back on our feet, the mean words started to come more often. One night, when he was drunk, he smashed the bottle over my head. When he realized the enjoyment that gave him, the physical abuse began to increase. He raped me numerous times. One time, he used his gun, threatening that this would remind me of what would happen if he caught me with another guy."

"You tried escaping by going to Kevin's tattoo shop?"

"Yes, his shop was close enough to where we lived that I could walk there within an hour."

"An hour's walk?"

"It wasn't that far in this small but big town." I sighed. "I was scared to leave Alex. I had nowhere to go. My parents haven't talked to me since high school. Where would I go? When I found the tattoo parlor, it was my saving grace. I prayed that someone would help me. Lucky for me, Kevin was that someone. He saw the signs, got me out, and saved my life."

"He did, and I'm fortunate. Alex would have killed you."

"He almost did," I whispered, his hand resting on my thigh, rubbing it soothingly.

"You want to go down to Florida this weekend? I can take you to my training class and one of my fights."

"I would like that, but I might be too scared or nervous to see the fight. I'm afraid that it'll bring on too many flashbacks."

"If you go, and it's too much, you could always wait for me backstage."

"What if I never get comfortable with it?" I asked nervously.

I heard him let out a deep sigh. "We'll find a way to get through it."

"What do we do now?" I asked, glancing up at Corey.

"Well, we need to chill out until I think the coast is clear, or we can take this bad boy down to Florida."

"Seriously?"

He smirked back at me. "Seriously. I have to be there in a few days anyway, and it's a three-day trip."

"Aren't you tired? What about food?" I asked.

"We can go nap and then be full sail ahead. That's if you want to be my co-captain?" he asked with a raised brow. I smirked and felt a bit daring, so I straddled his lap. His hands instinctively rested on my hips, and it felt right. A smile came over me as I stared down into his brown eyes.

"With pleasure." I kissed him roughly. I had this love-hate relationship with him. I hated what he had done and that he fought for a living, but I couldn't help how full my heart felt when I was with him. He had beat up Alex on my behalf. He said he loved me, but we have a messed-up relationship. "I still hate what you did."

"Because I fought for what's mine? You'll be mine forever, beautiful." His voice came out husky.

I leaned back, resting my full weight on him. One of his hands grabbed my arm, "Show me the scars?"

Tracing a few of the faded scars that I had tried so hard to heal or hide, they looked more natural than when they were fresher. "Those were self-inflicted."

Corey looked up at me without showing disgust. "Why

143

would you do that?"

"I was in a fucked-up state of mind, Corey," I started to explain as I got off his lap and started to walk away. I took a few steps before stopping, crossing my arms over my chest, and sniffed up some tears. I heard the chair creaking and could feel his towering strength behind me. His hands were gripping my biceps firmly, and it was comforting. "I felt more numb now than I did then."

"You felt numb recently?" The confusion was clear in his voice.

"Yes, because I didn't know what to think about what was happening. My body was numb to the emotions. I felt like this when I was with him. I feared that life was repeating itself, Corey. I feared that you were becoming him. I couldn't go through that again. I harmed myself to feel again, so that I was the one in control. Alex always controlled me, and I had no say in anything but this. A part of me wanted to end it all before he did so he wouldn't have the pleasure of doing it himself," I explained. Corey's posture stiffened at my words.

"I'm sorry I put you in that position. It was not my intention."

"Why did you attack him? That's what he wanted all along, and you fell right into his trap. Then, finding out from Kevin that you fight for a living made my heart sink. I thought history was repeating itself. I can't go through that again." I stood there, shaking my head no.

"I'm sorry I scared you. I saw red. Anger overruled me; all I could think about was what he had done to you. When he described the assault with the gun, that made me even more furious. I lost all control. In MMA, we teach control, and we have to do anger management. I lost my cool."

"You take anger management?" I asked, looking over my

shoulder at him.

"I go once a week. In MMA, it's not about anger. It's a sport no different than any other. We aren't going in there filled with rage, wanting to hurt our opponent purposefully. We go in there to fight, use proper techniques, and put that to use. It's like boxing. Do you think Muhammad Ali wanted to hurt all his opponents?"

"No."

"Right answer. I don't want to hurt them. Yes, injuries do happen, but we go to the gym to practice routines and maneuvers to use on one another. It does help get rage out."

"I'm sure it does."

"I feel that you have rage built up. You've bottled up so many emotions that you are about to explode." He read me like a newspaper. How'd he get to know me so well? "Going to a show and being able to scream will help relieve some of that tension. Maybe I can get you to do a few jabs."

"Are you going to take me to the gym with you?"

"Well, duh! You are stuck with me. I teach the pre-teens; they have the most anger."

I smiled and tugged at the hem of my shirt nervously. "I'd like that."

"Then I'll set it up."

"But Corey?"

"Yeah?"

"We have no food or clothes," I said. I heard him chuckle. "Why are you laughing?"

"We are having a heart-to-heart, and you are concerned about food?" He laughed again.

"Well, I'm getting hungry after all this commotion, and I'm an emotional eater, if you must know."

"Well, let's go see what we have." He winked, offered me his arm, and led me to the mini kitchen below deck. I leaned back against the table, watching him open cabinets to see what was available. "We've got protein bars and protein shakes."

"You eat that crap?"

"Yeah, I do. I get a heck of a workout at the gym and from my fights." He pulled down a white and blue jug that said ISO something on it. "And no milk."

"What now?" I asked, biting my bottom lip.

"Nap, then we will go from there." He grasped my hand, leading me to the smaller-sized bed that looked like no one had used it in ages. "That's if you are okay sharing a bed with me."

I rolled my eyes before I crawled up the bed and flopped onto my back. Corey removed his shirt while still standing at the end of the bed. He was so sexy. I had thought he was attractive since he walked into the parlor the first day. Now, I see this whole dark, protective side of him that I didn't see before. Alex was just barking up the wrong tree when he provoked Corey. But now that I'm with Corey, can I live with him knowing he will get hurt doing MMA? I'm sure he broke his nose fighting, not by walking into a door. I'm accustomed to being the patient at the hospital and not the person I loved. Wait...do I love him?

"You're staring," Corey said without looking up from tightening his pajama shorts. I hadn't even noticed he'd changed. Where'd his shorts come from?

"Deep in thought, sorry. You have clothes on board?"

"Just a spare outfit. You want the spare wife beater?"

"Nah, that'll be too cold for me."

Corey walked around the bed and slid in next to me, his arm

hanging around my waist. He tugged me closer to him until my body molded into his nicely. It felt so good to be wrapped in his embrace again. "Penny for your thoughts?"

I sighed and glanced at him. "You got a penny?"

"Put it on my tab."

"I didn't realize you had a dark, protective side. Also, you lied about your nose. Then I realized I was always the patient, the one injured, not Alex. Now, I'll be going to the hospital for your injuries. How often is it that bad?"

"That rarely happens. We have medics on staff to check us out post-match, so we don't have to go to the hospital unless it's a broken limb."

"How many times have you gone?"

"This year? Once, for my nose. Pretty good, considering it's April."

"You said you loved me. Why do you love me? Would you be mad if I don't say it back any time soon?"

"I love you because you complete me. The moment my eyes landed on you, my whole world stopped. You are a breath of fresh air and the calm before the storm. You are what occupies my mind the majority of the time. My heart skips a beat when I think of you, and my palms sweat when I'm with you. I won't be mad. You'll say it with time and only if it's true."

"Would you still love me if I can't stand watching you fight?"

"I'll love you even if you can't watch me fight. I'll understand."

"But for how long?"

"How long for what?"

"For you to realize you can have another girl that will support you more or be in the front row cheering you on?"

"And who says that's what I want in a girl?" He shifted our

positions to make eye contact with me. "You're overthinking everything, beautiful. You'd have to do a lot worse to get rid of me."

"Who said I would want to get rid of you?" I asked. His whole face was lit up with a smile.

"Good, I don't want to leave you. I want you to be mine forever." He whispered before I felt him kiss the top of my head. "Now get some sleep. The last couple of days have been rough. I barely got any sleep the last few nights."

I snuggled up closer to him for his body heat. The weather on the lake was a lot cooler than on land.

My mind wouldn't rest, and I kept asking myself why I was still here with Corey? I had promised myself that I would never again enter into a relationship with someone who showed an ounce of capacity for violence. But here I lay, next to Corey, who fought for a living and had just kicked the shit out of my ex. Yet, I was content. I couldn't fully describe all the emotions he made me feel. I felt like I was floating on cloud nine with him. He had me feeling giddy for the first time in my life. I was exploring parts of myself that I'd closed off from others and opened my heart up again. I have been torn down so many times in my past that he's my glimmer of hope. I'm afraid of losing him because I love how he makes me feel. Was this what love felt like? If so, I don't want to live without him.

"Get out of your head and get some rest," Corey mumbled. I glance up toward Corey to find his eyes pressed shut and his mouth curled into a smile.

"How'd you know?"

"You breathe differently when you fall asleep and aren't dead weight on me."

"Oh..."

"You still want to talk?" His dark eyes are now staring back at me.

"I don't know. You make me feel so many things I've never felt before, Corey. I have torn myself down so much, and I'm afraid I'll never get out of this hole I'm buried in. I met you, and now I can't imagine life without you. You make me feel alive and give me a glimmer of hope." I rambled on while I stared at the foot of the bed.

"I'm glad you feel something about me, and I didn't completely fuck this up."

I playfully smacked him. "I'm being serious, you jerk."

"Look, I know that as of right now, both of us are shaken up, and you're feeling fragile. We just had to be Bo and Luke Duke to escape that psycho. Do you think we can save the heavy talk for when we get to land?"

"Yes, and after we get some sleep." I agreed. I snuggled closer to him, my cheek pressed against the firmness of his bare chest. The subtle beating of his heart beneath my ear soothed me enough to calm my thoughts temporarily. Corey's arms tightened around me to hold me where I was. I didn't want to be anywhere other than where I was. Fearing Alex was hot on our tail and knowing he was out for revenge didn't make sleeping easy. Being on land, at Kevin's house or the tattoo parlor, was unsafe for us. There was no stopping Alex, and I had no real idea what he was capable of doing. I was not only fearful of what he would do to me, but I feared what he would do to Corey now that Corey made it clear that I was his. Alex now knows that Kevin may not get physical with him, but Corey will. Corey had no fear of Alex since he had his MMA training to help him deal with any threat.

Chapter Thirteen:

I must have zonked out because when my eyes slowly began to flutter open, I was very groggy. I rubbed my eyes, trying to clear my vision, then my eyes flung open. I didn't see or feel Corey beside me. Anxiety and panic overwhelmed my body. Where was Corey? I am alone on his boat.

I jumped out of bed and curled into the fetal position in the dark corner. Tears of fear were rolling out of my eyes. Alex must have found us. I'm caught now. I have nowhere to go and no way to protect myself. I am going to die here. I am going to be killed and tossed overboard. The police wouldn't find any trace of Corey or me. Kevin won't go looking for another week when we don't return from Florida. I'd be responsible for Corey's death.

Stomp. Stomp. Stomp. Was that footsteps I was hearing? Stomp. Stomp. Yes, that was certainly footsteps. Creak! That's the door. I ducked further down into the darkness, hoping that if it were Alex, he wouldn't be able to see me. From where I sat, I could make out the outline of a figure stepping into the doorway. Then, the person began to walk down the steps into the kitchen. I instantly knew it was Corey by the figure's features. He had plastic bags hanging from his hands. Corey was alive, and Alex hadn't found us!

"Melanie?" I heard Corey call out. I noticed he began to look around as if he was trying to see where I had gone since I was no longer in bed. I stood up from the darkness, the tears leaving streaks down my cheeks. "Baby, what's wrong?"

Before Corey could take another step closer, I dove over the bed, jumping into his embrace. He dropped the bags to catch me. I cried into his shoulder in relief that he was okay. His arms wrapped around me, holding me tight, and my fingers dug into his back.

Mumbling into his shoulder, I said, "You're alive."

"Of course, I'm alive. Are you okay?" He asked, concerned.

"Y-Y-Yes." Stammering out as I slid to my feet and wiped my eyes. "I have terrible anxiety issues when it comes to staying in new places. Even though I have been on your boat, I am not quite comfortable here. I freaked out when I woke up, and you weren't next to me. I thought Alex had found us, and you were a goner."

Corey's thumb wiped at the tears on my face, and he looked sad that I was crying. "He's gone, beautiful. He couldn't have found us this soon, even if he wanted to, sweetie. I'm sorry I spooked you. I didn't want to wake you, so I scheduled a grocery delivery with food items that would last us for the trip to Florida. I went to the pier to grab the delivery."

"They deliver to the pier?"

"Yep. We have a three to four-day trip down to Florida, depending on how many breaks we need to take."

"Let me help put this away," I said. I began to pick up the

bags he had dropped and helped put everything away. I was happy we were taking the boat instead of flying, and he was thoughtful enough to order food for us. I think sailing to Florida will give us a few days to recoup from what happened with my ex and get to know each other more intimately.

"How are you feeling now that you had a nap?"

"Hungry. And my heart is slowly trying to get back to a regular beat from my anxiety attack. What do you want to eat?"

"I ordered some donuts, and I can brew some coffee."

"Were you able to get any sleep?"

"I got some sleep. It was much better than snuggling up to my cellmate Bubba," he said, giving me a wink, and I chuckled. "But being in jail gave me lots of time to think about you and your ex."

I sat at the table while Corey began brewing coffee and making a donut tower. I knew the topic of Alex would come up, and Corey was putting a lot of thought into this. What was bugging him so much? "Melanie, do you still believe in love?"

What kind of question was that? After discovering the damage Alex had caused me, I am sure he is worried about my emotional state or if I was even ready to love again.

"Do I believe in love? Yes," I responded as Corey brought the plate with the tower of donuts to the table and slid into the seat across from me while we waited for the coffee to brew.

"Why did you love Alex? He is nothing like who or what I am."

"You two are quite the opposite of each other. I met Alex in high school. I was young and stupid then, Corey. I'm older now, so I see the world differently than I did then. I've experienced a lot more, too."

"Would you want kids? Or want to get married?"

I had no idea where this was coming from, but we had to talk about these things if we were going to have a future. "I guess I did want to get married and have kids. I wanted to live in a little cottage-sized house with kids and stay at home. That was what Alex promised he'd provide me. Alex turned my life upside down. I don't even know what I want anymore, Corey. I honestly did not think I could be sexually active because Alex had instilled this fear in me. But Corey, you have pushed me past that fear, and I'm grateful you have been patient with me. I don't think Alex ever asked if I was okay with what he was doing. He just took what he wanted, even if I said no. I'm scared that he knows that I ran off with you. I worry about what that means for you. I fear him killing the one man I'm falling for." Tears began to fill my eyes, slowly escaping from the corners. "I am trying so hard not to get attached to you because I fear the worst with Alex knowing about you. And I feel guilty because I brought you into this. You don't deserve the trouble that comes with being associated with me. You are risking your life because of me. I'm not worth your life. I am destined to be his bitch forever."

"No, you're not," Corey sternly said. His hands clenched into fists on the table. Oddly, the thought of him getting so angry and upset over Alex was a big turn-on. He was becoming so protective of me that I felt secure. He wanted to fight for me. He certainly wasn't shy about showing that he did love me. I think Corey needed to attend that anger management class to get this situation off his chest and to get help with this flare-up. The only problem was this wasn't going to be a one-time thing. Alex is a narcissistic man who will not take no for an answer. I know this won't be a one-time occurrence with him.

"He's mad that he doesn't have control over you anymore. He will never, and I mean never, lay another finger on you or me. He will not have the chance to kill either of us. Do not live in fear of this guy. I will not pressure you to have sex with me, given the trauma you have been through. When you are ready, I'll be ready. He will never know if and when we have sex. I mean, I do like to leave marks, though." He winked when he said this, and I felt my cheeks warming instantly. I had to break eye contact with him due to it. "Do you want to go back to that?"

"Fuck, no."

"Then, fight for yourself. Maybe meeting me was just what you needed."

"How so?" My eyebrow perked up, intrigued by what he meant by that.

"I can teach you how to defend yourself and fight for you."

"My rock'em sock'em robot."

Corey burst into laughter. "Good one. But, yes. Will you ever say you love me? Do you feel that way about me? Do you even think of a future with me? I worry that I messed it up by being so stupid, and letting my anger get the best of me. I also don't want to fight for us if you aren't feeling it with me."

I could tell that the thought I may not want to be with him was crushing his soul. I know how he must be feeling. The years I thought I loved Alex, only for him to continue to crush me down, was worse than it all. Alex chose and continues to choose violence. Alex diminished me; he ruined my life like he claimed I did his.

I reached across the table, resting my hands gently on his

ink-covered wrist. Corey glanced at my hands, then at my face. "Corey, I feel things about you that I wouldn't change for the world. I want us to work so badly. I fear saying those words again. I was in love with Alex and saw what he did to me. I will say it eventually, but not now. Please know the feelings are reciprocated, even if I don't express it verbally."

Our eyes connected, and a glimmer of hope showed in his eyes upon hearing me say that.

"Do you want to be married and have those kids? My condo in Florida isn't a cottage, and the house in Lancaster isn't very cottage-like, either. I wouldn't choose that house because Alex is too close for comfort."

"I thought you wanted to go to Florida since that's where your career is."

"I'm only going where my girl wants to go."

I smiled when he said, 'My girl.' He certainly was the one and way better for me than Alex. I honestly didn't think I'd fall for a guy like Corey, this ultimate badass covered with tattoos. My parents hated Alex for specific reasons, but they would have more reasons not to like Corey based on his physical appearance. Once you knew him, Corey was this amazing, down-to-earth guy.

A smile came on my face, "I'm thinking Florida, but Corey…"

"Not another but," he said with a chuckle. He leaned back on his side of the table, patiently waiting to get what I had to say.

"What about my car? A job? If you decide to break my heart?"

Corey burst into laughter. I glared at him. "I would never break your heart, beautiful. Secondly, the Volkswagen will never make the drive to Florida. Kevin will have to sell it.

Finally, you don't have to work if you don't want to. Go to college or do whatever you want until you figure it out. Be that stay-at-home wife until we have kids."

That all sounded great, and the smile on my face was pure. That's what my dream has always been: to be a stay-at-home mom. "How many kids do you want?"

Corey finished chewing his bite of donut before he responded. "Four."

"Whoa, you expect me to give birth four times?"

"Yep. The house I'm renting out is a five-bedroom house with three bathrooms. We'd have plenty of room."

"You'd kick that family out?"

"No, I'd give them lots of notice to find someplace new. I don't expect you to get pregnant right away."

"Very true," I said with a smile.

"Do you still want kids?"

I sighed, "I'm not sure, Corey. Alex killed my soul and extinguished the romance light within me. I need a lot of rebuilding, but you have re-lit this flame within me."

Corey smiled, and he reached across the table, holding my hand. "Well, I'm not planning on going anywhere and will be okay without kids."

Our breakfast was filled with discussions about our future, making my heart feel full that he wanted a future with me. Corey looked exhausted, but he kept plodding along.

"I'm going to go get this boat on the water. Care to join me?"

"I'll be up in a minute. I'll clean up and brew a new pot of coffee," I answered. Corey stepped in front of me, bent over to have his face mere inches in front of mine, and pressed his lips against mine roughly.

"I love you," he whispered and winked before I watched him

walk to the upper deck. I stood from the table, ridding it of our trash. I brewed the coffee, leaning against the counter, waiting for it to be ready.

Was I going to move to Florida? What about Kevin? If Corey and I leave at the same time, then that means he would be without a piercer. What about me? He's losing me. I felt terrible about leaving him without notice. I also felt bad making the move without some game plan. What if Corey dropped me on a dime? I'll be there with no car, job, or place. I had no backup plan when I was with Alex, and look at what happened. I felt like I had a chance for a better life with Corey and truly wanted this to work. I feared history repeating itself.

I poured the hot contents into the coffee mugs and filled them the rest of the way with creamer. I headed up to the captain's wheel, where Corey stood still with his back to me. I stepped beside him and rested his mug on the little table he had there.

"Thanks, beautiful," Corey said, taking a big gulp of the coffee. "I spoke with Kevin. He's closing the shop for a few days, and they will meet us in Florida. I figured that gives us extra protection for you, and while I'm working, you'll have someone there if flashbacks occur."

"You did? They're coming?!" I was shocked and happy. He cared enough about me to arrange for Kevin's family to be with me during this trying time. He wanted me to be comfortable.

"Yes, they are. I know you get anxious being alone in places you aren't comfortable with. You are also going to your first MMA fight on top of what just occurred. I am nervous about what I'm about to put you through. I want you surrounded by people that love and support you."

"You're nervous?"

"Yes, I am. I'm scared you'll leave me once and for all."

"I'd never do that!" I gasped as he glanced at me.

"We will have one open day, no work scheduled. You want to go to Disney World?"

"Seriously?" I asked excitedly.

Corey burst into laughter. "I take that as a yes since you were beyond excited when asked."

I blushed and grinned. I stood there sipping at my coffee, keeping Corey company for hours. We alternated between spending so many hours sailing, followed by so many hours cuddling in the bed, trying to catch up on sleep. I couldn't believe Corey made this long journey frequently for work. I didn't know anyone else I would want to make this trip with. We spent the time sailing and discussing things we probably wouldn't have any other time to discuss.

Chapter Fourteen:

Corey began to pilot the boat toward the various docking piers. Standing at the end of the pier, the family of three was waving, slowly getting bigger as we approached. From what I could see, Florida's coastline was stunning.

Corey pulled up perfectly to the pier. I was giddy that we had made the trip safely and we were still talking to each other. I hugged Corey tightly. He tossed the rope to Kevin, who tied it off like an expert. I was relieved to see land, but the sail here had such breathtaking views. I understood why Corey did it.

When it was safe, Corey lowered the ladder over the side so we could make our way to land. Corey helped me over, and I began to descend to the pier. Kevin grabbed my hand and tried to assist me to the pier. When Corey got to the bottom, Kevin helped him, too.

"Thanks for coming to get us," Corey said as I finished hugging Anita.

"No problem. We landed not long ago and already dropped our things off at the condo," Kevin said.

"I didn't bring anything." I glanced at Corey, and he smiled.

"Oh, yes, you did. I had them bring your whole wardrobe. Plus, I got you a special gift. Is it here or at the condo?" Corey asked Kevin and Anita. I was beyond confused as to what he could be talking about.

"Jack has it. He wanted one as well," Kevin said. Jack was all smiles when he handed me a black shirt. I looked at it questionably. I unrolled it to see my boyfriend's image printed on it, in his MMA fighting gear, and the words "Stay Down" written on it.

"A fan made this shirt and has been selling it online. My girl needs to represent me," Corey explained as I burst into laughter.

"Thanks for that," I said, hanging it over my arm as we walked to the car. Even down in Florida, Corey had a muscle car. Corey and I claimed the front seats, and he drove us to the apartment complex. I stared at the brick building. "Are you sure all of us will fit in this apartment of yours?" I asked curiously. I turned to look at Corey in the seat beside me.

"I'm positive. Don't you worry about a thing," Corey reassured me as he shut the car off. We all climbed out of the car and followed Corey up to this apartment he claimed would fit all of us. Needless to say, he was right. It was more of a loft or townhouse than anything because it had three bedrooms and a spacious layout.

"Holy crap! I didn't realize it was going to be a mansion of a condo," I said as I looked around the apartment.

"I told you we would all fit," Corey whispered as he shut the door behind us, locking the door for us. I noticed a pile of bags in the living room. The three other members of our party grabbed their bags and walked to the left side of the condo.

Chapter Fourteen:

"Where will I be staying if they get those two rooms?" I
asked.

"In my room," he said as I pulled my bottom lip between my
teeth. "We should grab a quick lunch before I need to be at
the venue," he said as I nodded. I wasn't sure why he needed
to be there this early, but it wasn't my place to question him.

"Can I grab a quick shower?" I asked as he turned around
to look at me again.

"Of course. Don't forget to wear my shirt." He winked at
me with a smile.

"What else would I wear?" I asked sarcastically. Corey led
me into the master bathroom, showing me how to work his
shower. I was in awe of this bathroom. It had a separate
Jacuzzi-type bathtub with a two-person shower, which was
beyond amazing.

"I'm probably going to order some pizza or Chinese. What
do you feel like having?"

"For pizza, I'll eat anything besides anchovies and pineapple.
If you order Chinese, I'll take noodles and some of that orange
chicken or Mandarin chicken," I said as he nodded.

"Got it." Corey gave me this half-assed Boy Scout salute
while leaving the bathroom. I wasn't far behind him to grab
some clean clothes.

I unzipped my suitcase, pulling out a pair of shorts to match
his shirt. I headed back into the bathroom, shutting the door
behind me for privacy. I showered, trying to wash away the
worries and nerves in anticipation of the fight.

I dressed and towel-dried my hair before locating the
kitchen for some takeout.

"I like your shirt," Corey teased. I smiled back and chuckled.
The five of us ate our lunch with very little chit-chat. I kept

glancing at the red circular clock hanging in his dining room. The time to leave was ticking closer and closer. I couldn't help biting my bottom lip or shaking my leg out of nervousness.

"I'm going to freshen up. Come on, Jack. Let's go change out of our pajamas," Anita said as she stood up, grabbing their plates. Jack followed suit behind her.

"Yeah, I should finish getting ready," I said.

"Can we share, or are you hogging the whole room?" Corey asked. Corey took a big gulp of the canned energy drink he held. He would probably need that to get through tonight's fight, considering we slept very little on the sail down.

"We can share for now." Corey chuckled.

I took care of my dishes, such as they were, before heading back into the master bedroom to finish getting ready as Corey stepped into the closet with me. "Do you wear your fighting gear there or change upon arrival?"

"I'll change into my gear there, but I always have to arrive dressed in business casual," Corey said as he pulled down the dress slacks, a button-up shirt, and a blueish blazer to match. Oddly, I couldn't wait to see him in that outfit.

"Why, though?"

"Company policy," he answered with a shrug. Corey slid past me to go shower and get dressed. I sighed and finished what I had started before heading to the living room.

I was the first one ready to go, so I glanced around his living room, looking at the details. I looked at what he had in his apartment, like his magazines and DVDs, before I crept over to the sliding glass door. I slowly pushed the blinds open, far enough to see a view almost identical to the one from the bedroom.

I pushed the door open and carefully stepped out onto the

patio. I walked over to the railing, looking out across the town, before looking down momentarily, then back up at the view, before I psyched myself out due to my fear of heights.

"Sweetie, we're leaving," Corey called as I looked back at him. I nodded, running a hand through my hair. He stepped out onto the patio with me. "You okay?"

"Yeah, maybe just a little nervous, is all," I replied truthfully.

"Everything will be okay, trust me. If it gets to be too much for you tonight, you can step out into the concession area or go backstage." Corey said as I nodded.

"I want to give this a shot, but what if I let you down?" I asked as I crossed my arms over my chest. I glanced down between us, hearing a soft chuckle come from him.

"You won't let me down. I understand the circumstances and that fighting isn't for everyone," Corey said as I glanced up at him.

"How would that affect us? I don't want you to decide between me and your career."

"What? I wouldn't ever put you or myself in that position. Even if you can't stand fighting, I would be just as happy if you supported me doing it," he said as I nodded. I think I could do that regardless. "Come on. I don't need to be late," he said. I stepped into the condo with him following me inside. We headed to Corey's car to leave for the venue where he would be performing tonight.

Chapter Fifteen:

⚬⚬⚬

I climbed out of the car, looking around the parking lot at all the different vehicles that were in the surrounding us. Then, I looked over all the various buildings in front of us.

Corey pulled the trunk open to grab his duffel bag. This building was not where I expected to be for an MMA fight. A bigger venue or arena was where I thought they would hold such an event. I pushed the door to the car shut right when Corey slammed the trunk with his one hand.

Corey reached out with his other hand and snagged my hand. His fingers intertwined with mine. I stared at his hand, then looked up at him as I bit my bottom lip. I walked beside Corey, holding tight to his hand as the other three walked behind us. I observed our surroundings as Corey led us into the building where we would be for the night. I saw fans already lining up outside the building near where we entered, calling his name. I glanced at him as I scooted closer to his embrace, unsure how to feel about everything. Hearing these people calling for my boyfriend was quite uncomfortable, but what else could I expect? They all wanted to meet him. He was a celebrity here, so wouldn't I do the same thing if I were a fan and wanted to meet them?

"You okay, baby?" Corey whispered as he broke his grip on my hand, slipping his arm around my shoulder to pull me closer into his embrace. I snuggled closer to him, my face dug into his chest and arms wrapped around his waist.

"Is it unsettling having those people calling your name or trying to get your attention?" I asked as I looked up at him. He reached out, grabbed the door handle, and pulled it open.

"Yes and no. That isn't the worst of it," Corey told me. I looked back at the fans and then ahead of us as he let me enter the building first, and he held the door open for the other people in our party. He stepped into the building, letting the door shut behind him as he walked past us. Corey led us through the building while I was eyeing everyone we were walking past to see if I recognized them as another fighter from the videos I had watched.

This was where he worked, where he spent his weekends and did his fighting. "Wait here. I'll be right back," Corey said as he entered a room. I looked over at Kevin and Anita, who were entertaining Jack, who was overly excited about the show. I couldn't help but smile at Jack's excitement. Jack looked up to Corey and loved that he knew Corey because of his status. Corey reappeared from the same room without his bag in tow. That must have been the locker room.

"Let me snag your passes and tickets." He reached out, gripping my hand again.

"Do you need your four passes?" the man behind the desk asked.

"Yep," Corey said as he stepped behind me, wrapping his

arms around my waist. The guy began to search through other passes, finding our four before he handed them over to Corey.

Corey led us to the auditorium where the caged octagon was set up. We walked down the ramp he would enter through later. My head was on a swivel, trying to observe my surroundings. I spun around in a circle, taking it all in. I was in awe and surprised at how much it looked like what I had seen on my phone when I had watched his fights.

"You want to get into the octagon?" Corey asked from behind me. I looked over my shoulder at him as my hand rested on the cold metal of the cage.

"Why would I?" I asked, perplexed as to why he offered.

"Jack, you want to get into the cage?" Corey asked. Jack's face lit up as he jumped in excitement.

"May I? May I?" Jack asked excitedly.

"If it's okay with your parents," Corey said as Jack looked at Kevin and Anita.

"It won't be anything new, so go ahead," Kevin said as Jack jumped more in his excitement. Corey picked the boy up, throwing him over his shoulder as Jack laughed and wiggled. Corey carried him into the octagon and ran laps around the caged ring.

Corey finally set Jack down at the entrance to the caged ring. Jack ran back into the caged-off area, and Corey chased him. Jack tripped, and Corey dove over him not to collide. Jack got up and jumped onto Corey. Corey screamed in pain.

"Pin him, Jack! He's down for the count!" Kevin yelled. Jack flipped to lie across Corey's body, and Kevin smacked at the cage.

"I'm not out yet. You think you can beat me, little boy?" Corey asked as Jack giggled. Corey went to town, tickling his sides. Jack was so full of giggles that Corey could stand up and pick Jack up with him. Corey tossed him in the air before catching him again, but the giggles escaped Jack's mouth like he wasn't afraid that Corey would drop or hurt him.

"Are you sure you don't want to get in? It might help you relax," Anita said, stepping up beside me.

"I don't know if I want to get in there with him. What if he hurts me?" I asked as I looked over at her, and she burst into laughter.

"Corey? Hurt you? Ha! Good one. He can't even hurt Jack, much less lay a finger on you. He won't mess with you. You were just on a boat with him for four days, and he didn't hurt you. Maybe getting into the ring might give you a sense of what it feels like to be in it and what he feels every night when he performs." Anita explained. I let out a sigh, knowing she was right. I walked to the cage entrance, walked up the few metal steps, and entered the cage.

"You decided to get in?" Corey asked as he walked over with Jack on his shoulders.

"She can be on my team," Jack said as he ran his hands through Corey's short hair. I turned to stand face to face with Corey, a smile on my face. Corey picked Jack off his shoulders, setting him down beside him.

I looked around the arena surrounding this ring, getting a different perspective. I couldn't imagine how this felt when everyone was in their seats, cheering or booing, or just plain out screaming. Jack ran to the edge, whispering something to Kevin through the cage. Kevin nodded before Jack ran out of the ring and up to his dad.

"Hey, Corey, are the public restrooms in the concessions open yet?" Kevin asked as Jack's leg was bent like he was holding it in.

"Not yet, but you can use the one in the back," Corey stated. Kevin nodded as he led Jack to where we had come from to use the bathroom. "How does it feel being the ring?" Corey asked as he brought me out of my zombie-like state.

"It's weird. I can't imagine the adrenaline rush you must get when these seats are filled," I honestly answered. I looked at how many seats filled the place, then back at him. "Don't you ever get nervous?"

"Every time. More so tonight with you in the crowd." I blushed at his answer.

"What is the ring made of? It seems sturdy but also like it would hurt when you fall," I said as I jumped a little when he chuckled. Corey explained how they built the ring and cage. It blew my mind. "Why do you put your body through this? All this has to hurt and take its toll on your body."

"It does hurt somewhat, and eventually, I will feel it more when I get older. As to why, I just love it. I know how to protect myself so it doesn't hurt as much, and I see the medics before and after matches to ensure my body is in tip-top shape. I also go to the gym and see doctors regularly." Corey explained it all to me.

"I just don't get enduring this pain. Do you like the pain?" I asked. I couldn't wrap my mind around this whole pain aspect.

"No, nobody likes pain. Think of it like getting a tattoo. It may be painful sometimes, but it's worth it in the end, isn't it?" He asked in a way that made sense as I nodded. "You may not understand the pain or why I do this, but there isn't much I can say to explain further what this is," he said as I nodded again.

I ran a hand through my hair because he was right. I couldn't understand the pain or why he would even want to endure it. I am sure this is due in part to the pain I had been through with my life and my ex.

"Corey, meeting time!" a man yelled who was on the stage. Corey nodded, and he turned to look at me and shrugged.

"I got to go, beautiful. I'll see you soon." He kissed my forehead as he climbed out of the ring, heading backstage to prepare for the night. I sat at the entrance to the ring. I may not understand this, but I knew I had to see what it was about.

"What do we do now?" I asked Kevin since Corey was gone, and it left just the four of us.

"We can go look at the concessions. After his meeting, he will probably have to start getting ready because the doors will open in about fifteen to thirty minutes," Kevin stated. I nodded as we headed to the concessions, seeing them preparing to open up. I headed to the bathroom with Anita before we joined Kevin and Jack again. "What do you want to eat?" Kevin asked.

"Popcorn!" Jack exclaimed. We were the first ones in line for the concession stand. We bought our drinks and snacks to eat throughout the show before we headed to our seats.

We were in the front row. I wasn't sure if I was ready to be this close to the action. Other fans began to fill up the rest of the seats, and there was one seat beside me that was still empty. Nerves began to sink in as the lights lowered, knowing the show was about to start. My leg bounced from nerves, the ice in my drink shaking with it as it rested on my knee, and I was lucky that none of it spilled out of the cup.

I was more anxious for Corey's match than anything, but watching the other matches would prepare me to see him fight. I felt someone plop into the seat beside me, making me jump out of my skin. I looked over to see just my man beside me.

Corey was wearing his black wife-beater and board shorts with random black designs. Corey had wrapped his hands and feet in tape, and his hair was gelled up into a Mohawk. I was impressed he could do that. I couldn't help but smile when I saw him, but I wondered what he was doing out here.

"What are you doing?" I whispered, trying not to bring attention to him as he smiled.

"Making sure you weren't freaking out." He wrapped his arm around me. "You seem too quiet. The boy beside you is yelling louder than you."

"I don't want to be a heckler, nor do I want to get killed today," I said as he smiled.

"They aren't going to come into the crowd to get you. And if they did that, do you know how many people we would have to go after?" Corey asked with a smile. The next fighter emerged from the back when the lights went out completely.

I felt Corey slide his hand into mine, interlacing our fingers as best as the tape allowed, and I gripped his hand tightly. I heard him groan a little from the pain of my squeezing so hard, I was presuming.

"Are you that scared of this?" his voice asked close to my ear.

I let loose a little as I bit my bottom lip. The second fighter made their way to the ring, and they climbed into the cage. Corey cupped his hand over his mouth, "BBBOOO! You suck!"

I nudged him and covered my face with my other hand, "Shut up!"

"BBBOOO!" I heard Jack joining in along with Corey and even doing the thumbs-down.

"You're a bad influence," I said as Corey smiled and laughed.

"It's okay to hate us or to heckle sometimes," Corey said as he kissed my cheek. Corey moved his hand to wrap around my shoulders, holding me, and sat there throughout the fight. I jumped, more like flinching during some of the connections.

Each time I cringed, Corey held me tighter, trying to soothe me. He kept telling me everything would be okay, but it was just a natural reaction. Corey sat out there with me for the whole fight and then through the following match. He kissed me on my temple, then whispered, "I got to go. My match is next."

I nodded as he kissed me on the lips before he went back to the changing rooms. I became more nervous, knowing that Corey's fight was next. I edged forward in my seat and moved my soda to the floor so I could rest my elbows on my knees. I put my hands over my mouth, awaiting this match.

His music hit as I looked to the stage, seeing the man who had just been sitting beside me walking out onto the stage like nothing had happened. I heard the little boy beside me screaming and watched him jumping to his feet in excitement. Corey walked along the ramp to the ring. He climbed into the ring and made a lap around it stone-faced. He stopped in front of where I sat and knelt.

My eyes connected with his serious brown eyes. I stepped forward and pressed my hands flat against the cage. He pressed his hands against mine, saying, "Don't worry, beautiful."

It was hard to understand him with his mouthguard in place. I felt tears fill my eyes out of fear. Another song started playing, and we watched the other fighter making his way to the cage.

"Be careful. Whatever you do, be safe."

Corey simply nodded and tried to give me a reassuring smile.

The mouthguard didn't help with any of this at all. He stood up, his brown eyes staring down at me intently. I trusted Corey. I stood there with my hands pressed against the cage. The ref signaled for Corey and the other fighter to meet in the center of the ring. They bumped fists, then backed up until the bell rang. They danced in a circle until the first punch was thrown.

I was so nervous about the hits and kicks. Watching their arms and legs swing, connecting or not. This back and forth continued for a while until it seemed like something snapped in Corey. He was a sweet man to me, but when a fist from his opponent connected with his cheek, it was like a switch flipped. Corey gripped the guy's leg, flipped the dude onto his back, and straddled him.

I forced my eyes shut as Alex gripped my legs and pulled them so I landed flat back on the cement patio. He straddled my waist and pinned my arms on either side of my head. I looked into his green eyes, illuminated with anger.

"Why are you out here in a two-piece bikini? Are you sleeping with the neighbors? Being the little slut you are? I knew you could never keep those legs shut. I'm going to show them who you truly belong to." Alex snarled. I was kicking the best I could and trying to keep my legs closed so he couldn't pry them open.

I opened my eyes, realizing I was still at the MMA fight, and looked at the party I was with, none of whom knew I had zoned out. I turned back to the fight taking place in the octagon.

Corey's arms were still swinging like crazy. He was going to town on his opponent.

Blood. There was blood. It hasn't even been five minutes. The ref called for it to stop and pulled Corey off his opponent.

Corey walked over to me and knelt. "Are you okay?"

I chuckled, "Am I okay?"

"I'm fine, beautiful. One more round and the guy will be out cold in a minute. Meet me in the back?"

I nodded my head. "Yes, I have to make sure you are truly okay. Any pain?"

"We will worry about that later, sweetie." He laughed, looked over his shoulder, and the ref signaled for the next round. He stood up and headed back to the middle of the octagon. I clenched at the ring's apron, observing every move to ensure he wasn't injured.

The ref signaled again, and the bell rang. It was over, and Corey had his hand raised in victory. I rushed toward where I would be granted access backstage. I rounded a corner, and Corey was rubbing at the back of his neck. I ran full speed and nearly tackled him to the ground.

Corey laughed and held me tight. "Are you okay?"

I wiped my eyes. A couple of tears had escaped my eyes. "I was scared for you, Corey, but it was such an adrenaline rush. Are you hurt?"

"Nope, he didn't get a single punch in. You want to come with me to collect payment and change?" Corey asked. I simply nodded. I think that I'd had enough fighting for tonight.

Corey cupped my hand, and I was nothing but smiles. "I enjoyed it tonight, Corey."

"Any flashbacks?" he asked curiously. I sighed, knowing he would ask that. "Are you afraid of me now?"

I stepped in front of Corey to stop him. "Yes, I had a couple of flashbacks, Corey. But-" I stepped closer to him and stared up at Corey. "I'm not afraid of you. I love you."

I jumped back a step with a gasp. I covered my mouth, shocked I had said it. Corey had this boyish smile come back to his face. "I love you too, beautiful."

He pulled me in for a big hug, and I loved this man. I followed Corey everywhere while he completed his routine of collecting payment and seeing the medic. I lounged in his locker room while he showered and redressed in his business casual outfit. He hugged me to his side while leading me outside. On our way toward the exit, he would stop to introduce me to fellow fighters and their wives or girlfriends.

We finally made it outside after meeting numerous people, all of whom I had already forgotten their names. This time, there were no fans surrounding the area. He sat down on the curb, and I sat down beside him. "You smoke?"

"Socially only, so I'll take one." He smiled as he handed me one out of the package. I held it between my lips, waiting on the lighter, and Corey flicked it on. He stuck it out to light mine first, then lit his own. I took a long draw. "So, those flashbacks? Anything particular?"

I exhaled the smoke, glancing at Corey, who did the same. "I thought back to one summer. I was wearing a bikini by our poolside, and he thought I was sleeping with the neighbors. He grabbed my legs, flipped me to my back, pinned my arms above my head, and raped me on the patio."

Silence fell around us as we both took a couple of drags from our cigarettes, and I'm sure it had to settle in that I was raped multiple times by Alex.

"Were you sleeping with the neighbors?" I glared at him for even asking. "Stupid question."

"Yep," I agreed, taking another hit. "You smoke after every fight?"

174

"Yeah, it helps ease the pain." He answered as he took a long drag of his cigarette. "Would you want to come again? I don't want you to come and just think of him the whole time."

I took a long drag. "I didn't think of him the whole time. It did bring back unpleasant memories."

"Are you going to want to come support me? I feel horrible that I'm inflicting this on you. If you don't want to come, you don't have to."

"I'll come when I feel like it. I enjoyed myself tonight, Corey. I can come to watch it again. Just a warning, it might affect my sleep, though."

"I don't want to do that to you." He couldn't even look at me. He took a long drag, "I'm no better than him, huh?"

I looked up at the night sky. "You are way better."

"I bring you into this environment. You are trying to get away from violence, and here I am, promoting it." Corey shook his head.

"I love you, Corey. I wouldn't change that for the world."

"You don't think I'm violent? Mad at me for promoting fighting?"

"Not anymore." I took another long drag when I felt someone step up to us. I looked over my shoulder, noticing that the rest of our little Florida household had joined us. I tossed half of the cigarette down and stomped it out. Corey helped me to my feet. He cupped my hand and led us back to the muscle car. He drove us to the condo in a gated apartment complex, which made me feel more secure.

Corey led me into our bedroom, and he tossed his bag aside. I climbed into the bed after kicking off my shoes. I stared at Corey, who pulled his shirt over his head. Corey tossed that aside before crawling from the foot of the bed to lay beside me.

On top of flashbacks from tonight, my anxieties were high from being someplace new. Thoughts and fears of my ex finding me here were pulling at me. It didn't help that I was experiencing flashbacks from the event tonight. Alex's image staring back at me was prominent.

I felt Corey's arms wrap around me, pulling me tightly into his embrace. My head rested against the curve of his neck as his two arms wrapped around my body. I felt safe being this close to him. I closed my eyes, snuggled closer to him, and relaxed enough to fall asleep. His heartbeat echoing in his chest soothed me to sleep.

Chapter Sixteen

The following day, I was the only one in Corey's gigantic bed. I shot up to a sitting position and began to panic. I looked around the room to see that I was truly alone.

I slowly pulled the blanket back, letting my feet slide from under the covers. I tip-toed toward the bathroom and then the closet, peeking into each, clearing them of anything suspicious. No one seemed to be in there.

I searched my duffel bag for anything I could use as a weapon and found my perfume. It may not be much, but it would sting whoever I sprayed in the eyes. With my heart beating loudly in my ears, I realized chatter and laughter were coming from the living room. I slowly slid down the wall as I concluded I was safe. I heard footsteps coming down the hallway, and I saw Corey step through the door, making me jump a little closer to the wall.

"What are you doing, and why do you have your perfume in your hand? Did you fart or something?" he asked as I blushed at the mention of farting.

"No, it's just that I got scared, and this was the most dangerous weapon I could find."

"Are you going to stink them to death with sweet pea?"

"How do you even know what sweet pea is?"

"That doesn't matter. Why were you scared?" Corey asked. I shrugged, not looking at him as he let out a sigh. Corey reached for my hand, pulling me over to sit on the massive bed with him. "Talk to me, Melanie."

"I'm still adjusting to being somewhere new. I don't feel secure enough yet and don't have a way to protect myself. Logically, I know Alex is far from here, but I'm guessing that watching the fights gave me a few more flashbacks than I thought that amplified my anxieties," I said truthfully, feeling him kiss the side of my head.

"You're in the safest place you can be. Alex has no idea where I live or that you are even in Florida. No one has access to the parking lot gate without a key card, and the same goes for the front door. If you don't have a key card, you have to buzz up to the apartment, and someone must let you in. We have a twenty-four-hour watch team and security guards on the premises, plus I am here to protect you. I have a bat under my bed along with a gun securely hidden somewhere in this apartment, and just so you know, we are near it right now," he said as I looked at him. "Plus, you saw how lethal my hands can be."

"Have you ever used a gun before?"

"No, and I won't use it unless I have to," Corey said as I nodded. "Do you feel safe now?"

"To be honest, I think I felt safer last night when you held me," I said, knowing I was blushing. I kept my eyes focused on my lap.

"I'm glad I was of service. Now, how about you put your perfume away? I have the day off, so I thought we could go to Disney World," he said as I looked at him, smiling brightly.

"Really?" I asked in excitement.

"Yes, and you can all get Mickey or Minnie ears. Unlike you guys, I want Goofy ears," Corey said as I chuckled.

"You will be my Goofy for the day," I said as he smiled. I leaned in to give him a quick peck on the cheek before I stood up. I hurried into the closet, putting the perfume away before dragging my bag into the bathroom. I took a quick shower and prepared for the day ahead of me.

Considering how long we would be outside, moving, twisting, walking, and doing other fun things at the park, I knew I should wear comfy shoes and clothes. I walked back into the room as I finished wrapping the last of the holder around the ponytail I had made. Corey pulled Jack onto his back for a piggyback ride.

"You want a piggyback ride, too? I can carry both of you," Corey asked as I chuckled.

"I doubt you could, but thanks for the offer," I said as I put my hands in my pockets. "Are we all ready to go?" I asked as I looked over everyone, who nodded in unison with excitement. We all headed out of the apartment complex to the car, and Corey drove us to the amusement park.

Jack got more excited the closer we got to Disney World, and I was trying my best to hold in my excitement, too. Corey paid for parking before he pulled forward, following the other cars to find an empty spot close to the tram to take us to the park's entrance. We climbed out individually, Corey meeting me on the passenger's side, where he slid his hand into mine. We walked as a group to the tram and waited for our turn to claim a row of seats. We rode it to the front entrance of the park. When allowed, we climbed off the tram and found each other after the big rush of the crowd.

"Jack, always hold onto one of our hands and never let go, okay?" Anita said as she knelt to give him the little lecture.

"Okay, mom," he said as he grabbed her hand.

We followed the rest of the crowd, and we must have looked strange with Kevin, Anita, and Jack linked by their hands, and then Corey and I were coupled by ours. We got in line behind the crowd at the entrance, waiting for our turn to go through the turnstiles to get into the actual park.

"Are you excited?" Corey asked as he moved his hands to rest on my hips.

"Beyond excited. I have never been here before, and I am ecstatic. Would you judge me if I was a little too eager about seeing the characters or something ridiculous like that?" I asked, interested in how he would answer.

"Absolutely not. That would make me love you even more."

"Are we going to see Mickey and Minnie today?" Jack asked.

"Yep. We will go to their houses first," Anita said.

"We get to go into their houses?" I asked enthusiastically as the other three adults looked at me, "What?"

Corey laughed good-naturedly at me. "Yes, sweetie. They each have their own house."

I smiled, and the line slowly moved to let us into the park.

"Off to Mickey and Minnie's places we go." Corey looked at the map he had grabbed. We were letting him be the tour guide and find where we wanted to go. We went under the railway and made a sharp left.

I gasped and felt oddly emotional. There, in front of me, was Cinderella's castle. It was so pretty and magical. I stopped in my tracks, my hands cupping over my mouth.

"It's so magical," I whispered. Corey slid his arm around my waist.

"Wait until you get closer and walk through it."

"You can?!" I looked at him, shocked. Corey gave me his boyish smile, his hand gripping mine, and he tugged me along. Main Street was busy with too many gift shops and delicious sweets to count. As we approached the castle, hired photographers greeted us.

We posed in various positions as a group or individuals. I had to have a classic couple's photo with Corey, and the photographer insisted she get one of us kissing. I noticed Anita had her phone out and was also taking pictures of us. Leave it to Anita to be our biggest fan. She would most likely drop those into my messages later.

"I love you," I whispered again.

"I love you, too. Is this everything you imagined it to be?"

"Yes, and then some." I smiled as Kevin shoved Corey, moving our group to the next attraction. We walked over the drawbridge and through the belly of the castle.

My head was on a swivel as I took everything in. This place was so different from what I had expected. Everywhere you turned, you saw other guests with backpacks and a map in their hands, all with their Mickey ears. I had never seen so many Mickey symbols in my life. We entered the little kids' area with a mini roller coaster and a bunch of rides designated for kids Jack's age.

"Now for Mickey's house," Corey said. Our hands swung between our bodies as we walked through the kids' area to a replica cartoon-looking house that was an orangish color with white trim. "Are you ready to meet Mickey?"

I smiled at Corey and chuckled, "No, I'm not."

We stepped into the house. The first room we entered was the living room. The whole place had this realistic vibe with a cartoonish aspect to it. There was a recliner couch, a coffee table, a television playing old-time Mickey cartoons, and little accessories like a vase with flowers. I had my phone out, taking more photos than I needed. I sat down on the couch, soaking in what the room felt like. Corey stepped in front of me, and I looked up into his brown eyes with a smile.

"You want to take your picture?" Corey asked. I couldn't find the words to answer, simply nodding. He pulled me to my feet and slid into where I had just sat. I gasped, and he joked, "You thought you would get a solo picture? I want pictures, too."

I snickered and rolled my eyes at him. Corey pulled me onto his lap and handed his phone to Kevin, who willingly took the photo for us.

"May I get a solo picture now?"

"Absolutely. We have to document our first trip to Disney together."

"Well, not alone. We've got a posse with us," I nodded at our mini tribe. "Regardless, I am having fun."

"Me too, but we will be breaking away soon to have our lunch date."

"We are?" I was shocked.

Corey chuckled at the expression on my face. "We are. I made reservations at the Blue Lagoon."

"Where's that? And when did you manage to do that?"

"Don't worry about it," Corey said.

Jack ran up to us and tugged at our arms. "Come on! The line is getting long, and we still have the whole park to explore."

We got up from the couch, following close behind Jack through the rest of the makeshift house. A long line had formed to meet Mickey, and we lined up in a room that showcased his garden. They had an animatronic gopher 'stealing' carrots to keep guests entertained while they waited. I stood in front of Corey, watching the carrots disappear. The gopher appeared laughing, and then the carrots reappeared for it to happen again.

We moved through the rest of the house until we entered a dark room. Standing in the middle of the room under a spotlight was Mickey Mouse with an employee on either side. Corey stepped behind me, his hands holding my hips, and he tugged me back to press against his muscled body. We watched Kevin, Anita, and Jack pose with the famous mouse. Then, they took pictures of Jack with Mickey, followed by one of Anita and Kevin with Mickey.

The trio stepped aside so Corey and I could have our pictures taken. We stood on either side of the mouse for the first picture. Corey stepped aside to let me take a solo photo with Mickey. We walked out of that building and went next door, hoping to repeat the process at Minnie's house, but Minnie wasn't available. I guess she wasn't out visiting the park yet.

We exited her house back into the kids' area. Jack excitedly pointed at the roller coaster. "Can we ride that?"

"I am not a big ride person. Kevin?" Anita asked, looking at her husband.

"I'll go," I volunteered, glancing at Corey. "I'll only be at Disney once, so I have to fit in as much fun as possible."

"Count me in," Corey chimed in. We followed close behind the excited seven-year-old. The line was shorter than Mickey's house, and we practically walked onto the coaster. Corey sat beside Jack in the front row while I got the second row to myself.

Corey and I went on the roller coaster and multiple other rides with Jack in the kids' section. Kevin pulled Jack away to explore Pluto's doghouse so we could go on our lunch date at the Blue Lagoon.

"I guess that's what it will be like to have kids," Corey said as he swung our hands.

"I guess so. But our kids, pffffft."

Corey chuckled. "Especially if they take after me."

"Why do you say that?"

"I was a daredevil as a kid. I would jump off the roof, slide down the stairs, and go to house parties."

"A real rebel."

"So says the girl that ran away to be with the love of her life."

"Ouch," I said, cupping my hand over my heart. "Maybe our kids will be a little rebellious if they take after either of us. But you know what we'll have? Street smarts. We know all the tricks in the book to beat them at the game."

"Very true. So, does that mean you are open to having kids?" Corey asked as he pulled me into his embrace.

I was pressed firmly against his hard frame, staring up into his brown eyes. I bit my lip. I wasn't sure what I thought about having kids. However, a part of me wanted them. I was holding on to my dream of a big wedding, walking down the aisle wearing a white dress with a long, queen-length train. Deep down, I wished for that. But I think I lost hope, given my situation with Alex. My future with him was so dark that I didn't see any light at the end of the tunnel.

Yet after everything I've been through, I'm standing in the

happiest place on earth with the man I love. I don't know what our future holds. All I know is that he makes me happy.

"You're taking a long time to answer, beautiful." He pressed his forehead against mine.

"I love you, Corey," escaped my mouth, and he smiled brightly.

"I love you, too, but that didn't answer my question."

"I don't have an answer, Corey. I think deep down, I want kids. But right now, I'm not sure if I want to start thinking that far into the future." Corey nodded his understanding. He gave me a soft kiss.

"I understand. Come on, beautiful. We don't want to be late." He led me to the fanciest restaurant I had ever stepped foot in. One of the water rides surrounded the restaurant, with boats that would float by occasionally, which was a little unsettling.

Corey pulled the white metal chair out for me and slid it back in when I sat. I looked over the menu, which was challenging to read in the dim lighting to set the mood. I kept glancing up at Corey from the menu. "How'd you know to reserve this?"

"I've got friends. Plus, you know that I can pull some strings around here."

"You can?" I asked to close my menu.

"I am a big deal down here. You don't gotta worry about a thing," Corey said when the waitress came to collect our orders.

We filled the meal with in-depth conversation, finding more common ground. I felt that we were truly connected. The food was served in small portions that left us feeling hungry. After Corey paid the tab, we walked out of the darkened restaurant into the bright sunlight.

"Now that I overspent on a pea, why don't we get a churro?" he joked.

"I've never had a churro."

"You're joking, right?"

"No. Is that a bad thing?" I asked as he stared at me.

"Yes, it is. Come on. We will find one and eat it on the way to the Eiffel Tower."

"The Eiffel Tower is in Paris, Corey, not Disney World."

Corey burst into laughter. "Yes, the Eiffel Tower is in Paris, but Disney has these pavilions for foreign countries. One was designed to be like France, complete with a replica of the Eiffel Tower. It'll be like traveling the world without leaving home."

His fingers interlaced with mine as our hands swung a little between our bodies. Everything seemed to be in slow motion as we walked down road-sized paths. The crowds of other customers, the subtle music, the horse-drawn carriages, the storefronts, and everything in the amusement park seemed so magical. Corey pulled me into a short line to a little red fair cart with various snack options. Even though we had just eaten, I was still hungry. The portion sizes at that restaurant were not worth the value.

Corey bought two churros. They were long sticks of fried dough covered in cinnamon sugar goodness. Where has this been my whole life? We ate while he led the way to this France-like place he swore by. You couldn't miss the Eiffel Tower. I stopped dead in my tracks to stare at the monument. My mouth had dropped open in awe at Cinderella's castle, but my jaw was on the ground this time. It was breathtaking even though it wasn't as big as the real one.

"It's beautiful, isn't it?" Corey whispered. I smiled as I looked at him.

"Beyond beautiful."

"You want a picture?"

I nodded as I turned around to pose for a picture with the tower behind me. Corey and I switched places so I could take a photo of him.

"You want a selfie?"

"You want to take a selfie?" I chuckled as I stepped up next to him. He pressed his lips to my cheek for the picture. "Hopelessly romantic, taking cute pictures, are we?"

"You know it. I love you. What do you say we kidnap Jack and take him on some real rides? Kevin and Anita won't take him out of that kiddie place because neither likes rides."

"Sounds good. I'm more than ready. I've never done this, so I'm up for anything," I said. I wanted to experience it all. Corey texted Kevin while we wandered around, waiting to hear where they were.

We picked Jack up at the Tarzan treehouse while Kevin and Anita went on their own adult adventure. We took Jack on as many big rides as possible until the sun set on the horizon. We beelined to the front entrance to claim spots for the Main Street parade, followed by fireworks.

Jack sat on the curb, with us adults surrounding him, the crowd filling in around us for the event. Corey's arms wrapped around my waist, pulling me tightly back against his hard chest. I felt secure and safe. I'd had such a wonderful day.

I began to reflect on the day with Corey and with Jack. We made great parents, if I do say so myself. We bought Mickey ice cream for everyone and went on more rides than I could count. Corey and I were still kids at heart. Maybe I had loved today because I missed being a kid. My whole childhood wasn't that great. I ran away to be with Alex and ruined my life.

Here it comes. Did I want to be a mom? Using Jack as our guinea pig today, Corey and I had proven we were good at it. He would be a wonderful dad. Even if I weren't ready to be intimate with Corey yet, there would come a time when it would be possible.

"You need to get out of your head. The parade is about to begin," Corey whispered in his deep voice. How has he come to know me so well he knew I was absorbed in my thoughts?

I looked over my shoulder at Corey. "I want kids."

Corey smiled and kissed the curve of my neck. "You tell me when you are ready to start trying, and I'll be there."

"You're that easy?"

"I'm a man. Of course, I'm that easy. With a girl as sexy as you, I'm ready all the time." He growled, and it was the sexiest sound I'd ever heard.

"I'll be ready when you put a ring on my finger, Mr. Mathison."

"Sounds like the best time to start," Corey said, giving the curve of my neck another kiss. Music began to play over the sound system, announcing the parade was coming down the street. I snuggled closer to Corey, knowing our future would start when we made the ultimate commitment to each other.

The parade approached us. I snuggled back against Corey to soak in his body heat. The first thing that greeted us was a marching band from southern Georgia. Following behind them were the various characters and floats. The smile on my face was permanent, no matter what was happening.

The last float had Mickey and Minnie Mouse on it, their hands waving at guests that lined both sides of the street. An usher released the rope holding us back to allow guests access to the street after the parade ended. We followed the crowd of guests toward the castle, lit with various colors. Light-hearted music blared over the sound system, making you feel like you were in a Disney movie.

"We never got our ears!" I remembered, and I looked at Corey.

He laughed. "Kevin?"

I turned my attention to Kevin as he pulled a navy blue bag with the Cinderella castle on it out of his backpack. He removed a hat with Mickey's ears and gave it to Jack. Then he pulled out a Goofy hat, handing the green hat to Corey. I chuckled in disbelief as Corey plopped the hat on his head.

I rolled my eyes when Kevin handed me a princess-style Minnie ears. Princess? I looked it over before I smiled.

"I had to get the princess hat for my princess." Corey whispered, "I'll be your jester."

I chuckled as I put the ears on my head. "You certainly are goofy, my big Rock'em Sock'em."

I grinned as he gave me his biggest smile. "I love how that nickname stuck."

A woman's voice came over the sound system, speaking about never giving up on your dreams. I don't know how they did it, but the park made it seem like Tinkerbell was flying around the castle. The first of the fireworks was set off with a big bang. The show was amazing, from the fireworks to the music and colors that danced on the castle. The people I was with made it even better.

After the grand finale, the area began to clear out. I turned around to face Corey. My hands fell flat on his chest, and his hands locked around my waist. I stared up into his deep brown eyes. I didn't want this day to end.

"What now?" I asked, and he smiled.

"There's some rides we missed if you want to hit more. Everyone usually leaves at this time of night, so the lines are shorter."

"What about Kevin, Anita, and Jack?" I looked around and couldn't see them anywhere.

"Probably got lost in the crowd. They will need to head back to the condo soon. We wore Jack out today. What do you say? Alone time with me without a kid? We got to practice being parents, but now we can have some solo time."

"Sounds great, but I want to hit the Haunted Mansion, puh-lease!"

He nodded and led us through the traffic of people heading in the opposite direction to the black and white mansion with little to no line-up. I happily smiled as I began speed-walking through the metal barricades to the entrance. Upon arriving at the front door, the employee in a black and green maid's dress allowed us into the big elevator with the other patrons.

Maybe it was my morbid side, but this was my favorite ride. Corey seemed to like it just as much. I soaked it all in. At the end of the ride, Corey snapped a picture of us in the mirror with the ghost. We took the escalator out of the ride and came outside to a dark sky.

"I loved that ride more than I thought I would." Corey's hand gripped mine, leading me through the park to a different ride. "This better not be 'It's a Small World.'"

"No, I wouldn't torture myself with that. It's the Peter Pan ride."

"Peter Pan has his own ride?"

Corey burst into laughter at my excitement. He nodded as

we waited in the short line before climbing onto the sailboat. This ride has to be the second-best one of the whole day.

After hitting about five other rides, we decided to call it a night because tomorrow would be a busy day. Corey still had to attend his anger management class, teach, and end the day with a fight. Corey laced his fingers with mine as we walked through the amusement park to the castle, still lit with pretty pinks and purples. I tugged at his arm to stop and walked up to the wood barrier, staring at the castle.

I pulled out my cell phone to snap a picture as another memory of the day. Sliding the phone into my butt pocket, I turned around to find Corey down on one knee.

My eyebrow rose. "Your shoe untied?"

Corey shook his head, his hand sliding out of his pocket. What was in his pocket? His hand flipped over to expose a little black box.

"You can't, Corey." I shook my head no as he nodded his head yes. His fingers flicked open the top part of the box, exposing a silver band holding a diamond.

"Marry me, please, Melanie?"

Tears of happiness began sliding down my cheeks. I couldn't believe he was proposing to me right now, after everything we had been through since meeting. Much less right here in front of Cinderella's castle.

"Yes, Corey." I nodded as I accepted his proposal. Corey jumped to his feet to slide the ring onto my finger. He pressed his forehead against mine, a big smile planted on his face.

"You've made me the happiest man alive, beautiful. I love you, Melanie." He said softly before his lips softly pressed against mine for a sensual kiss. Flashes of light sparkled in the darkness, like stars twinkling in the night.

"Now we have to stop and pick up our pictures. I had it arranged for photographers to be here to capture the proposal."

"What if I had said no?" I chuckled and could tell he didn't think it was as funny as I did.

"Not funny, Melanie," he said when he finally chuckled. We posed for a couple more photos before he led me up Main Street to pay for prints of the pictures we had taken of us throughout the day. We opted for a few more of the proposal than the others because we had lots of those on our phones. He led me back to his car, opening the passenger door for me. I sat on the black and red leather seat, staring in disbelief at the ring resting on my finger. I was engaged.

The driver's door opening grabbed my attention. "You're going to be mine forever, princess."

Corey gave me a wink before flicking the ignition, causing the car to roar to life. I was going to be his forever. I loved the idea. A smile spread over my face at the thought. Once he pulled out of the parking lot, his hand reached to hold mine while his sports car sped through traffic to his apartment complex.

We let ourselves into the condo that was pitch black. We tried to be quiet as we went to the master bedroom, where we tried to settle in for the night. Corey lay in his basketball shorts, his hands propping his head up, staring out the windows. I emerged from his closet wearing his wife beater and basketball shorts. I sheepishly dove under the covers so I wouldn't be seen.

"Hey, beautiful. I love you," Corey said as his arm wrapped around me, pulling me closer until I couldn't get closer to his tattooed body. "I'm beyond happy you said yes. I want to spend every second of every day with you."

"Me too." I had surprised myself when I said yes, but I loved Corey and wanted to be his. He was the one for me, I could tell.

"Get some rest, baby girl. We have another long, full day ahead of us tomorrow."

"Okay," I softly said as I forced my eyes shut, trying to allow sleep to consume my body. It took longer for sleep to overcome me due to the excitement from the day, but at least I was going to get some rest before the next day.

Chapter Seventeen

The sun's rays beamed through the windows and landed directly in my eyes. Regardless of whether my eyes were open or closed, the brightness disturbed the peaceful sleep I was enjoying. I groaned at my displeasure at being woken up, and I rubbed my eyes and began to roll onto my back to wake Corey.

The bed was empty again, and I started to panic that I was alone in his condo. I wondered where he could be rather than when an attack would happen. I sat up in the bed, giving the room one last look when I heard the shower turn on. My head snapped around to look at the connecting bathroom. He must be taking a shower.

My mind at ease, I lay back down. Corey was enjoying a nice morning shower, probably to help him wake up. If he were like me, he was likely still exhausted from yesterday's excitement. I felt for him because he had a full day of work ahead of him. Me? I was just tagging along for the ride. I pulled the blanket over my body, cuddling under it a little longer while I listened to the sounds of the water from the connecting room. I should have gotten up to see who else was awake in the condo, knowing their routine at home. Should I make breakfast or brew coffee? I wasn't sure where anything was in his kitchen, but surely there was no harm in looking through the cupboards.

I got up from the bed, quietly moved out to the kitchen, and flicked the overhead light on so I could see what I was doing. From what I could see, Corey and I were the only two up, but we were also the last to go to bed. I spotted the coffee maker on the counter. The first spot to check was the cabinet above it. Lo and behold, there were the filters and small canisters of coffee grounds.

I began to prepare the machine to brew the magical brown adult juice when I heard the patter of someone walking down the hall. I looked to where the sound came from, making out the subtle shape of Corey in the darkness. Corey's hair was tousled from being toweled dry. The black wife beater he wore defined his upper body, and the skintight blue jeans hugged his heavily muscled thighs. He was carrying a pair of boots as he came around the corner to join me in the kitchen.

"I hope I didn't wake you." He dropped the boots at the condo's front door before stepping further into the kitchen, standing behind me.

I flicked the machine on to start brewing the contents. "Nah, the dang sun was in my eyes."

"I'm sorry, love. So, what do you want to do today?"

"I have choices?" I asked with a raised brow.

I turned around to face him. Corey rested his hands against the counter on either side of me while he towered over me.

"Yep, it's all up to you. I need to be at anger management at eight, my teenager class at ten, and a personal training session at one. I have to be at the venue at four. I have enough time between the teenager session and mine to have lunch with you. You can tag along with me or go with Kevin and his family to the beach or whatever they had planned today."

I turned to look at the hallway that led toward the guest rooms. I felt horrible I had not been spending time with Kevin and his family. I also wanted to go with Corey to see his daily life. If this was going to work between us, I had to know what that included. Corey was the man I loved, and this was his life.

"Would Kevin be upset if I opted to go with you?"

Corey laughed. "I don't think Kevin would care if you flew to the moon. Kevin is enjoying some quality time with his family. Let him have that. So, you'll be mine all day?"

"Yep. No getting rid of me now." I waggled my fingers, showing him the ring he had given me the night before.

"Man, that ring looks good on your hand." He stole a quick kiss from me. "I'm going to put my boots on. You may want to freshen up."

I nodded as I pushed off the counter and followed him out of the kitchen. The coffee needed some time to finish brewing anyway. I went to our room, digging through my bag to decide what to wear. I had a few choices. Most were already dirty from the last couple of days.

I pulled on a pair of longer jean shorts with fading rips and the A Day To Remember shirt that Corey had bought me.

I ran a brush through my hair, applied a layer of deodorant, and spritzed a couple of sprays of Sweet Pea onto my body. I exited the room with my purse and phone, ready to go on a dime's notice. I rested my personal belongings on the counter when I entered the kitchen. Corey stood in front of the coffee pot, pouring the dark liquid into two coffee mugs.

"Thank you, Corey," I said as I stepped into the kitchen to grab my cup. Corey retrieved the creamer from the refrigerator and poured some into both cups. "Do we have time for breakfast?"

"Not a big one. I may stop at a McDonald's on the way. You okay with an egg McMuffin?"

"I'm beyond okay with that. I love McDonalds," I said, sipping from my mug. The hot liquid sent a jolt of energy through my body. "Do you need to go pack your bag?"

"Yeah. With today's agenda, it will probably be a couple of bags." He sighed, scratching at the back of his head.

"I'm sorry that you're tired. We shouldn't have stayed out so late."

Corey glared at me. "Along with thank you, you need to stop saying sorry. I'm an adult, Melanie, and I chose to stay out late with you. I'm fine. I loved every minute of our day yesterday."

Corey took a big gulp of his coffee. He headed out of the kitchen, and I was right behind him. I got comfortable sitting on his bed, holding my cup of coffee while I watched Corey toss a couple of bags onto the bed.

I slowly sipped my coffee, watching Corey shove things into the bags. He zipped up the bags, pulled them onto his shoulders, and led me out of the room. He tossed his bags by the door before returning to the kitchen. I leaned against the doorframe, watching as he topped off his coffee cup.

"We should eat some breakfast here. We're already planning on eating lunch out." I suggested. Corey glanced at me momentarily. I stepped into the kitchen, beginning to go through the cupboards, and saw how bare they were.

"With what food, sweetheart?" he asked.

"You don't keep your stuff stocked?"

"No, I usually get a delivery with essentials the day I roll in for my fights."

"Why did you keep both places, Corey? Between the cost of renting this place, traveling back and forth, and everything else?" I asked, not understanding why he would do that.

"Lancaster is where Kevin and my adopted family live. My parents may not live locally in Lancaster, but they hated that I was states away. I would be much closer to my parents if I got a house in Lancaster."

"Are you still close to your parents? I haven't heard you talk to them on the phone or seen you texting with them since we met."

He took a swig of his coffee, probably to buy some time before answering. "I still talk to them every month. I just have been through a lot of shit with them, and for my mental health, I try to keep my distance from them."

I was interested in discovering what his parents had done that warranted needing to distance himself from them. No one's parents were perfect, but he had to have endured something critical to cause him to limit contact with them.

"Do you want any more coffee, or are you ready to go?" he asked, swiftly transitioning from talking about his parents.

"I'm ready to go." I dumped the remains of my coffee down the drain before setting my cup upside down in the sink. I picked up my belongings and followed him out of the condo, pausing as he locked up after us. "You don't like talking about your parents?"

Our hands swung lightly between our bodies while we

walked down the long corridor. "You can say I take after my dad. We have the same taste in music and outlook on life. My mother, she's a tough nut to crack."

"You're a momma's boy?"

"Eh, not really. But I guess, as the mom, she has such a soft spot for her boys. She wasn't happy when she found out I had turned to MMA. She thinks it's too reckless, and I'm going to get seriously hurt."

"She has reasons to be fearful, Corey. You came home with a broken nose."

He opened the exit door into the parking lot, steering the way to his car. "Injuries do happen. I just want to feel supported. They cut me off from many things in college because I chose a career they disapproved of. We don't see eye to eye, so I feel that they will never support my decisions."

I could see where he was coming from but couldn't tell him how to feel. His parents may have done bad things in the past, but my relationship with my parents was no better. I had no contact at all with them. I can't imagine how hard it must be having parents who want to be in your life but constantly nagging over your every decision, not being there for you in whatever you decide. How can they love you but not support you?

"I'm sorry, Corey. Do they know about us?" I asked, looking at my ring while he pulled my door open for me.

"I have mentioned you to them. My mom didn't seem too thrilled."

I felt like I had been punched in the gut when he said that. His mom hadn't even met me yet and didn't like the idea of us being together. I got into the car, staring blankly out the passenger window. Suddenly, I didn't want to talk about this with him anymore. The car purred to life moments later and then started to move out of the parking spot.

"Why isn't your mom happy? She hasn't even met me." I spoke softly.

"My mom is upset she hasn't met you yet. She has this idea about who is perfect for her little boy. Her standards are pretty high."

"You think I can win her over? Honestly, give it to me straight, and don't sugarcoat it, Corey."

Corey glanced toward me. "Absolutely not."

Another punch to my gut. "Why's that?"

"Because I picked you, and she doesn't trust my judgment. That's the only reason why."

I had this defeated feeling in the pit of my stomach the whole drive toward his anger management class. I was so upset I didn't even ask him to stop for breakfast because I couldn't force myself to eat when my anxiety was acting up like this. Upon arriving, it looked like we were the last two to enter the large open room. A long table filled with refreshments was to one side of the room, and a circle of chairs sat a few feet away. I felt like I had stepped into an AA meeting.

I stuck close to Corey's side, my arms wrapped around his muscular arm, feeling out of my comfort zone. He led us to the refreshment table, where we poured another cup of coffee and picked a doughnut. I certainly needed some food to help offset all the acid from this much coffee. Corey led me to the circle of red chairs, and I slid into the seat beside him. I slowly nibbled at the powdered donut I had chosen while the rest of the participants filled the seats. A man in business attire slid into the last empty chair with a clipboard.

I grabbed Corey's hand, clenching it tightly, nervous about

sitting in on this meeting. Corey tried to soothe me by rubbing circles on the back of my hand with his thumb. The mediator introduced himself and brought the meeting to order. He asked if anyone would like to start the session by expressing how their week had passed. Corey lifted his hand to draw attention to himself and for permission.

"Go ahead, Corey. Thank you for offering." The mediator nodded toward us. I glanced at Corey, unsure of what he was about to say or express.

"Hi, I'm Corey. I usually have excellent control of my anger and teach my students to control theirs. This past week, my anger got the best of me." He glanced at me and mouthed, 'I'm sorry' before he continued, "Recently, a man who had done horrible things to the woman I love approached me. He deliberately provoked me, and he got the response he wanted. I saw red and attacked. I couldn't stop myself. I was so angry with him for what he had done to the woman I loved. I ended up arrested for assault, but the charges were dropped because it was ruled self-defense."

I couldn't believe he shared that with everyone. I was embarrassed that I was sitting here, knowing I was the girl in the story. It was emotional to relive the roller coaster ride of last week with total strangers. It was too much to think about what had occurred and to hear Corey express how his anger got the best of him.

"Wow, Corey. What could you have done differently?" the mediator asked.

"Nothing. He did everything right." Another man stepped in, saying, "If a guy had assaulted or caused harm to a woman, he deserved to get his ass beat."

I chuckled and blushed a little at myself as many other

members agreed with the man.

"I could have handled it differently instead of instantly beating the shit out of him. I could have thrown him off the premises or something." Corey shrugged.

"Corey, fuck that. Yes, anger overcomes you, but don't dwell on it. You did the right thing," the same man said. He got up from his chair, coming over to pat Corey on the shoulder. He asked me, "Are you the lucky girl?" I shyly nodded. "Nice to meet you. Corey is a great man. That's the first time I have ever heard him admit his anger got the best of him."

I smiled. "Corey is a great man. I love him so much."

The mediator tried to get people to help figure out what Corey could have done differently to control the anger that had consumed him. I sat there listening to people throw out suggestions about what Corey could have done differently in the heat of the moment. I relaxed in my chair, holding the cup of coffee that was still half full and my other hand gripping Corey's. I was glad I had tagged along to see what these meetings entailed. After the meeting had adjourned, I hugged Corey's muscular arm while he chatted with a few other class members. Corey truly knew these people. I guess they must have all built a bond while attending these classes every week together for however long.

"We need to get going. I have my teenage class in forty-five minutes," Corey whispered.

I nodded, allowing him to lead the way out of the building to the car parked in the adjacent lot. He drove us to the training facility that was in the downtown area. The training facility was in this run-down industrial-style building. The metal roll-down garage door was closed at that moment. I looked at my surroundings, unsure why there was a training facility here, of all places. Corey led me to a red door that he pulled open. Stepping in before him, I suddenly became overwhelmed by the noise.

There were the sounds of bags being punched and speed bags swinging, fans whirring, music blaring, and people bouncing in the ring. I was so overwhelmed with the sound factor that I couldn't even think. Corey slid his hand back into mine, leading further into the building, seeing that a few people were already working out. He led me to bleacher seating, set to one side, and pointed where he wanted me to sit. I slid into the third row, giving me a good vantage point, while Corey disappeared between the various pieces of equipment in the building. I saw him fist-bumping a few people along the way before disappearing into another room. I assumed it was the dressing room, and when he returned a short time later, he was in his ring gear.

I sat back and crossed my legs, watching Corey climb into the ring with this Mario guy he had told me about. He shook hands with the guy before stretching his body to prepare for whatever he had in mind for his class. I wanted to know more about what they taught in MMA. Mario called for the boys to enter the ring with Corey. I could barely understand what Corey was saying over all the other noise in the training facility. Based on what I could hear, Corey instructed the boys about discipline and controlling their anger. He told them that fighting wasn't about hurting your opponent. Corey paired the kids up to practice some of the moves. He climbed out and leaned against the ropes, watching the kids run the drills.

Two boys began to get too physical, yells erupting between the two. One speared the other, slammed him to the ground, and began to get reckless in his swings. Corey dove into the ring, pulling one kid off the other, and shoved him toward the ropes.

"Walk it off!" he yelled.

The kid climbed under the bottom rope and jumped off the apron. The kid walked in my direction while Corey squatted beside the victim, listening to what he had to say. Corey went to find the other kid, listening to what he had to say about the altercation. Corey brought the two together. Of course, he did it directly in front of the bleacher I was sitting on.

"You two need to resolve whatever issues you have. Do not let your anger or emotions control you when you go into a fight. Are you mad at him for dating your girl?" Corey asked, looking at the aggressor.

"Yes," the boy said. "That's my woman."

"Talk to him like a man. You don't need to swing your hands to show your dominance. MMA is not about hurting others. Take your emotions out of it. You two need to talk it out before you step back into my ring." Corey gently shoved them away from the class to walk it off while they talked. Corey returned to the rest of his class, where no further interruptions or fights broke out. Corey spoke to each kid when the class was dismissed, asking if they had any questions. Corey climbed out of the ring and approached me. "You want to come learn a few things?"

Corey gave me his trademark smile, making it hard to tell him no. I stood up, clasping the hand he offered and stepping off the bleachers. I was nervous about trying any of the moves I had seen him teaching his students because I had never thrown a punch in my life. He led me to an area filled with equipment, where he slid gloves over my hands before putting these padded ovals on his hands. He instructed me on how to

204

punch the pads, and he called the shots.

I was so glad he had pulled me out of my comfort zone to do this. I felt energized, and I was releasing so much of the bottled-up anger I had in me. Even though it was Corey, I kept swinging my arms, trying to let free whatever anger and anxiety I had pent up inside me. He even took me into the ring after helping slide a padded helmet on my head before he pulled one onto his head. Corey grabbed my head, bumping our foreheads, forcing me to look into his eyes.

"Let it all out. Don't hold back. You cannot hurt me."

I did not expect him to say that, but he had to have known I had all this tension in me. He went on to instruct me on where or how to kick correctly. Corey spent at least an hour with me and allowed me to beat on him. After an hour of working out with him, I was out of breath. I sat on the bottom row of the bleachers, and Corey tossed me a water bottle. He plopped down beside me, downing half a bottle in one shot.

"Thank you for letting me try that," I said, rather pleased with myself. I took another long drink of water and glanced at him.

"No need to thank me. You needed to release that anger you had, and you also needed to learn how to defend yourself." He smiled as he drank some more of his water.

"I love how you separated those two boys earlier," I commented as he smiled wider.

"In MMA, it's not about our emotions. We don't do this to take out all of our anger and frustrations on an opponent. I think teenagers have it the hardest because your hormones cause you to feel everything a lot deeper, and you go through so many changes, making you forget yourself." I smirked. I could sit here forever and listen to him talk about the teaching career he is so passionate about. "I know when I was a teenager, I was angry at everyone and everything. These two fought over a girl they were both interested in. Is that worth breaking a bone over?"

I chuckled, "I don't know, is it?"

"Wrong person to ask." He outright laughed as he finished up his water. "I've got to go do a few things, and then I'll be right back."

I nodded as I continued to sip my water, waiting for him to return so we could leave the gym. I wouldn't mind returning with him to learn more about fighting and release the anger and tension I had built up.

After observing Corey in training today with the teenagers, I knew that Corey's brand of violence didn't go past the octagon. I had no longer feared that he'd snap someday and use that strength against me. Later that afternoon, Kevin, Anita, and Jack opted to go sightseeing tonight instead of accompanying us to the fight.

"Are you going to be okay on your own here?" Corey escorted me to the front-row seat next to the octagon's entrance. He squatted down on the walkway that connected backstage to the octagon. I looked from the caged ring to him.

"I hope so. I wish that I had someone here, but I should be fine. I can always make a run for it if I need to."

"That's why I picked this spot," Corey said with a smile.

"Thanks for looking out for me." I smiled back.

"That's what fiancés do. I gotta change, do my weigh-in, and some promo photos. Doors open in fifteen minutes, and the show will be on in thirty."

"Get going, Rock'em, Sock'em," I said, smiling. I climbed to stand on my seat, and I was finally his height, even though he was kneeling on the stage. I planted a rough kiss on his lips. "Be safe for me."

Corey held back a moan. "I will be if you promise I get more of those."

With a wink, Corey stood to his towering height of six foot three. I climbed off my seat and sat down. My legs automatically crossed at the ankles, and I pulled out my phone to pass the time. The eruption of music blaring through the sound system and the stampede of people pouring into the arena, along with their chatter, added to the anticipation of tonight's fights.

Corey's music was the first to play when it got to show time. I jumped to my feet and pressed myself against the steel cage. Corey did a lap around the inside before he stepped in front of me and placed his hand flat against mine, the steel cage the only thing separating us.

"I got this, beautiful. I've fought this guy before and won. I'll be fine. You relax for me, okay?" he asked as I stared deep into his dark brown eyes.

"I'll try my best." I tried to speak confidently. New music started playing, and his opponent entered the arena. Corey looked over his shoulder at the other fighter. Corey had his hair spiked like the last time I watched his fight. He wore a pair of white trunks with black designs, and his gloves were different from his previous fight.

I backed away and returned to my seat while he prepped for his fight. He walked to the center of the octagon, bumping fists with the opponent before walking backward to his corner. My hands cupped over my mouth, intensely watching them begin their attacks. Corey started to knee his opponent in his rib cage.

Images of Alex above me popped into my head, his legs relentlessly kicking at my limp body. I curled into a fetal position as memories flooded my mind, visions of Alex consuming my brain.

"You worthless piece of shit! You can't even get rid of a wine stain. Didn't your mom ever teach you how to clean up after yourself? This place is a pigsty." Alex's voice was ringing in my ears. Tears began escaping my eyes. I clenched them shut, trying to push the sound of his voice and images out of my mind. My mind was clouded with the memory of Alex hovering above me and the pain radiating from my abdominal area. With every single kick from Alex, my abdomen throbbed more.

My breathing became heavy as I became a captive in the flashback.

It's just memories. Five things. I hear people screaming. They are rooting. The bell! I heard it ring. I hear clapping. I feel the plastic stadium chair. There's a presence. Someone is hovering over me. It's Alex. He found me!

"Baby. Can you hear me?" Corey's strong, deep voice broke through to me. I lifted my head to look at the man I recognized. Tears rolled down from my eyes. Corey's face was beaten and bloodied, worse than I could imagine. More tears escaped at how hurt he was. "Are you okay, Melanie?"

All I could do was shake my head no. Corey didn't hesitate to scoop me up into a fireman's hold and rush me backstage. He set me down on my feet when we entered his changing room.

"What happened?" I whispered.

"You zoned out and went into a full panic attack. I lost my focus because I saw you freaking out and lost the fight." His voice held anger. "That's it. I can't bring you any more. I can't risk losing any more matches or putting you through this. Seeing you sitting there in tears and frozen in fear distracted me from my fight."

"Well, I'm sorry I'm insane and caused you to lose! I guess your winning streak is more important than some stupid girl!" I yelled at him as I stormed out of the room. I followed the red illuminated signs that read "EXIT" to escape the building.

Upon leaving the building, I headed toward the intersection I saw ahead of me. I pulled out my phone and texted Anita to ask if she knew Corey's address. Instead of sending the address, she shared her location. Clicking on the site, I saw it was a twenty-minute walk. I huffed as I kept my head hung low, watching my phone as I headed in her direction, and tried to think of what I had on me that could be used as a weapon if someone attacked me.

I approached the apartment complex and snuck in when someone exited the building. I went to Corey's condo, knocking on the door, hoping Anita would answer and not Kevin. Without exchanging a word, Anita opened the door to let me in as I moved past her to go to the room Corey and I were sharing.

I changed into Corey's MMA shirt he had bought me, feeling oddly comfortable rocking this shirt with some boy-short underwear. I sat cross-legged next to the floor-to-ceiling glass window with an amazing view. Streetlights illuminated the street below, the moon's reflection shone on the horizon, the ocean gleaming like glass. I stared at the view, trying to ease my mind about what had occurred tonight at the venue.

I began worrying when hours passed, and Corey still hadn't returned home. His opponent had beaten him badly during their match. Maybe he had been sent to the hospital. My thoughts became more concerned for Corey. I heard the sound of steps coming closer to the room. I looked over my shoulder in time to see the door being pushed open and Corey stepping through the doorway. I could make out half of his body with the light from the hallway.

"You're still up," he said, tossing his bag aside.

"My mom said never go to bed angry. We were both really pissed off when I left," I said. I looked back out the window. "I'm sorry I caused you to lose. It was my fault."

"It was worth the loss. You are worth more to me than one damn fight. To be honest, I had won three matches against the guy. He probably needed that one win, don't you think?" His words were soft, trying to make me feel better. "But I don't want to impose my career on you. It's not right or fair to bring you into that environment knowing you will react the same way every time."

Corey walked further into the room, and I looked at him.

"You still want to be with me? Even if I can't come to your shows?"

"And why wouldn't I want to be with you?"

"Because I'm broken."

Corey scoffed. He walked over to the nightstand and flicked the lamp on. My eyes were squinting due to the sudden brightness in the room. Corey walked back over, removing his shirt in the process. My eyebrow raised, wondering what he was doing. Corey turned his back to me.

On his tricep was a freshly inked tattoo, but I recognized the design. It was the half skull-half heart design I had been working on the day he walked into the Dead Soul Tattoo shop. I scrambled to my feet for a better look at the fresh tattoo that took up most of the back of his arm. My fingers hovered as I traced the outline in the air over it in pure shock.

"Corey," I softly spoke, tears blurring my vision from happiness.

"You'll forever be mine." He looked over his shoulder at me, and our eyes locked. He turned around to grab my hands, pulling me to the bed. He sat on the corner and pulled me to stand between his legs.

"You know how stupid you are?" I scolded him. "Isn't the first rule of dating to not get your significant other's inked name on you?"

"It's not your name, though. It's your artwork." He corrected me with his boyish smile, but with his badly swollen lips, it wasn't much of a smile.

"You want ice for those lips or your nose?"

"Nah, I already took some pain medicine and iced it while I got inked," he answered.

I stepped back from him, looking down at my legs. "You see them?"

"See what?" he asked in confusion.

"The scars."

I glanced at Corey as he looked over my legs. "I only see one. How'd that happen?"

"He pushed me down the stairs," I responded, figuring he could put the rest of the pieces together. I bit my bottom lip as I lifted my shirt just enough to show the scarring on my rib cage and abdominal area. "This was what I had flashbacks about tonight. He was kicking the shit out of me. A rib punctured my lung, and it was filling with fluids. They had to go in and drain it."

Corey reached out and pulled me closer as his arms locked around my body. "You are the sexiest woman in the world, and I'm lucky you are mine. But put some shorts on before bed because you'll drive me crazy all night if you don't."

"Even if I looked like Edward Scissorhands with all these scars?"

"You're the sexiest Edward Scissorhands I've ever seen."

I playfully smacked him before I straddled his lap and rested my hands on his shoulders.

"I wouldn't do that, baby. Not if you aren't sure."

"If Alex finds out, we're both dead," I said.

Corey rolled his eyes, saying, "I like to leave my mark. And as much as I would love for this to happen, and you're hot as hell sitting on my lap, I think you're too vulnerable tonight."

"But-" I began to argue when he gave me a rough, deep kiss. I moaned against his lips. I loved how he made me feel and wanted more. As much as I wanted to be angry at Corey for denying me, he was right. After tonight's fight and my panic attack, I think that we both wanted sex, but it would be all wrong. "After that kiss, you can still say no?"

"Yes. I am sore from losing, and I won't perform well. You want to come soak in the tub with me?" he asked. I bit my bottom lip as I debated my answer. I was ready to expose myself for sex but now doubted being able to do it for a soak in the tub.

"Will we both fit?"

"I'm positive."

"I'm sorry you lost your fight. Did you break your nose again?"

"Fortunately, no. Busted lips and cracked ribs."

"Do you hate me? Am I banned from ringside now?"

"No. I still want my girl there. I was being selfish when I blamed you. It's not all about winning, and you are way more important than any fight," he said, his hands gripping my thighs tightly. "I was thinking it might be a good idea to have security sit with you and escort you out if things escalate to the point that it becomes too much."

"You can do that?"

Corey chuckled. "Yes, I can do that. You are worth it. I'll talk with Richie in the morning to get it arranged for my next fight in two weeks. That gives us plenty of time to move our lives from Pennsylvania to Florida."

"Excuse me, what?" My mind was baffled by what he had just said. "Move our lives down here?"

"Talk in the bath?"

"No, Corey. You can't swoon me out of this. Shouldn't I be a part of this conversation?" I jumped off his lap to walk to the enormous window.

"Would you have said no?"

"No, but..." I trailed off, staring off out at the dark horizon. I felt him step up behind me, and his hands rested on my shoulders, trying to comfort me. "What about my life back home? I have a job there. What about Kevin?"

"You think that Kevin can't find someone? You worked for free, so you did him a huge favor."

"I have no job security here, Corey. How can I help pay for things?"

"Did I ask you to help pay for things?" He waited for an answer as I looked over my shoulder at him. "No, I didn't. You're mine, and I take care of what is mine. I get paid well for fighting. Your belongings are already here. We just need to fly back and pack my house. Once we pack my house, we put it on the market. The sale will help us out financially. Then, if you want, you can go to college, take a break from working to find yourself, or flip burgers for all I care."

"I don't know, Corey. I'll be too dependent on you."

"You would be if you wanted to be the stay-at-home mom you've always dreamed of." His whispers sent shivers down my spine. He had a point. "I was hoping it would be less of a discussion with you about the idea."

"I wish we had discussed it more before you decided for both of us."

"We can talk about it more over breakfast. We've both had a long day, and I need to soak my bones." Corey headed to the connected bathroom, leaving me staring at the night sky. Corey was already trying to make the best decisions for us as a couple. He had gone to jail for me, for goodness sake. As much as I loved Pennsylvania, I would love to live in Florida. This place was so luxurious compared to what I'm used to. But I feel like I'd lose my mind if I were stuck in this condo all day without something useful to do.

I could hear the water running to fill the tub and looked over at the connecting door. I walked across the room, slowly edging my way into the bathroom to see Corey lying in the white glazed tub. His head hung back, eyes shut, and the water was mid-chest.

"I'd go insane staying in the condo all day."

"You can join a gym, do whatever you've always wanted. You won't be a prisoner here." He responded without opening his eyes.

I crossed the bathroom, moving to sit on the toilet to watch him soak out the pain. My mind was floundering with so many thoughts on different topics. I was overwhelmed with the idea of moving to Florida at a moment's notice. My mind was more flustered that Corey was naked in front of me, and it was bringing back fond memories of the BBQ.

"This is so sudden, Corey, especially after everything we've recently gone through. Are you sure you want to live with me?" I leaned forward on my knees and pressed my mouth against my hands.

"Of course, I want to live with you. What happened between us only made us stronger. We will have disagreements, just like we will have laughter and moments when we cry. Relationships have ups and downs. It's not all sunshine and roses."

"What if we want to break up?"

"Doubtful, but if it occurs, you are always safe with me. I'll protect you until you get on your feet. I don't see me ever not loving you."

"Are you sure? Even if we break our hearts, can I stay here? Wouldn't that make matters worse?"

"Isn't life about taking risks? Can you honestly tell me you want to go back to Pennsylvania and risk Alex killing you? You know there's no stopping him. He wants control over you and doesn't have it anymore."

"If I wanted to stay there, would you?"

Corey let out a deep sigh. "Yes, I would. I will follow you wherever you want to go. Would I be happy about it? Not necessarily. I can't keep getting thrown in jail." Corey sat up straighter in the tub, showing me more of his hard body. "I'm getting out. If you don't want to see me naked, then turn away."

I turned my body to face the opposite direction while he got situated. I peeked over my shoulder just in time to see him tying the gray towel around his waist. Water was still rolling down his chiseled upper body, and his hip dents were perfectly defined, leading to the covered pelvic area.

"You've got a lot of calls to make in the morning," I pointed out.

"I do. Tomorrow, we have a lot of work ahead of us."

"We?"

"Yes, we. Kevin and his family need a ride to the airport. Then, on the way home, we stop anywhere you want so you can grab some job applications to make you feel more secure. Also, I've got phone calls to make."

"Job applications?"

"Yes, you said you had no job security, money, or anything else. So, it hit me while I was soaking that maybe we can find some places with the 'Now hiring' signs in the window so you can grab applications. Maybe that will help you feel less worried about moving here if you have job leads. Wouldn't that help make you feel better?" He stepped between my knees, and I looked up at him, our eyes connecting. "We need sleep. Today was a super long day, and tomorrow will be just as busy. We've both got too much on our minds. I think I see smoke coming out of your ears."

I rolled my eyes, but he was right. I liked Corey's idea of picking up job applications on the way home from the airport. I could fill them out and return them sooner rather than later. At least I could start the process of getting a job. That way, when we settle into our lives here, I will have interviews or be hired already. I stood up, following him into the other room. Corey headed into the closet while I went and slid into the enormous bed. I lay on my side, staring at the closet door, waiting for him to emerge.

Was I ready for this move? What if no one hired me anywhere? I would be unemployed, reliant on Corey, and by myself. I always wanted to be a stay-at-home mom, but we aren't married yet or to the point of having kids. I should be working to help Corey, yet the thought of working together in a relationship is new to me. I have to get myself used to a new place. Florida is an entirely different environment than what I am used to. I have no car, so when I get a job, it'll have to be somewhere close, within walking distance, or on the bus route. What is the closest bus route here? Or should I go back to school? Having a degree would be nice. I'm opening a new chapter in my life, and I have no idea what to write in it.

Corey emerged from the closet wearing a pair of snug black basketball shorts low on his hips, and he tightened the strings to keep them on. He walked around the room, flicking the lights off before I felt the bed dip when he climbed in. I rolled over to face my fiancé. I scooted closer to him, and his arms instinctively wrapped around me. I pressed my face against his warm chest. The subtle beating of his heart echoing through his chest caused a smile to spread across my lips.

"Corey, how will I get to work without a car?"

"On the days I need the car, I can drop you off and pick you up. If I don't need the car, you can take it. I'll have Kevin sell that old Volkswagen. We can make this work. I would do anything to keep you with me. I will follow you to the moon and back. I want this to last forever," he said, his lips pressing to the top of my head.

I wanted this to last forever, too. I began to think of our future together. I wanted that house with the kids and everything that went with it, just like I had always wished for as a little girl. Corey had me hoping and dreaming again. Everything seemed so perfect in a twisted way.

"If Kevin and his family leave tomorrow, when do we leave?"

"We leave on Monday. I couldn't book us all on the same flight, and sailing back would take too long. We're on a time crunch to get back here. I gotta train and practice for my next fight because it's for the belt."

"The belt?" I asked with a raised brow. Corey's manly laugh made me smile.

"Yes, in the fighting world, we have titles. They want me to fight the champion in two weeks for the belt. I haven't had an opportunity to fight and win a belt in months, and they told me tonight after you left. I was on a winning streak until tonight."

"Yeah, when your bad luck charm was there."

"Hey! You aren't bad luck," he said, taking offense at my words.

"You lost because of me, Corey."

"How do you know I wouldn't have lost anyway?"

"You said yourself that you had won against him three previous times."

"So?" Corey shrugged. "No more talking. We need sleep. You'll have applications to fill out, and we have a long week ahead of us to pack things."

"Okay. I love you," I mumbled. It still seemed so strange, but good to say that to him. Given recent events, I realized he cared so much about me due to his actions. Alex would have never gone through what Corey had for me. Alex lost his love for me years before I left. I snuggled closer to Corey, closing my eyes and hoping for a long night's rest.

Chapter Eighteen

I stood in the guest room of Corey's house. The flaps were wide open, and the box stood empty. I looked around the room, wondering what needed packing. It seemed pointless to bring anything because Corey already had doubles of everything in Florida, or there was no room for it in the condo. I began stripping the sheets off the bed. Maybe we could bring these with us for one of the guest rooms. I started folding the sheets and blankets to fit them in the moving box.

Today was only the first day of packing. I began browsing through Corey's belongings in the room and tossing what I thought was unnecessary to pack. Corey was hard at work in his main bedroom since that probably had the most items needing to be boxed up. I moved on to the next guest room, repeating my actions. I carried the box down the stairs and taped it shut before placing it by the front door. I opened another box and began to pack up the vinyl records in the living room. Checking out each record as I grabbed it, I loved Corey's taste in music. We had so much in common it was no wonder we were drawn to each other.

"Make sure you put bubble wrap around that one," Corey said, causing me to jump. I looked over my shoulder to see him carrying a box down the steps.

"Well, duh, it's Foreigner. They deserve double wrapping." I put it down to safely wrap up later. "I started a pile of things that can be sold by the front door. You know we will have to ask Kevin and Anita to sell everything, right?"

"I know. That's why we are in a rush to pack, so we know what we have to sell," Corey said, placing the box in his grip on top of the one I had finished. "But I have something I want to show you."

Corey walked through the living room, signaling for me to follow him. I trailed him to the room on the main floor with the closed door I had never looked in before. Corey slowly turned the knob and pushed the door open to expose various display cases filled with numerous gold and black championship belts, along with a lot of career-inspired awards. My gaze slowly looked over all of it. Corey moved aside as I entered the room to get a better look.

"You won all of these?" I asked surprise in my voice. My finger traced over the design etched in gold plating on one of the belts.

"Yes, but these are replicas of the real thing. It doesn't freak you out?" he asked, resting against the door frame. I shook my head as I stepped further into the room to look at a different belt.

"The only thing that freaks me out is that you have a stack of MMA magazines, whereas most men would have a stack of Playboys," I teased, glancing up at Corey from the stack of magazines.

Corey let loose a hearty laugh. "I had a stack of those too but pawned them in college because I needed groceries. Are you hungry? I can order up some lunch."

"Sounds delicious."

"I was thinking about Chinese food," he said.

"Chow Mein and coconut shrimp, please."

"Do you want to split an order of orange chicken with me?"

"Of course." I followed Corey to the living room and plopped onto the couch for a much-needed break. I pulled a stack of applications on my lap to fill them out while Corey placed our order. Corey walked out of the kitchen with his phone in hand, punching away at the screen when the doorbell chimed. At first, I glared at Corey, who looked confused about who was at the door. I began to panic because neither of us knew who it could be. The last time someone came to the door, it was the police, so of course, I had to make a joke. "You didn't kill Alex this time, did you?"

"If I did, they wouldn't find the body," Corey said with a wicked grin. The doorbell chimed again. Whoever was at the front door was getting impatient. Corey put his phone on the coffee table before crossing the room and peering through the peephole. Corey jumped back and suddenly became very nervous.

"What's wrong?" I scooted forward and stood up.

"It's my parents."

"Your parents?! Why are they here?" I asked loudly. Suddenly, I was the nervous one.

"About that…"

"Corey! Did you invite them and not tell me?"

"Well…" he hedged.

I glared at him, placing my hands on my hips.

"I invited them over for dinner but told them I had nothing here to cook because we were packing to move to Florida. My mom went on this rant about how she hadn't met you yet and they could help pack. Also, if I were moving to Florida, they wanted to see me before I made the big move."

"You could have warned me!" I said, throwing one of the couch pillows at him.

"I was going to, but they weren't supposed to be here until much later. I thought I had more time to prepare you."

The doorbell rang again.

"They can't see me like this." I looked down at the pajamas I wore. They were sweaty and very worn with stains and rips.

"Go change."

"All I brought was pajamas because I thought we weren't leaving the house."

"Grab something out of my clothes. My mom is very impatient, so you better get moving," Corey said.

A knock came to the door this time. "Corey! I know you're in there with that sweet girl of yours. Open up!"

I walked over to where Corey stood. I gave him a gentle kiss. "I'm still mad at you for planning this without telling me. I didn't want to meet your folks this way."

"I know, beautiful. But, you had to meet them sometime."

"I know."

Another knock rattled the door. "Corey Anthony Mathison! We've got milk and eggs. I don't want them to spoil. Open this door now."

I snickered. "Your mom used your full name, Corey Anthony. You're in big trouble."

"Shut up! Go change." He shoved me playfully toward the stairs.

I bolted up the stairs, letting him answer the door. I hurried into our bedroom to rummage through my duffel bag filled with the few pieces of clothes I owned. I tried to pull an outfit together that would impress his parents. I was beyond nervous about meeting Corey's parents and couldn't even think straight. I found a pair of black pajama shorts that could pass as regular shorts. I had no proper shirts, so I rifled through Corey's shirts hanging in the closet. Wifebeater, wifebeater, long-sleeved dress shirt... Aha! A plain white, short-sleeved shirt. The cut was a bit lower than I wanted, and it might show some of my cleavage, but I had no other choice. I pulled it off the hanger, headed straight into the bathroom, and switched clothes. I pulled my hair out of the messy bun, giving it a good shake. I sprayed myself with my Sweet Pea perfume to hide the musky smell of sweat.

I pulled up my big girl panties and bravely left the bedroom. I tiptoed to the top of the staircase, peering down to the main floor, trying to hear Corey's conversation with his parents. Maybe I would be lucky enough to see what they looked like before joining them. I quietly crept down the steps, trying not to draw attention to myself. I got to the bottom step, and the butterflies in my stomach took flight like they were jacked up on coffee. I couldn't believe I was about to meet his parents.

I walked around the corner to find Corey sitting on the coffee table facing the couch. From where I stood, I saw his parents taking up the couch. His dad had a receding hairline, strands brushed over the top of his head to try and hide it. Is that a sweater vest he's wearing? His mom had shoulder-length brown hair, a metal clip holding it back. She wore a dress shirt with a jean skirt.

"Hey, beautiful," Corey said, drawing everyone's attention to me. I shyly stepped further into the room, instantly regretting my outfit choice. I walked over to stand beside Corey, and he tugged me to sit on his leg.

"Mr. and Mrs. Mathison. It's a pleasure to meet you finally," I nervously said, pushing a loose strand of hair out of my face.

"Well, aren't you darling? Corey, you picked a good one. She seems so wholesome. You should have become that doctor," Mrs. Mathison said, playfully smacking her son's leg.

"Whatever he chooses to do, I'll still love and support him," I said, looking at Corey with a smile. He smiled, too, as he pulled me even closer to him.

"You two must be starving. Why don't you come into the kitchen and help me prepare our supper, Melanie? That way, I can get to know you better."

"But the–"

"The men can do the packing and heavy lifting while we're in the kitchen. Those championship belts weigh a ton. Plus, the U-Haul has to get all packed up so we can leave in the morning." I looked at her, puzzled. Corey hadn't informed me about this development, but it had also slipped his mind about his parents coming over. "Charles and I are driving it to Florida because we don't want Corey missing his fight." She chattered away as she led me into the kitchen. "Have you ever made homemade noodles?"

"No, but it sounds time-consuming."

"Oh, it is." She pulled a Tupperware container from the tote bag on the table. When she opened the Tupperware, layers of noodles filled the container. "I took the liberty of making them already. What's your specialty?"

"I don't really have one. When I cooked, my ex wanted simple meals. He thought he needed light meals because he ate so late and close to bed that big meals would make him fat." My nervousness made me give her the details.

"Oh, dear. Corey learned a lot of tricks from me. As long as you know the basics, you can learn. Are you good at measuring?"

"That I can do," I confidently said as she handed me a list of things to start measuring.

"Are you okay with Corey's job?"

I looked over my shoulder, his mom's back to me as she laid noodles flat in the cookware. I turned around, focusing on watching her as she created the layers of the lasagna. Was I okay with him fighting? What kind of question is that?'

"I'm taking that as a no because you went silent."

I sighed and turned to lean back against the counter. "I'm going to support Corey, no matter what. He loves MMA and is good at it. It's not my place to discourage him or tell him no. I'm not comfortable with the idea, but I love Corey."

"I don't like it personally. I go crazy worrying about my son. I think he knows that and continues to do it because he knows it drives me nuts. I prefer that piercing job he had over this fighting. Are you one of those fangirls he talked about?"

Fangirls? Are those the girls screaming for him? Has he been with them or told his mom about them? Am I a rebound for him? He said he was on dating sites. All the questions bounced around in my head, filling me with doubts for the moment.

"No, ma'am. We met at his piercing job."

"You're into that too? No wonder," she said with a chuckle. "He got that from Charles. He was big into Poison and Foreigner. Were you a client?"

"Actually, no. I was the receptionist at the tattoo parlor."

"Receptionist? So, you didn't do any piercings or tattooing?"

"Well, I drew designs for some of the tattoos. That was about it." I shrugged.

"That is a bit of a relief."

"How did you and Charles meet?" I asked, needing to change the subject while we finished making the lasagna. A smile came across her lips as she began to tell me about how she met her husband and their dating history, making the whole meal prep go faster, and I didn't have to answer fifty questions. I popped the lasagna into the oven to cook and followed his mom into the living room, where more boxes had appeared while we made supper.

"Forty-five minutes until dinner will be ready. What can we do to help?" his mom asked.

"Do you want to help us load more boxes into the U-Haul? We need to leave early in the morning," Charles said.

"Absolutely," his mom confidently said. His mom seemed like a planner. She went into great detail about their planned route to Florida and what to do with the furniture if it didn't sell.

Before I knew it, the timer in the kitchen went off, so she excused herself to pull out dinner. Corey tightened his grip on my hand, pulling it into his lap and rubbing his thumb over the back of it. His dad began to talk about his university days, about moving in and out of the dorms. I hadn't gone to university, so I was intrigued by sorority houses and dorm life.

"Did you go to those house parties, too?" I asked Corey.

"I went to a few." All of a sudden, he seemed uncomfortable with my question and tried to shrug it off, and I felt him stiffening up.

"That's where he met Stephanie," his mom called from the kitchen. She walked into the living room, drying her hands with a dish rag. "That Stephanie was something else."

"Stephanie?" I asked with an arched brow, then looked at Corey. He couldn't look at me and stared pointedly at the cup in his hand.

"Corey's ex. They were engaged, but Corey ended it for some unknown reason." His mom shrugged. Corey finished the rest of his drink in one gulp and crushed the can in his fist. She looked at him and continued. "I don't know why you went back to fighting. If you had never started fighting, you would already be settled with a beautiful wife and kids. That fighting career has consumed your life. What's wrong with taking some time for yourself? I was looking forward to you marrying Stephanie. She had a career, a nice sports car, and a future. She wanted kids."

I could tell Corey was getting furious. I was offended because his mom raved about how great Stephanie was, comparing her to me and finding me lacking. I had no idea about his history with Stephanie or the damage she had caused. Corey still wanted to have kids someday, so maybe being with Stephanie hadn't changed his mind. There was no way I would sit here and listen to this any longer. I had to put an end to it for Corey's sake as well as my own. I'd had enough.

"I do apologize, Mr. And Mrs. Mathison. It's been a long day, but I think it would be best for you to head home and rest for your trip."

"We were planning on sleeping here," Mrs. Mathison stated.

"I think it's for the best that you don't, ma'am."

"What about dinner?"

"Look," I said, pulling my wallet from my purse. "I suggest

you take this $20 and go buy yourself dinner. And if you don't go, I'll throw you out myself," I growled.

"What's your problem?" she snarled right back at me.

"My problem is that you don't see how you've upset your son. I may not know how much this Stephanie chick hurt Corey, but if you can't support his fighting career, then you need to leave. He's your fucking son. If he loves what he does, then be happy for him. Not everyone gets that chance. Not only did you upset and disrespect your son in his own home, you disrespected me. And honestly, if you can't accept me, I hope you are gone when I return from the bathroom. So now, if you would excuse me." I stomped up the stairs to the master bedroom and plopped on the edge of the bed, waiting for enough time to pass before heading back downstairs.

I heard someone clear their throat and looked at the doorway to find Corey standing there. He started walking toward me, dropping down beside me on the mattress. We sat in silence for a moment. I didn't know where to begin right now.

"They left." He spoke to me in a quiet voice.

I nodded my head. "I'm glad. You don't deserve to be treated that way, regardless of how much help we need. We have other people we can ask to give us a hand."

"Thank you for sticking up for me and taking a stand against them. I promised myself I would bite my tongue to have their help."

"Who was Stephanie?"

Taking a deep breath, Corey slowly exhaled while pushing his fingers through his hair. "She was six years younger than me and a huge fan. My mom needed a job, and the boss lady interviewing her mentioned our last names were the same.

Mom said she would see that I took her daughter out on a date. That guaranteed my mom the job. I went on one date with Stephanie, for my mom's sake, but I didn't feel there was a connection. Stephanie kept putting more and more pressure on me for another date, so I agreed. My mom thought things were going so well between us and started to plan this wedding on our behalf. On one date, I got drunk, and things got out of hand. Stephanie ended up at my place, and I called it quits afterward. My mom lost her job because of the whole fiasco. A month later, Stephanie called me crying and said she was pregnant. I felt bad for leaving her if she was pregnant, so I went back to her. I took her to the OB/GYN appointment I scheduled, only to find nothing on the ultrasound. Stephanie had told a blatant lie to get me back. My mom still hates that I fight due to injuries. She would rather see me settle down and get married to have those grandkids she is dying for."

I stared straight ahead at the floor, trying to understand what he was saying. The silence was thick between us. I didn't know what to think or say.

"I didn't say anything because I had closed myself off for a long time. It was a dark period of my life. I spiraled into a deep depression and focused on my career. I became unstoppable. I haven't been beaten since then. Well, there was this once."

He got a tiny smile with that one. "I'm sorry, Corey. I'm not like her at all."

"Don't be sorry. And I know you're nothing like Stephanie. Now that my parents are gone, are you hungry?"

"Corey, I'm starving, but your mom made that lasagna out of anger. I've got a better idea." I got up to retrieve my phone and called Kevin. "Kevin, bring Anita and Jack to Corey's. We need help."

229

With a click of the phone, I set it back on the dresser. Corey laughed. "That's all you say to him?"

"Straight forward and to the point. Now, go pick us up some pizza and beer. We've got work to do," I sternly said. Corey got up and stepped in front of me. I stared up at his brown eyes. "I'm neither pizza nor beer."

"You aren't, but you are all mine." His voice was growly as his hands gripped my hips, tugging me firmly against his frame. His lips crashed roughly against mine, and moans escaped us both. "I love it when you take control, babes. Maybe later, I can show you how much I truly love your bossy side."

Being tugged close enough to feel the bulge formed in his pants had me groaning. I knew what he was getting at. He winked and walked out of the room. I sighed and followed behind him a few moments later. While Corey was gone to pick up the beer and pizza, I tossed the dinner his mom had cooked into the garbage with glee, heading outside to the nearly full U-Haul. As I stood there, I reworked everything in my head. Could we fit everything? We could tow Corey's car, but what about the larger pieces of furniture?

Scratching the back of my head, I began to doubt this would work. The sound of a car coming down the street drew my attention. Looking toward the sound, I saw Kevin's car roll up.

Kevin parked alongside the curb before he crossed the grassy front yard. "What's the plan?"

Kevin stood beside me with arms crossed over his chest and stared into the U-Haul with me. I glanced at him momentarily, trying to figure that out myself.

"I was originally thinking we could load all the furniture into this truck, but I didn't realize how little room we had left."

I sighed.

"Why are you taking it?" Anita asked while Jack climbed into the back of the truck.

"Corey has plans for all of it. We have to make the drive ourselves now. That's the only way it's going to work. We'll have to leave soon to make it in time for his fight." As I took the time to explain what was happening, they didn't even question me.

"Corey will be back soon with pizza and beer."

"Let's go see the damage." Kevin turned on his heel to go into the house. I showed him what still had to be loaded and returned to the truck as Corey rolled up. I jokingly said, "Speaking of the devil, he appears."

"Hey, man. Thanks for showing up at the last minute." Corey said, smacking at Kevin's hand before pulling him into a one-handed bro hug.

"That's what best friends do. Why don't we eat while we unload, and the girls can plan the route?" Kevin filled Corey in.

"Route?" Confusion was evident in Corey's voice. His brow became furrowed when he looked at me.

"Yep. Change in plans. You and I are going on a road trip." I winked as I turned on my heel, and before I got too far, my arm was in a firm grip, and Corey pulled me backward. I was pressed firmly into Corey's embrace, and a hard bulge pressed firmly against my ass.

"The only trip I want to take is the one that will lead me to that sweet pussy of yours," Corey growled into my ear, his hand rubbing between my legs. "My cock will drive into this tight pussy, full speed ahead." His hand rubbed me through my shorts, making me want to drag him upstairs right now.

231

"Melanie!" Anita called from inside the house. I didn't want to pry out of Corey's grip, but we couldn't be too suspicious.

"You'll control my stick shift later," Corey growled outside my ear before I broke from his embrace and rushed inside before Anita came looking for me.

"What happened with the parents?" Anita asked, but I only glared at her. "Right. His mom's big mouth?"

"Nailed it," I said as I put the pizza down. I grabbed myself a slice to eat while I went to grab my phone from upstairs. "Anita, did you know about Stephanie?"

The expression on Anita's had me chuckling to myself, and I took it to mean she didn't want to discuss the bitch. I turned to my phone, taking her hint. I looked at my map app, seeing how long the drive would take from here to his condo. The app estimated at least fifteen hours nonstop, so I took it to mean we needed two days max. We would get to Florida much earlier than I had expected, leaving us time to take care of any other business.

I called and reserved a room for tonight since we wouldn't have a bed to sleep in. Next, I called U-Haul to book the tow bar to take Corey's car down to Florida behind the truck. Anita helped file paperwork to sign my car and the house over to them, giving them permission to seek or make important decisions on our behalf while we were out of town.

Corey strolled in through the front door with Kevin behind him. Both men had beads of sweat on their foreheads from the hard labor of unloading and reloading the U-Haul.

"We need to go to the U-Haul store tonight," I spoke openly.

"Why? I'm exhausted and ready for bed."

"We need to tow your car somehow," I answered, looking up at Corey from where I sat cross-legged on the floor.

Corey sighed while pushing his hand through his sweaty, short brown locks. "Can't we do it in the morning?"

As much as I wanted to argue with him, he looked exhausted, more than after his fights. He was right. After a hot shower and a good night's rest, we could hook up his car and hit the road in the morning.

"Or how about we drive your car down in a couple of days? We would love to come to your championship fight," Kevin suggested, making it the best option.

"We have a winner," Corey said, pointing at Kevin. I chuckled and rolled my eyes at how ridiculous he was. "Sorry to cut this short," Corey said, "but we've gotta find a place to crash."

"We've got a room at Red Roof Inn," I announced.

"I hear they have the best continental breakfast," Anita piped up.

"Count me in," Corey said, offering his hand to pull me to my feet. He tugged me against his frame, his hands cupping my ass. "Anywhere my woman is at, I'll be happy."

Shivers went down my spine when he said things like that. He pulled me tighter to his hard frame. His lips crashed hard into mine, tasting like pizza, beer, and sweat.

Breaking the kiss, I stared into his dark brown eyes, butterflies filling my stomach like the first time I met him. I would be his, all his, for the rest of my life. It hit me then that we were actually doing this: moving in together and getting married.

"Are you ready to go, beautiful?" he asked, his fingers tangling in my hair. He tugged my head to the side, kissing my neck lightly. "I can't wait any longer to get you undressed and screaming my name."

I held back a moan. He led me out of the house behind

Kevin's little family. Corey locked up his house for the last time and handed the keys over to Kevin. We gave out hugs and said our goodbyes. Corey planted his hand on my ass to give me an extra oomph to help me climb into the raised truck. I had my legs slightly spread, trying to take the next step, when I felt his fingers slip under the hem of my shorts and begin to press against my clit. I gripped the handlebar tightly so I wouldn't fall back.

"Fuck, you're wet for me, baby." He groaned from beneath me as he rubbed his fingers over my clit. I threw my head back, moaning, unable to stop him. "Shit, get in. I need to taste that pussy."

I hurriedly got the rest of the way into the truck as he jumped in the driver's seat. Corey drove the big box truck over to the white building with red trim, where I had reserved a room for the night. I headed into the lobby to check us in, returned with two keycards, and led Corey to the room on the second floor.

I swiped the card, opening the red door. The king-sized bed was the first thing I saw in the room. The bed had a hideous patterned comforter, but I didn't care what it looked like, only that it was there for us to use. Corey pushed past me, tossed our bags to the floor, and gripped my hands, pulling me to him.

"I need my tongue on that pussy." He growled into my ear. He pulled me towards the bed, tugging me to sit on the edge of the hard mattress. "You are going to be mine tonight."

His lips attacked mine roughly, his hands fumbling with the hem of my shirt.

"C-C-Corey, what if I'm not ready?" I stuttered out.

"We'll use the color system. Red means stop, yellow means

slow down," Corey explained, and it seemed simple enough to understand. Corey's lips attached themselves to the curve of my neck, nipping and sucking as his hands roamed under my shirt. Nimble fingers started roaming across my stomach to slowly rise higher to massage my breasts through the satin and lace of my bra.

I sat up to help him pull the shirt over my head, and he flung the fabric aside without a care in the world. His fingers were quick to unhook the clasps of my bra, the straps sliding down my arms and off my fingertips. When my breasts were free from the garment, Corey groaned with pleasure while my cheeks burned from blushing.

I couldn't look at him because of my embarrassment. Corey gripped my chin, turning me to face him. His lips crashed against mine in a rough kiss. He leaned forward, lowering me back to lay on the bed. Corey left a trail of kisses down my body. I bit my bottom lip, anticipating what he would do next. The pleasure of his lips gently sucking at my puckered nipples left me moaning. He lavished attention on one nipple, then the other, keeping his hands gliding over my skin while his mouth worshiped. His hands roamed ahead of his lips, over my abdomen, quickly undoing the jean shorts I had on. Gripping the fabric, he tugged the shorts down my legs with my thong in one swift movement, throwing them over his shoulder. I shifted up the bed until I reached the pillows, Corey's eyes devouring me as my breasts bounced with every movement.

"Fuck, this is all mine?" The rumble of his voice reached somewhere deep inside me, making me feel a rush of moisture. I watched as he licked his lips. He stared at me with a hungry, lust-filled look. Climbing back onto the bed, he positioned himself between my thighs and dipped down between them. Resting my legs over his shoulders, he stared up the length of my body, his brown eyes meeting mine.

He was not about to...Oh, my god! His tongue was sliding along my slit to circle my clit. My back arched off the bed, my breath caught in my throat, and my fingers clawed at the comforter.

"Moan for me, baby. I want to hear all those sexy noises," he demanded as his tongue went back to pleasuring the most sensitive part of my body. Moans escaped my lips from the pleasure he was causing. His finger dipped into my wet pussy, adding to the pleasure.

"Yellow!" I screamed. Corey slid the finger out, his tongue continuing to inflict pleasure.

"Just want to make you cum before I fuck you senseless and fully claim you as mine," he growled.

Corey sat back on his legs, sliding the finger back into me. I willed my body to relax, trying not to think of my experiences with Alex.

"That's it, baby. It's me, Corey. My finger is the one buried deep in that wet pussy of yours."

Corey towered over my body, whispering in my ear. Thoughts of Alex left my mind with every word Corey whispered. One finger turned to two, pumping hard and fast. Scissoring to spread my pussy, getting me ready for him.

"So tight. My dick won't fit in this tight pussy of yours." He continued thrusting his fingers inside me, giving me dirty talk that made me wetter. My walls tightened around his fingers, and I was panting from pleasure. "Shit, baby. You going to cum all over my fingers?"

Words failed me, so I simply moaned my reply to him. He

dove back between my legs, sliding his tongue along my clit until I orgasmed. I stared at Corey standing at the end of the bed, stripping out of his clothes while I lay there, basking in my pleasure high.

Once he had stripped off his clothes, I could see Corey was right about one thing. His cock was a lot bigger than Alex and what I was used to. Corey slid between my legs, resting my thighs over his hips, and I felt his cock teasing at my pussy. Swallowing big gulps of air, I could feel the dull pain of being stretched to accommodate his size. Corey gripped the headboard for leverage as he began to thrust into me. Even though it felt good, flashbacks of Alex hovering over me flooded my mind.

"Red!" I cried out. Corey immediately stopped and climbed off me. I curled up, tears and sobs escaping. I felt horrible, calling a stop in the middle of what had initially been amazing, and now I was embarrassed.

"What's wrong?" Corey asked, kneeling at the side of the bed with his forehead pressed against mine.

"Flashbacks." I was whimpering, trying to suck up the tears that had already escaped. "I tried to push them out of my mind, but they came rushing back in."

"What can I do to make you forget him and make you all mine?"

My brain wrestled through so many solutions as it tried to kick the flashbacks back to hell where they belonged.

"Could we try another position?" I suggested. Corey's face lit up, a devilish, lusty smile coming over his handsome face.

"Get on all fours, beautiful," he said as he stepped back to give me room to get into position. I rolled to my stomach and then pushed onto my hands and knees. His hands slowly ran down my spine and over my ass. Nudging my legs open a little more, he positioned himself against my pussy and eased back in.

"Corey, please, I want more." No more ugly memories flooded my brain, only pleasure. I wasn't above begging.

I yelped out in a mixture of pain and pleasure. Corey's fingers dug into the skin on my sides, his grip tight, as his hips pounded against my ass. The sound of skin slapping skin filled the room.

I clawed at the bed underneath me. Corey was able to thrust deeper and felt so much larger in this position. No flashbacks of Alex entered my mind. Moans of pleasure escaped my lips every time Corey entered my body.

Corey pulled out, his breathing fast and his chest covered in sweat. He slid up the bed to sit, placing his back against the headboard, grabbed me under the arms, and pulled me to sit in his lap, my back to his chest, his cock easily sliding back into my soaking pussy. My muscles began to convulse around his thick cock. Corey wrapped his arms around me to keep me sitting in his lap. He slid his hands up to grab my tits and hold on.

"I am about to cum into your tight pussy," he growled into my ear. "Rock your hips for me, baby."

Rocking my hips as he instructed, pleasure began intensifying from the slow movements. Corey dropped one hand from my breast to dip between my legs, his fingers pressing against my clit, adding the right amount of pressure to the sensitive nub.

"You're so wet, baby. I want to cum in you, truly mark you as mine. You need to cum with me, beautiful."

Corey began to bite at my neck, which would leave a visible

mark for sure. My head fell back against his shoulder, eyes clenched shut from pleasure.

"Cum, beautiful. Cum with me," Corey rasped into my ear.

"Corey!!" I cried out, my hips continuing to rock against him as I rode out my orgasm. His fingers dug into my skin, and his teeth bit roughly into the flesh of my neck. He held me tight to him, and I could feel his cum pulse deep inside my pussy, leaving me panting from the ecstasy I had just experienced. I got to my knees and flopped face forward onto the bed, staring back at Corey. He held himself in a plank position over my naked body, balancing on his hands near my shoulders.

"Now you are mine," he growled before giving me a rough kiss. He climbed off the bed to retrieve our clothes and get a washcloth to clean us up.

Chapter Nineteen

Our trip to Florida took longer than expected due to the U-Haul's inability to go higher speeds. The hours passed faster than either of us realized, our conversations flowing easily from one topic to another. Corey made me so happy, and I forgot all about my past. For once, I was excited about my future.

Arriving at our first stop in Florida and stepping out of the U-Haul, I could smell the salty ocean air from here. Walking around the front of the truck, I stared at the rundown industrial building housing the MMA training center. I let out a sigh and glanced at Corey.

"Do they need all this furniture?" I asked, uncertain if Corey's donation would go to good use.

"Most definitely. Most of these teenage boys bunk in the back room. A lot of them are homeless with nowhere to go. Mario would rather they crash here than wind up with the wrong crowd."

Corey was confident that the boys and the center would

need this furniture. Aside from the one class I had sat in on, I didn't know any of these kids. Corey's fingers entwined with mine as he led us into the building. I could hear the sounds of fists hitting punching bags, fans, and music entering my eardrums, just like last time.

"Mario!" Corey called out. The older trainer turned in the squared ring and leaned against the ropes. "I've got that furniture I promised you."

"Great, we cleaned out some rooms in the back. Mikey and Josh, help the man," Mario called out to the two teenage boys who were punching the speed bags. The two boys followed us back outside to the boxed truck. I stood aside, watching them unload all the bulky items and carry them back inside.

My stomach began to grumble. I was ready to get home so we could eat and relax. Corey walked out with a long face, and I looked at him, puzzled as to why he was so upset.

"What's with the long face?"

"I've got to fight tonight."

"Tonight?" I was shocked.

"Yep. Antonio's wife gave birth today, and he backed out to spend time with his family."

I huffed out a breath. "Well, I can't blame him. Any chance we can go eat first?"

Corey laughed. "We've got plenty of time for that, beautiful." Corey led me to the passenger side and boosted me into my seat. "I don't think we're returning this U-Haul. I get to grab that ass of yours every time you get in."

I rolled my eyes at him before I slammed the door shut. Corey hopped in and drove us to his condo. We had another two days with the truck, so we didn't rush to bring any boxes up.

Corey ordered us some Del Taco for delivery. While we waited for the food, we showered, and he packed for tonight's fight. I sat on the bed, watching him make multiple trips to and from the closet. He looked damn good in his navy blue suit.

"Are you coming tonight? If you're too tired, you don't have to."

"I'm coming tonight, but only if you want me there."

Corey's gaze raised to me from his bag. "Of course, I want my girl there."

I smiled as he walked around the end of the bed to stand in front of me. My legs widened to allow him room to stand between them, and my arms wrapped around his neck when he leaned down. I was so in love with this man. He closed the distance between our lips, giving me a deep kiss.

"I can't wait to marry you, and then you'll truly be mine forever." He spoke against my lips and gave them a little nip. I loved hearing him say I was his. When Alex had said it, it scared me and grossed me out. I jumped off the bed to change into a different outfit that was more suitable for tonight. Corey voice interrupted my thoughts. "We need to go shopping for you."

"No, we don't," I argued back.

"Yes, you do need to go shopping. As my girl, you need to be dressed differently. Dresses, skirts, maybe even heels." He raised his eyebrows suggestively with each suggestion.

I looked down at my outfit of choice, feeling saddened my wardrobe was not up to the standards of his job. I went quiet as I continued getting ready. Corey must have known that I had taken offense to his words. Stepping behind me, his arms snaking around my waist, he tugged me back against his solid frame.

"I didn't mean to offend you, beautiful. I'd much rather you be naked with me between those legs of yours, but my work has standards. Even I have to follow the dress code." His words were muffled against my skin as he kissed the curve of my neck. "But you in dresses will distract me from my fight."

I loved the attention he gave me, and it made me feel attractive, special, and loved. Giving my ear lobe one last nibble, he slid past me to grab his dress shoes. I finished pulling the band around my hair and joined him in the bedroom. Once we had eaten and finished dressing, we collected Corey's bags and my purse to head out for the night.

Corey drove us to the venue, where fans were lined up outside the back entrance, calling his name when they saw him approaching. Anxiety rose, making me tighten my grip on his arm as we walked past all the fans. He led me to his dressing room, where I stayed while he checked in.

"I need to go do my promo shots. Do you want to come with me or head to your seat?" Corey asked, undoing the zipper on his bag.

"I'll go to my normal seat. See you out there." I winked before I found my way out of the room and to my seat by the octagon. I slid into the front row aisle seat next to the cage entrance. Corey made sure this specific seat was reserved for me at every show due to my issues.

Soon, the rumbling noise in the venue intensified, and the bleachers vibrated and shook as fans began stumbling in by the hundreds. My eyes were scanning the crowd of fans still filling in. My eyes landed on one particular face straight across the octagon from me. The ten-foot silver cage may have blurred my vision, but this person was the spitting image of Alex.

My posture stiffened, and I froze. I couldn't move, couldn't scream, nothing. I didn't know a single soul around me to help snap me out of this petrified state either.

Even as Corey's music hit, I was stuck staring at the man, and oddly, he was staring back at me.

"Melanie! Melanie!" Hands were gripping both my shoulders, snapping out of my trance. My eyes locked with Corey's brown eyes. "What happened?"

"Alex," I whispered. Corey turned around, and his head snapped back when he saw the same guy.

"Mikey!" he yelled, waving the teenage fighter from his class over. "Escort her to my locker room and make sure no one comes in or out."

Corey pointed aggressively in Mikey's face to get his point across. I'd never seen Corey be so enraged. Mikey escorted me to the changing room, where he watched the fight on his phone while I paced around the small room.

Alex had found us. But how? We'd made sure not to leave traces of ourselves when we left Pennsylvania. It couldn't be him, could it? We left no trail. Corey can't go assault happy down here. He'd ruin his career.

I was out of my mind, worried about what could happen, when a rhythmic knock came at the door. Mikey pulled it open a half inch, just enough for him to peek out and see who was there before he stepped aside to pull it open the rest of the way. Corey slid in, not a drop of blood on him. Covered in sweat, he wore a worried expression on his face.

"You're free to go, Mikey. See you on Tuesday," Corey instructed as Mikey saw himself out.

"How'd he find me?" I asked after the door clicked shut.

"I don't know, but we need to take a detour home so we won't lead him straight to our residence. Even though he won't pass all our security measures, I want to take precautions."

Corey grabbed his outfit, beelining into the separate bathroom to change in privacy. He returned, wearing his business attire, and shoved his fight gear into his bag. He flung his bag onto his shoulder and offered me his hand.

Corey firmly gripped my hip, holding me close as we made our way to his muscle car. He held my door open for me, walked around, and tossed his bag into the back seat before he climbed in.

The engine roared to life, and Corey sped out of the parking lot. His so-called detour was an hour long with multiple turns. He finally turned into the condo parking lot and used his keycard to gain access. No cars were behind us trying to follow us, which was a good sign.

We headed up to his apartment. I followed him into the bedroom, where he tossed the duffel bag aside and led me into the bathroom. We both slowly stripped out of our clothing and stepped into the shower.

I stepped back, trying to give Corey more room, only to be pressed against his body, arms snaking around my waist to hold me close. We stood under the flow of the water, letting it massage my head, and I shut my eyes. Alex's haunting eyes stared back at me.

My eyes snapped open. Corey tightened his grip on me, and I felt him give the curve of my neck a soft kiss. We stood in the shower in complete silence for what seemed like forever. Corey reached around me to shut the water off and reached out for our towels.

I wrapped mine around my body while he tied one around his waist before he stepped out of the tub, offering his hand to me. We went into the closet, locating and putting on our pajamas.

I climbed into the bed and lay on my side to watch Corey punch away at his phone. I was unsure what he was doing but presumed it had to be business. When he finished, Corey dropped his phone on the dresser and ran his hands over his face. He turned to look at me, and his long face turned into a smile when he saw me.

"We should get some sleep. We've had another long day." He climbed into the bed beside me. His arm snaked around my waist, pulling me into his hard frame. My face buried into his chest, his arms locked around me, and the beating of his heart through his chest reassured me. I closed my eyes, wanting to get some sleep, but behind closed eyes, I couldn't get rid of the haunting images of Alex and some of the numerous attacks he had made on me.

I wanted to forget Alex. He was my past. I needed to put him behind me and move on. Why did he continue to haunt me and dredge up bad memories I wanted to forget? Why couldn't he let me go because I would never be his again? I scooted up the bed as best I could and slammed my lips against Corey's.

I rolled on top of him, straddling his hips as I hovered over him, placing rough kisses on his lips. His hands gripped my hips, fingers digging into my skin. I rocked my hips hard against his, making my intentions loud and clear, showing him exactly what I wanted from him. I broke the intense kiss and sat back, making sure I was pressed hard against his pelvis. My fingers trace his defined abs, running my fingers along the lines of his six-pack, then down to the elastic of his boxers.

"Corey, make me forget," I begged with a harsh exhale.

Corey's hands traveled up under my shirt, exposing my ass and letting him know I wasn't wearing any underwear.

"Fuck. I'll make you forget your name, beautiful." His words were raspy, and I felt his hands shift lower to grab tightly onto my ass. Lifting his hips, he pressed his semi-erect cock against my pussy. Moaning, I tugged at his boxers to free his cock, which was growing harder by the second. I gasped, seeing the sheer size of him again. He was certainly doing a great job of making me forget about Alex. Wrapping my hand around his impressive size, I positioned his hard length where I wanted him then I slid onto his big cock.

I gasped with every inch that disappeared inside me. His fingers dug harder into the cheeks of my ass, and I gasped from the stretching sensation. I pressed my hands flat against his chest for support as I worked my hips, swiveling and riding him. I loved being the one in control of our pleasure. With Alex, he had never let me be in control of the sex or anything in our lives. I began to grind on Corey faster, the sensation of my orgasm building higher and faster within my core.

Corey's hands moved from my ass so that he gripped my hips, hanging on so hard I knew there would be bruises left behind that I would gladly wear. I whimpered as he began to slam up into me roughly, managing to move my body easily. Corey was grunting with pleasure. It did feel good, but I wasn't in control anymore. Thoughts and memories of Alex consumed my mind.

"Red!" I cried. I pulled myself off Corey's cock before jumping off the bed, running toward the bathroom. Tears streamed from my eyes, and I wiped my cheeks, brushing away the stray tears that fell profusely. I felt one of Corey's hands gently grip my wrist and turn me around to face him.

He pressed his forehead against mine.

"Sorry, baby. I couldn't take the teasing anymore. I wanted to pound into that tight pussy of yours," he apologized.

"The problem is Alex always controlled the sex. I loved being in control of you just now," I told Corey, and he nodded his understanding.

"I understand, beautiful. Do you want to go back to bed?" he asked, and I shook my head no. His eyebrow raised, staring at me with confusion. "What do you want to do then?"

"Finish fucking me senseless?" I asked as he growled. He picked me up and slammed my back against the wall, his body easily holding me there. His hands planted on either side of me as he slammed his still-hard dick back into me. I don't think I would ever fully adjust to his size. Corey's lips attacked my neck as he began to pound into me. With every thrust, I would slam back against the wall.

"Fuck, Melanie. You're all mine. You'll always be mine. From now on, remember this cock pounding into this tight pussy of yours is all you need." His low voice growled into my ear.

I whimpered and moaned as he continued to roughly pound into me, snapping his hips at the end of each hard thrust. "Do you want to finish what you started?"

I raised an eyebrow as he carried me to the bed, rocking my hips with each step. I wanted to feel his cock thrusting into me. Corey gave my butt a quick spank for acting up. He sat on the edge of the bed and laid back. I smiled, instantly knowing what he wanted me to do. He was letting go of control so I could finish what I had started. Once again, I planted my hands on his muscled pecs for support as I began to ride his cock. I alternated between hard and fast, and then

I would slow down to tease him. I began to slide off his cock, until just the tip was inside, then slammed back down on it, forcing myself to take the pleasure with the pain. His moans of approval filled the room, along with my gasps of pleasure.

"I'm going to cum." Corey's warning spurred me on as I slammed back down on his cock about five more times before his fingers clawed at my skin, and he arched off the bed, shooting his load deep inside me. When his spasm ended, he stated, "Fuck, you didn't cum yet."

Corey threw me down on the bed beside him, and he dove between my legs. His tongue pressed against my swollen clit as his fingers slid easily into my pussy, filled with his cum. Arching my back off the bed from the sensations he evoked, my fingers tangled in his hair as he worked his magic. After just a few moments, I cried out in pleasure, an intense orgasm ripping through my center.

Corey hovered above me, pressing his lips gently against my neck. "I love you, beautiful. I can't wait to spend forever with you. You'll be mine and only mine."

Why did he say that? It flipped a switch deep inside and turned me on. Corey planted a sensual, lingering kiss on my lips, and I watched as he headed to the bathroom to clean up. I got comfortable on the bed, waiting for him to return with a washcloth for me and the cuddles I knew that would follow.

Corey lay beside me, tugging me against his solid frame. I snuggled up closer to him, needing to feel the comfort of being secure in his grip. I had to feel safe.

Corey locked his arms behind me to hold me in close. "You've had a tough night. I thought I would drop you off at the mall tomorrow morning with my credit card and let you shop until you drop. Pick up dresses, heels, make-up, and anything you want at Hot Topic or the lingerie shop. That satin bra of yours seems a few years old, and it's not doing the best job holding in those perky breasts of yours. Fuck, I love your tits."

"Need a cold shower?" I laughed as he smiled.

"Only if you want some shower sex." With a wink from him, I blushed profusely.

"What if he's there?" I changed the subject. Without saying his name, Corey knew who I meant.

"Call me, but you have a hell of a right hook."

"I'm scared to be alone."

"I need to help the guys at the gym rearrange the furniture we donated and unload the U-Haul."

I didn't think I would be much help with unloading or unpacking. I felt out of my mind with worry and knew I wasn't very good company. I needed to make some friends of my own. Maybe there were some girlfriends or wives of the fighters I could get to know. Maybe some retail therapy would help bring back some semblance of a normal life. I closed my eyes, scooting closer to Corey whenever an image of Alex appeared. Slowly, my eyes closed, and sleep welcomed me.

The next morning, I awoke to the smell of pancakes and coffee. I slid out of bed and followed the delicious smells, spotting breakfast on the table. The grumbling of my stomach told me not to ask questions.

"I figured we would both need a big breakfast for the day ahead of us," Corey said as he stepped out of the kitchen with two coffee mugs.

I took a good, hard look at him. He looked like every woman's wet dream. He must have known I was getting turned on, too. He wore navy blue dress pants, a matching blazer, and a white button-up with a couple of buttons open at his throat. I could see a hint of his tattoos peeking out from underneath the edge of his sleeves. He slouched in the chair like I imagined a mafia boss would if he were making a deal.

I sat across from him, trying to push away thoughts of riding him while he sat at the table. I picked up the fork and began to poke at the scrambled eggs.

"Kevin and Anita can't make it this weekend. Something unexpected came up, so they are going to have my car shipped down," Corey said nonchalantly.

"Is everyone okay?" I asked, concerned about my friends.

"Yeah, I guess a pipe burst at the tattoo parlor. The repairs took up a lot of funds, so they can't afford the trip right now." Corey's explanation made more sense now.

"Oh," I softly said. I felt bad about their rotten luck and wished that they could come. I needed someone with me at the fight, especially since Alex was taunting us.

"I hired Mikey as your quasi-bodyguard for Saturday. He will protect you if I can't be by your side."

I almost choked on my food as I replied, "What?"

"Mikey is the most hot-tempered kid in my class and also the strongest. He can easily take Alex down with one well-placed punch. I need someone beside you ringside in case you can't handle it and to protect you while I focus on my career."

"Corey, that's a bit much."

"Not to me, it's not. I can't worry about you while trying to focus on my fight. Look what happened last time, and this fight is for the belt."

I tossed my fork down. I suddenly didn't have the stomach to eat anymore. I sat back in the chair, upset that he would hire someone to sit with me. I wasn't a child who needed a babysitter.

"Please don't be angry with me, but look how you react when he shows up. I can't take the chance of you freaking out or him taking you away from me. I can't let him lay a finger on the love of my life."

"Conversation over, Corey. I'd like to go to the mall now," I demanded.

I stomped to the bedroom to slip on a pair of shorts and grab my purse. By the time I returned, Corey had stepped over to the condo's front door. I pushed past him to head down to his car. I sat in the passenger seat in disbelief that he hired someone to babysit me. Was I his fiancé or his child?

Corey drove me to the mall in complete silence. He stopped at the mall's entrance, handing me a credit card. I knew I would have to spend the right amount of time window-shopping, even if I had no intention of buying a single thing. There was a pretty good chance that not using the card would likely cause another disagreement, but I understand his intention to care for me. I loved Corey and that he could provide for me and our future family. But I was feeling too clingy and dependent on him, and I hated that.

Stopping by a store's window, I notice the dress hanging on display. It was a little pricey, and I couldn't burden Corey more than I already had. I went into the store, figuring I'd try the dress on just for shits and giggles.

The dress fit perfectly and flattered me in all the right areas. The only issue was that it showed the scars on my legs. Otherwise, I couldn't find anything wrong with it except the price tag. Before I removed it from my body, I took a selfie of myself in it and sent it over to Corey.

'I adore this dress.' I added to the message. I dropped my phone back in my purse as I removed the dress, placed it back on the hanger, and left it for the associate to place back on the shelf.

I continued strolling through the three-story mall, glancing at the many different stores. I'd never been in a mall so big before. As I got onto the escalator to go up a floor, I began to feel uneasy and anxious, the hairs standing up on the back of my neck. These feelings were sudden and came out of nowhere. Looking around my surroundings, I didn't recognize anyone. How was I supposed to? I've only lived in Florida for two days.

Pushing the feelings aside, I kept on walking, trying on various dresses and articles of clothing that caught my eye. I even went into a shoe shop to try on high heels. The last stop was Victoria's Secret. I had an associate measure me properly for a bra and help me find two flattering types. One was for intimate moments, and one was for everyday wear.

I went into their connected perfume shop, where I found lip gloss and a new perfume to add to my handbasket. Corey won this battle, and I did end up purchasing something today on his card. Maybe I didn't go overboard the way he hoped for and buy everything he wanted me to get, but it was a start. Wandering through the mall, I went to the food court, hoping to find a place that served smoothies.

I stopped in the middle of the mall when I saw him, the six-foot-tall dark-haired man who had ruined my life. My breathing started to come in shallow but sharp gasps. I froze in time where I stood, but he was moving at regular speed. I forced myself to turn around and dart for safety. My feet moved as fast as they could, but I didn't know where to go for safety. My eyes searched the area for anywhere I could hide.

I saw a sign for the bathrooms. I'll be safe there, I hope. I took off running down the hall and slid around the corner. I dove into the family room, where mothers would feed their kids quietly, or families could change their baby's diapers. The corner stall was empty, and I locked the door behind me.

I pressed my back against the wall and slid down the slick tiles to squat in the corner of the stall. Pulling my phone out of my handbag, I noticed my hands were still shaking from panic. I slid open the screen and pressed the button with Corey's name. I did that relatively simple task, then put him on speaker.

"Hey, beautiful. You done already?"

"He's here."

"Who, baby?" Corey asked. How could he not know who I was talking about?

"Alex. He's here. I'm locked in the bathroom." Wiping at my eyes, I caught a few tears threatening to escape.

"Stay there. I'm on my way, and I'll be there in ten." The screen went black, letting me know he had disconnected the call. I pushed my phone back into my handbag. I had to leave this place because families needed this stall more than I did. I needed to be strong and face my fears. I stood up, letting out a huff of frustrated air.

I let myself out, moving slower than I had entered the room. I was trying to keep my guard up, my head swiveling to look around me. If I ran into him, I wanted to be ready to put up a fight. This mall was so big that he had to have moved on to a different section of the mall.

I headed toward where I had seen him before, hoping he had moved on. I had my phone in my hand, ready to call Corey or the cops. Arriving at a back hallway with an exit sign over it, I was grabbed from behind and slammed against the wall when I turned to go down it, leaving me gasping at the sudden blunt force of my back hitting the wall. My eyes met with Alex's angry green ones. His forearm pressed across my throat to hold me in place, anger flitting across his face.

"You little piece of shit! Think that you can just up and move? Who do you think you are? Don't you know that you are mine and no one else's?"

I hoped my clothes covered the marks Corey had left and Alex wouldn't notice. Meanwhile, I was left gasping for air. "Come with me. If you don't, you can say goodbye to that nut head of a boy toy."

Fuming that he was threatening Corey, I swung my leg up and ended up kneeing him right in his crotch. Alex's arm fell from my throat as he grabbed his nuts and dropped to the ground. To add insult to injury, I kicked him in the guts for good measure. I ran down the hall and barged out of the building's emergency door into the bright sunlight.

Running down the sidewalk that wrapped around the mall, I bumped into a hard body. Arms snaked around my waist to stop me from getting away, and I screamed and began to kick and hit for all I was worth. All I could think of was that Alex had caught me again, and I couldn't let him get his hands on me or take me away from Corey.

"Melanie, it's me!" Corey's loud voice finally cut through my panic, settling me down. He spun me around so I could see his handsome face. I jumped into his embrace, wrapping my arms and legs around him. I was lucky he was as strong as could be and had good balance. My arms wrapped tightly around his neck, and my legs gripped his hips. I wasn't about to let go of my savior. Crying into his shoulder, I was so relieved he had found me.

Corey said nothing as he carried me to the car. I felt drained and helpless. Maybe I did need that babysitter for his fight, after all. With quiet filling the car, we drove home.

We entered the building and went up to the condo. I went into the bedroom, tossing the bags from Victoria's Secret that I had somehow managed to hold onto the bed, and planted myself on the corner of the mattress to stare out the floor-to-ceiling window.

Corey left me to my solitude. Hours had passed, but it only seemed like minutes. I heard the creaking of the floor behind me from Corey coming down the hall. I was fortunate he gave me the time and space to decompress. He stopped at the door to lean a shoulder on the frame, and I glanced over at him, then back out the window.

"Are you ready to talk now, Melanie?"

Corey walked farther into the room, and when I checked for him again, he was sitting on the corner opposite me. I had been so absorbed in the view outside the window that I hadn't felt the bed move.

"Corey, why are you with me?" I all but spit my question at him.

"Because I'm in love with you."

"Why, though? What do you see in me that I don't? Our relationship has been one fuck-up after another, thanks to my ex and me."

"Aren't most relationships rough in the beginning? Isn't true love worth fighting for?"

"It is, but why stay with me, Corey? Alex isn't going to let me go." With tears stinging my eyes, I looked back at the view beyond the windows again. "I'm bound to live in hell for the rest of my life."

"Well, guess I'll be in hell, too."

I laughed. "You were going there before you even met me, I'm sure."

"Hey!"

We both laughed at that. "Corey, you deserve someone who isn't a hot mess."

"And why do you think that?"

I heard him get up and didn't expect him to sit next to me with his thigh pressed into mine. I looked at him, our eyes connecting. I ticked off on my fingers as I told him, "You are charming, funny, sexy as fuck, and protective as can be. You have awesome taste in music and a great sense of style. Any lady would be lucky to have you."

"And you are the lucky lady that got me." He lightly jabbed me in the leg to make his point.

Why must he be so charming? "I still don't understand why you picked me, Corey. I have nothing to offer to this relationship."

"Can you cook? Could you be open with me? Communicate more? Support my career? So far, you have shown that you are real and feel things. You communicate with me when things get too heavy, and you support me in everything I want to do. I say, 'Let's sail to Pennsylvania,' you're right there with me. That's all I want in my girl."

"But I have some bad attributes."

"The only thing I don't like is this pain in the ass ex of yours. He doesn't know what is coming."

"He pinned me against the wall at the mall and threatened to take you out," I mumbled, looking back outside.

Corey laughed. "I would sure as hell would love to see him try." Corey scooted even closer and pulled me into his lap with little to no effort. "I'm sorry I wasn't there to protect you. I should have gone with you today. Did you find anything to buy? I saw the Victoria's Secret bags, and that's it."

"That's all I bought."

"I am already getting very good visual images. But, so that you know, you did buy more."

"No, I didn't."

"Sure you did. Go check the living room."

I pushed off his lap to do as he suggested. When I walked into the room, scattered on the couch and sticking out of assorted bags were the various articles of clothing, shoes, and anything I had shown interest in during the day. Confusion hit me. How the hell did he manage to get these? I had so many questions running through my mind.

I looked at Corey, who had just stepped into the room and sat on the armrest with a shit-eating grin on his handsome face.

"How'd, where'd...Corey, I'm really confused."

"I knew that you wouldn't buy anything for yourself today. I am merely surprised you bought something from Victoria's Secret and that the card I gave you worked."

"What?"

"I hadn't used that card in months and thought I'd canceled it," he laughed as my mouth fell agape in shock. "I kind of went to the mall to find that red dress you not so subtly sent me in a text. I got a raging boner from the picture, and I knew you had to have it. I followed the map of texts you sent and picked up what I thought was nice."

"I can't believe you did this." Shaking my head in disbelief, I picked up the red dress I had tried on first today.

"That dress is going to cause a lot of trouble. It probably won't last a day. I'll end up ripping it from your body and fucking you senseless."

"This one is short enough where you don't have to." I winked. "I also didn't like this one because it showed off the scars on my legs."

"No one will be close enough to see them, just me. I have bigger fish to fry if anyone else gets that close."

"I won't ever be with another man."

"You are one special girl. I still have to fight that ex of yours off with a ten-foot pole." Oddly, that visual got a smile out of me. "Give me a little teaser. Try that dress on for me with some new undergarments."

I took the red dress to the other room, switching from my everyday underwear to the lacy bra and thong set. Then, I pulled the red dress over my head. I tugged it down my body, the fabric hugging my curves perfectly. I looked at myself in the mirror, adjusting it to lay just right, the hem covering as many scars as possible. I still felt vulnerable with some of them showing, but I also felt extremely sexy. I shyly walked down the hallway to see Corey sitting in the dimly lit living room, reclining in the chair with his legs spread just a little.

Corey's eyes roamed over my body, his hand brushing over the top of his pants. I was close enough to hear a moan escape him. He repositioned himself in the chair and reached out for my hand. He pulled me closer to him, and I straddled his lap.

"I love this dress. Would you wear it Saturday, please?" he begged.

"It's not too much?"

"Fuck, yes, it's too much. I will be beating every man who

looks at you but damn, girl. I need to see you in this after I win." His fingers dug into my thighs, and I leaned back on his legs, pressing against his pelvis. "And you were right. There's no need to rip this one off if I wanted to fuck that tight pussy of yours."

Shivers ran down my spine, his hands rubbing seductively up and down my thighs. I stared down into his brown eyes; flashbacks of Alex's green eyes unexpectedly flashed before me. Jumping off Corey, I stumbled back a few steps.

"What's wrong?" he asked, worry in his voice.

"Flashbacks. I can't, not like that." Shaking my head. "I usually can, but staring into your eyes brought back memories of him assaulting me today."

"Turn around, babes. Back that ass up onto my dick," he suggested. I had to think about it for a moment. I realized that this idea of Corey's just might work. I slowly walked back over to him, stepping close, then turning to put my back toward him. His hand nudged my legs open, roaming up my inner thigh to tease the tender skin. Biting my bottom lip in anticipation of what his fingers were about to do, only to hear him moan, "A thong baby? Shit."

His fingers brushed the thin strip of fabric aside before gently rubbing against my clit. I threw my head back in pleasure, moaning audibly. His finger slipped into my wet pussy, my hips rocking against the single digit, making him moan, too. The sounds of him undoing his pants came from behind me. Corey nudged me forward as he stood up, our bodies pressed against each other, making me feel even more turned on.

"Fuck, girl. You're getting wetter. Do I do that to you?" he moaned beside my ear. I looked over my shoulder at him, biting my bottom lip. "Shit girl, you can have this cock whenever you want."

Arching my back slightly to press my ass against his pelvis, I heard a low groan. He sat back down and pulled me onto his lap, my legs on the outside of his. Corey's hand slid between our bodies, helping guide his big dick into my slick pussy. I slowly gasped as every inch of his cock slid into my body until he filled me up. I gripped tightly onto the armrests as I rose on my tiptoes until just the tip was left, then slammed myself back down, seating him fully. Repeating the movements, I moaned every time I forcefully sat down on his lap. Corey's fingers dug deep into my hips, helping guide me and set the pace of the thrusts.

"Shit, this is all mine, baby. Are you going to cum like this?"

I simply moaned. His hand slipped around my body, between my legs, and his fingers added a slight pressure to my clit. I flung my head back to rest against his shoulder. "I'm going to cum, Corey."

"Cum, baby. Cum all over this cock," he whispered into my ear, sending me over the edge. I orgasmed, my core squeezing his cock tightly, prolonging the pleasure. Shortly after, my body went limp from pleasure overload. Corey held me tight, working his hips to thrust up into my body, causing me to whimper with more cries of pleasure and dig my nails into the armrest until I heard him growl from reaching his peak. "Fuck, girl. This is still my pussy."

"All yours, handsome," I whispered in reply. I couldn't move. I continued to sit in his lap, feeling tired but in the best way possible. Somehow, Corey scooped me up and carried me into the other room. He undressed the two of us, then carried me into the shower. His arms locked around my waist, holding me tight to his frame as the water from the shower rolled down our bodies. The water rinsed away the smell of sex and helped me forget the day's bad memories by washing them down the drain.

After drying off, we dressed for the night. I sat there, fastening the strap on the heels around my ankles. I stood up, trying to keep my balance on the stiletto heels. I stumbled over to the closet where Corey was getting dressed, standing with his back to me. He wore a black business casual suit, a dark gray button-up shirt underneath, and black dress shoes. He turned around, still buttoning his right cuff, his lips curled up in a smile.

"Hmm, this dress teases as much as that red one," Corey said as he gripped my hips and tugged me close to him. "Either way, you are sexy as fuck, babes."

Corey crashed his lips against mine and pulled me even closer to him. "Come on, beautiful. I can't be late." He gave me a slow, sensual kiss. His fingers entwined with mine as he led me downstairs to his car. I vowed to wait in his dressing room tonight since I didn't want to risk encountering my ex. Tonight wasn't an important fight, as Corey was just filling in.

Chapter Twenty

Over the last week, we had a few run-ins with Alex, but they were sporadic. The coincidence that he was at the same place we were at made us think he was following us or had someone working with him to keep track of us.

Finally, the night for his belt fight arrived. Corey pulled the car around the back of the building. Security from the venue approached the vehicle and opened my door. Corey walked on the other side of me, sandwiching us between two men who would provide my protection when Corey wasn't with me. I felt guilty that I had put Corey in the position of always being ready for combat.

Corey's grip never broke or loosened. Entering his private dressing room, he triple-locked the door and tossed aside the duffel with his gear.

"Here are the rules for tonight. Mikey will accompany you ringside and stay by your side the whole time. You are not to be left alone, ever. I'm third on the card tonight, and we will immediately bounce after I finish my match."

"What if I have to use the bathroom?" I chuckled, his glare making me realize he was not in the mood for jokes. "Sorry, bad habit. I make jokes during stressful situations."

"No worries." He gave me a wink as he began to pull his gear out of his bag and remove the suit he wore. I lounged on the couch and watched the show he put on for me as he changed.

"I hope you win tonight."

"I will with my lucky charm here dressed in red, my favorite color."

A rhythmic knock came at the door, followed by a pause, then a couple more raps. Corey began to undo the gold locks and opened the door for Mikey. I sat there like a child as Corey gave him clear instructions regarding tonight. Mikey offered his arm, led me out to my designated seat, and he plopped into the seat beside me. He whipped out his iPhone and began typing away, the subtle tapping noises agitating me. It wasn't his fault he was bored, stuck here with me when he'd rather be where all the action was. After all, who wants to be stuck babysitting a grown-ass adult?

I noticed the arena filling with fans buzzing with adrenaline and chatter. My eyes gazed at the crowd. I knew Alex had to be here, but I hadn't spotted him yet. Maybe he took the hint and was leaving us alone.

A sense of relief came over me at the thought that maybe he wouldn't show. The first two fights went as planned, and then Corey's match was announced as his entrance theme blasted from the speakers. Corey emerged from backstage, a towel thrown over his head, dressed in his trademark black and white shorts. He bounced down the ramp and into the octagon. I stood up and stepped closer to the cage. My fingers slid through the metal links and hooked on them.

Corey squatted inside the cage, and our hands pressed against each other's through the fencing. "I love you, beautiful."

"I love you, too. Knock'em dead, Corey."

He smiled as best as he could around the plastic in his mouth, then stood to his full height. Corey ripped the towel from his head with a single swoop of his hand and tossed it in a bundle by his feet. A blast of music played, and his opponent came from backstage with the belt around his waist and handed it over to the referee.

The referee walked around the octagon, holding the belt up high for the audience to see, then passed it out of the cage. He called the two fighters to the center of the cage to remind them of the rules before they tapped fists and signaled for the bell to start the match. Biting my lip hard, I tasted copper from drawing blood. I was engrossed in the fight, cheering for Corey to win, and thus far, his opponent had yet to land a hit.

Suddenly, a chill ran down my spine, causing my whole body to shiver. That feeling only came over me when I knew eyes were watching me. I scoped out the crowd again, sweeping my gaze over the crowd, back and forth, until I saw him sitting directly across the arena, eyes locked on me. Reflexively, I stepped back from the cage, my flight response kicking in. I swallowed a big gulp of air, and for once, Mikey wasn't on his damn phone.

"Are you okay?" Mikey rested his hand on my shoulder, and I felt him step closer beside me. I looked at him and shook my head. Mikey followed my glare to Alex, who stared at me intensely with an evil grin on his face. "That him?"

"Yes." The single word was barely audible, my voice catching in my throat. The bell rang at that moment, signaling the first round was over. Corey approached the cage, squatting down in front of me. Without even saying a word, Corey's expression hardened. He knew how to read me well enough to tell when something was wrong. "He's here."

Corey stuck his hand up, pressing it against the cage. I took the hint, pressing mine against his. "I'm almost done. Mikey, take her to the locker room and secure the door. This chump won't last another round," Corey confidently told Mikey as he stood. He looked taller than usual, being in the ring.

Mikey grabbed my hand and led me to Corey's private locker room. Mikey twisted all three locks on the door, latching them tight, and stood near the door on his phone. You never know what teenagers are looking at on these damn phones nowadays.

I paced in front of the couch nervously. I hated being unable to watch Corey win the belt or being there to support him. I was nervous, not knowing what Alex's next move would be. He was here somewhere, his focus on me, not the fight. He was sending a message, making me aware that he wouldn't go away or give up. I heard a rhythmic knocking on the door that I didn't recognize, so I knew it wasn't Corey.

I glared at Mikey, nerves filling my body with curiosity about who was at the door. Mikey began to undo the locks, slowly pulling the door open. I still couldn't see who it was since the door only opened a crack. Mikey stepped aside and pulled the door the rest of the way open, revealing Alex at the door. Why would Mikey open the door for him?

My heart beat faster, my feet began to propel me backward until my legs hit the couch, and I fell back on it. Alex handed Mikey a wad of cash that looked to be all hundreds. Mikey started to count the hundred-dollar bills. Shoving the wad of cash into his pocket, he slipped out the door, leaving me completely alone with Alex. Fuck you, Mikey. Wait until Corey finds out.

"Melanie, Melanie, Melanie. I am tired of playing this little cat-and-mouse game. I'm here to take you home," Alex said, stepping further into the room.

"I'm not going anywhere with you. I'm not yours anymore," I grated out.

Alex gave an evil laugh, saying, "You are being delusional. You've always been mine. Are you going to throw away everything we've had for some fighter? Do you think that he won't hurt you? Do you not see how he attacks his opponents or how he even attacked me in Pennsylvania? Wait, you were there at his house when he got arrested. You know just as well as I do that he is a violent man. He's no different than me."

Anger boiled up in me with every word he said. He stood in front of me, confident he was right, offering his hand to help me stand. I slapped it away and snarled at him, "I'm not going anywhere with you."

"Are you going to put up a fight? If you don't come easily, I'll drag you out of here by this pretty hair, kicking and screaming," Alex said, his fingers grasping my long auburn hair. He lowered himself to a squat and stuck his face into mine. "Oh my, look at that. A hickey. Do you not remember what I promised to do if you were to have sex with someone other than me?"

He stood back up, pushing the dark gray blazer back to expose the silver Smith and Wesson gun resting in the holster on his belt. I stared at the gun, knowing this was when he would kill me. I was so focused on the gun that I jerked when the door exploded inward. Relief overwhelmed me when I saw Corey standing in the doorway, his chest rising and falling with each labored breath. He was seething with anger, and I swear I saw steam coming from his nose like you would see from a bull. He threw the gold belt resting on his shoulder to the ground, his glare landing on Alex.

"You're a dead man. You do not mess with my girl," Corey said through gritted teeth.

"Oh, thank God you are here. Who should I start with, hmm? Should I kill him now, Melanie, or make him watch me torment then kill you?" Alex asked as he turned to look back at me.

"What are you talking about?" Corey asked, stepping into the room.

"Well, Mr. Superhero, it looks like Melanie broke one of my rules. This pussy is mine and only mine." Alex pointed the gun at me, "I just don't know who I should kill first."

"No one is going to get killed today," Corey snarled. "The only thing that is going to happen is you are going to get your ass handed to you again."

I froze where I was, my life flashing before my eyes. I felt for sure that this would clearly be the end. Alex had plotted and planned everything out perfectly. Alex had brought his gun with the intent of harming Corey and me. I knew Corey was trying to hold back from getting physical, trying not to trigger any flashbacks or instill any fear in me. I zoned out what words they were throwing at each other. I looked at Corey, making eye contact with him. I loved him so much, especially the little sparkle in his eyes. I loved Corey's protective side and knew he would do anything for me.

Anger overcame me. Alex was determined to ruin my future.

I was so sick and tired of him thinking he owned me. Alex's sick and twisted need to control me is infuriating. He needed to control everything I did to ensure I wouldn't do any better than him. I don't know why Alex treats me like he does. It was like he wanted to continue to control my life even if I wasn't in it.

With Alex's back to me, I knew he wouldn't see me coming. Using my momentum, I raced forward, wrapped my arms around his waist, and tackled him, sending our bodies flying to the floor. I climbed on top of him, all sense of self-control gone. I remembered the few self-defense lessons I had with Corey and let loose. My arms began to swing. My hands were going numb from connecting with his face repeatedly. I was screaming at the top of my lungs. I released all the anger and built-up fear inside me due to this man.

I felt arms wrap around my waist, pulling me off Alex. I continued to scream. My arms were still swinging but not making contact, so I kicked out as someone picked me up. Tears began to stream down my face as I was carried out of the room. When they set on my feet, I immediately collapsed to my knees, sobbing intensely.

I felt a hand rest on the arch of my back, and someone moved super close to me. My body tensed, not sure who it was.

"You're okay, beautiful. I'm right here. Let's get out of here," Corey's subtle, husky voice whispered soothingly in my ear.

I nodded, wiped my eyes, and slowly got to my feet with his help. His arm wrapped tightly around me, lending me the support I needed to walk. We walked past the changing room, slowing long enough to glance in. Alex was now tied to the chair, bleeding profusely from his head and face.

Had I done that? Looking in shock at my hands, I saw

my knuckles were bloodied and throbbed in pain with each beat of my heart. Ignoring his routine, Corey led me outside while wearing his fighting gear. I knew the medics hadn't checked Corey like usual after his fight. I tucked my dress under me and sat on a cement parking block with my arms wrapped around my legs. My mind was completely blank, the numbness taking over.

I heard the flick of a lighter, and a lit cigarette came into view. I snatched the lit cigarette between shaking fingers and took a long drag, filling my lungs with the nicotine. I had lost complete control, and this cigarette would help take the edge off.

"I snapped, Corey. What the hell happened to me? Did I do all of that damage to Alex?" I stared blankly at the black asphalt below me.

"Nah, Alex and I exchanged a few words, and I got some jabs in. You helped beat him bloody as well. You got in some really good shots, too."

"Am I going to get arrested?" I took another drag of the cigarette. "I don't want to go to jail."

"No jail time for you since it will be self-defense, but the police are coming. You need to bring yourself back to the here and now, though, so you can answer their questions."

"I'm just as bad as him, Corey. What happened to me?"

"You got revenge. You stood up for yourself, and I'm proud of you."

"I got upset with you when you beat him, and now I've done the same thing. I'm a hypocrite."

Corey laughed softly. "You're not a hypocrite. He got what he deserved. How do you feel?"

"Great for beating him up but oddly numb. My hands hurt

so bad."

Corey pulled one hand at a time into his lap, inspecting them closely to get a better idea of how badly I'd damaged them. "We'll get you checked out by our medics after these smokes."

"I may need a second one."

"Girl, you'll probably need a whole pack after that." We both laughed, silence filling the air until we could hear the sirens of the police cars pulling into the parking lot of the venue. Stomping out the rest of my cigarette, Corey gently gripped my hands to help me get to my feet.

The officers escorted us back inside the building, following us to the medic's office. I sat on the table, my head hung low, and the doctor held my hands. He examined my knuckles before he went to retrieve a few things.

"We have a few questions about your relationship with the victim," the first officer said.

"He wasn't the victim. He was the predator," Corey corrected. Corey crossed his arms over his chest, watching sternly as the doctor took care of cleaning my bloody knuckles.

"Start at the beginning, please." The officer flipped open his notepad and clicked his pen to start writing the details.

The doctor bandaged my hands while I explained everything as best as possible. I gave them the history between Alex and me, explaining how he treated me and the restraining order in place. I answered any further questions the officer had for me and then gave him my contact information. As Corey helped me off the medic's table, his arm snaked around my waist and gripped my hip. He pulled me closer into his protective embrace while the officer jotted down a few more particulars for his case files. Behind him, we saw Alex, locked up in handcuffs, being escorted past the door to a waiting patrol car by two officers.

Alex was under arrest and would have charges that would keep him in jail for the night. That meant I should sleep easier. But why did I feel guilty? I had beat the shit out of him, and he ended up being the one in jail. Somehow, it didn't feel right. I should be the one cuffed and stuffed. Knowing Alex, he would find a way out of jail. He always ends up knowing someone powerful and wealthy enough to pull strings for him.

"You two are free to go. I have all the information that I need. Thank you for your patience and sticking around." The officer flicked his notepad shut before he was on his way. He stood outside the room chatting with a fellow officer, possibly exchanging information.

"Let's get you home." Corey's words were the sweetest ones I'd heard tonight.

"I need a shower. I'm covered in blood."

"My locker room is a bit of a mess, and I'm worried it'll cause you too much distress. Can it wait until we get home?"

"I'd rather get cleaned up here than ride in your car like this. I'm sure you want to wash up, too."

Corey groaned his displeasure as he led me to the room where the fight had occurred. The only visible damage was to the coffee table and some rope that hung off the chair. Flashbacks hit me hard, the incident too fresh in my mind. I stood in the doorway, trying to think of what had taken over me and made me lose control. Stepping into the room behind Corey, I stayed within arm's reach of him. I needed his closeness to feel secure again. Never before had I felt so vulnerable and yet guilty at the same time. I couldn't understand why Corey stayed with me after I snapped. What if I had done that to him?

I entered the attached bathroom with him, stripped off the red dress, and stepped under the hot, running water. The water spraying down massaged my scalp before I felt Corey step up behind me. His arms snaked around me, tugging me into his embrace. Even being comfortable locked up tight in Corey's arms, my mind continued to race. I tried to remember what I thought or felt in the heat of the moment. Immense guilt kept hitting me about Alex in the back of a cop car and me being free. Why did I feel bad for him after all the pain and suffering he had caused me and the ones I loved?

The shower was short and was over before I knew it. I wrapped a towel around me and followed Corey to the messy locker room. I cringed that I had to put this dress back on, but I had no other clothes with me. Corey pulled on his suit from before the match and threw the duffel bag over his shoulder. I'm sure the gold belt he had won tonight weighed it down. His opponent probably took one hell of a beating during the second round when he let loose his fury to quickly end the match, knowing I was scared and alone backstage. Corey couldn't have known Mikey had switched sides and that Alex was holding me hostage to my memories and emotions.

My arms hugged his muscular bicep while we walked down the long, dark hallway to the parking lot. We were among the last to leave the venue, Corey's car being the only one parked out back. Popping open a red and white cigarette package, Corey extended it toward me, and I jumped at the chance for another one.

I put the white stick between my lips as Corey lit it. Taking a long drag, we slowly walked the short distance to his car. I stomped out what remained of the cigarette butt before stepping into the muscle car.

My hand rested in Corey's lap, and his hand firmly gripped mine on the drive home. The radio was turned off for a change, filling the car with a comfortable silence. I didn't need long, elaborate conversations with Corey to know he loved me or to be happy. Being together in the silence made us content. I felt that we were destined to be together forever. Contentment settled over us during the ten-minute drive home.

Corey scanned his parking pass to allow the black metal gate to retract into the building, allowing him to pull into the parking lot. He parked the sports car in his assigned spot and led me to our condo. The condo held all his belongings now – things that were here originally, plus boxes from his home in Pennsylvania. I wasn't sure what we would do with this much stuff, but after this past week, the boxes could wait a little bit. Maybe unpacking a few of them tomorrow would take my mind off of the troubles clouding my thoughts.

I went into the bedroom behind Corey. Our thoughts were so in tune that we both wanted the same thing. Leaving him to do his thing, I stood in the closet, pulled the red dress up my body and over my head, and dropped it on the floor. The dress desperately needed to be washed as it was probably hiding droplets of blood that seemed to blend into the fabric. I slid the wedged heels off my feet and stepped over the pooled-up dress. I pulled one of Corey's oversized t-shirts over my head, which made me feel more comfortable than any of my pajamas would have.

I walked back into the bedroom, heading straight for the bed, where I belly-flopped onto it. I needed comfort after tonight. I crawled up the bed and slipped under the thick comforter. I rolled onto my side, watching the closet, seeing

Corey's shadow as he unpacked his bag and changed out of his suit into his pajamas.

If I knew Corey like I thought I did, he would walk out in just basketball shorts as his pajamas. A few minutes later, he proved me right. Corey flicked off the closet's light, and the moon's shining aura illuminated the room. His upper body was exposed, showing off all the multi-colored tattoos covering his arms and neck. The random tattoo around his belly button always drew my eyes. Corey's chest and six-pack abs were defined for days, his shorts resting snuggly on his hips, which showed off the hip dents that dove beneath his waistband toward his pelvis.

Corey leaned onto the bed with a knee and crawled over the end of the bed to lay beside me. "I don't think you'll need the comforter tonight."

I smirked at him. "I needed something wrapped around me while I waited for you."

I scooted closer, his arms inching around me to hold me snugly. I relaxed to fit against his hard body. I felt his lips press against the top of my head. "I love you, baby. I'm going to be right here all night. You're safe."

I gave a short nod as I scooted even closer, my head pressed against his chest so I could hear his heart echoing through his body. It soothed me to listen to his heart's soft, pulsing beat. I closed my eyes and tried to relax enough to get to a point where I could fall asleep. Images haunted my brain with my eyes shut. Corey's grip tightened around me automatically, like he instinctively knew that I had terrible images coming to me. The night brought on restless sleep for both of us, though Corey didn't seem to care that we would have these sleepless nights together.

Chapter Twenty-One

Corey's Point of View-

I woke up before Melanie, so I lay there, gently running my fingers through the length of her hair as I watched her sleep. She needed as much sleep as possible after last night's events, but Melanie was stronger than she knew. I loved her so much and was fortunate to wake up every morning with her pressed against me. She was all mine, and it would continue to be that way. Alex was locked up for good, thanks to all the charges to be pressed against him. There was no way he could talk his way out of a Florida jail. He had no one influential enough down here to pull strings and get him out.

I wanted to marry Melanie sooner rather than later. She deserved to have something to look forward to. She'd moved her whole life down here, leaving her job and any friends behind, to be in Florida for my job. I'm sure being away from the crazy lunatic of an ex was the biggest pro, but she changed her whole life for me. Mrs. Mathison has a nice ring to it, and it certainly puts a smile on my face. She would be mine forever when they announced us as husband and wife.

I don't know what kind of wedding she would like, nor how many people would come. Kevin and his family would be there for us in a heartbeat. We would need them as witnesses to sign our marriage license. My mom would be livid if I tied the knot without consulting her, even if I didn't always agree with my parents. As for Melanie's parents, she hasn't seen or spoken to them since high school because of her ex.

While I was thinking about this, Melanie rolled onto her side and now faces me. I could hear the soft, subtle sound of her snoring. She finally fell into a deep sleep after a couple of hours. I slid out of bed without disturbing her and went into the closet to pull on an outfit for the day. I went into the kitchen, brewing coffee and waiting for my girl to wake up. I stood on the balcony, watching the sun rise, trying to think how I could reach out to people I didn't know and whom Melanie had lost contact with.

Sipping the hot contents in the mug, I tried to think of how to find someone you didn't know anything about. Maybe a private investigator? MARIO! I screamed at myself when I remembered that Mario worked in the field of investigation for thirty-some years before retiring and focusing on MMA to spend his free time. I wonder if he has time to do me this big favor. I bolted inside, grabbed my keys, and sped to the boxing facility. I HAD to get there before he opened up shop and became too busy to talk.

I jerked the gear shift to park and jumped out of the car. I jogged around the car and pushed the side door to the gym open. Silence greeted me.

"Mario!" I called out.

"You got a lot of nerve showing up right now, Corey. After

277

the mess you made last night, you're lucky I'm not kicking you to the curb." His soft, old voice carried across the gym.

"You won't do that, I'm your best fighter," I said cockily with a smile.

"What do you want? You only show up this early if you need something." Mario stepped around the practice ring and leaned against the post.

"I need you to do an investigation for me."

"On your girl?"

"How'd you know?" I asked. He gave me this glance like I was stupid. "Right, last night. She lost contact with her family in high school, and I want her family to be at our wedding."

"I can do that, but you've got work to do for me."

"Trade?"

"Yes. You need to do all the paperwork regarding last night. I also need any information you have about Melanie and her family. Write them a letter and an invitation to the wedding."

"We haven't set a date."

"Don't tell me." He shrugged and walked off.

"You'll do it?"

"Give me two weeks, and I guarantee you'll be in contact with them." I smiled big as I turned on my heels to go back home. "And Corey?"

I stopped in my tracks, my back still to Mario, unsure what he needed from me. I knew he was pissed with me, and he had every right to be. "Yes?"

"We lost Mikey last night."

"I kind of figured that," I thought with a roll of my eye.

"His things were gone this morning with a note saying that he had come into a lot of money and couldn't stand you as a teacher anymore." Mario further explained.

How much more did Alex offer him? It doesn't matter. I paid him to guard Melanie, and Alex paid him to spy on us, so he got double the amount for what? Being an asshole teenager. He used us both for his gain. Let him find his own way. Hopefully, he will use that cash for something beneficial.

"You want me to start recruiting again?"

"No, he was the next best thing after you. You've been my best fighter yet, Corey. Mikey had the flame. We need to get these others up to his standards." Mario said as I could hear him patting at the ring.

I left Mario behind, sure that Melanie would be awake by now. I stopped to pick up some breakfast for her and me. I returned to the condo to find Melanie standing at the railing on the balcony. She had pulled her hair up into one of those messy bun thingies. She wore one of my shirts that barely covered her ass, and she leaned forward against the hideous red banister. Her beauty always caused my heart to skip a beat. Pushing my front door shut behind me, I set the bags of pancake platters on the dining room table.

I stepped into the doorway of the sliding glass door. "Hey, beautiful. I brought breakfast back."

"What was so important that you had to sneak out?"

Her stare was icy, and she was angered. I would be, too, if I were in her position. "I had to clear some things up with Mario about last night. Mario had filled my phone with a shit ton of texts and calls, so I went to see him."

"It couldn't wait? I woke up alone. Oddly, I wasn't scared and didn't have an anxiety attack." She softly spoke, looking out in the distance. A smile crept on my face that she felt safe and secure when she woke up this morning alone was a great sign.

"I'm sorry you woke up alone, beautiful. I didn't want to disturb your sleep. I'm beyond happy to hear you weren't scared or panicked when you woke up. I bet you are hungry, though. I brought breakfast."

Her sigh was heavy with pain and disappointment that I had let her down, but I hoped that when she found out why I had disappeared, she would forget all about this. I outstretched my arm, giving her my killer smile.

Melanie huffed before she gripped my hand and let me lead her to the dining room table. I pulled out her chair before sliding it in when she sat down. She had me biting back an audible moan with her ass right in my face, no underwear in sight.

I walked around the table to sit down and handed her a platter. If I had my way, she would need the energy. I peeled off the plastic lid and began to dive in.

I could barely eat when my dick was throbbing for attention, and my pants were restricting me, making the pain worse. Eating and staring at her, I hungered for something that wasn't on my plate. Pushing myself back from the table, I strutted around the table and over to her.

She looked up at me with a confused expression. I grabbed the back of her chair, twirling her around to face me, my free hand tangling in that long auburn hair. Tugging her head back slightly, I dove in for a rough kiss.

Moans of pleasure vibrated against my lips, and my hand held her head still as I pressed a trail of kisses down her neck. Letting go of her hair, my hands gripped the neckline, ripped the shirt down the middle, and tugged it from her body. Even though it was my shirt, it needed to be gone right now. I found out how wrong I was about the no underwear.

Her naked body was sitting in front of me, a lacy baby blue thong barely hiding her pussy. I went back to leaving a trail of kisses down her tanned skin. My tongue flicked over one of the sensitive buds of her breasts before repeating the action on the other. I held her tits in my hands to marvel at what bounty was mine to enjoy.

I kissed down her body until I got to between her legs, my fingers pushed the tiny string aside, and I slid my tongue along her exposed slit to find her clit. She was already soaking wet, and I planned on making her wetter. I didn't want to stop feasting. My tongue continued to pick up her sweet juices. I slid to my feet, bending over, and used the armrests to hold myself over her.

"I want to fuck you over the table." Giving her another rough kiss, I moaned deep in her mouth. She quickly got up, leaned over, and pressed her stomach against the black marble, giving me a view of her perfect ass. I dropped my pants, grabbed my dick, and nudged her legs open, sliding my cock deep into her pussy in one thrust. I started slow and long, then picked up the pace until I could hear my balls slapping against her clit.

I pulled out and collapsed back into the chair. Grabbing her by the hips, I pulled her to sit in my lap, her back to my chest, my hands holding onto her tits. Taking the hint, she rode my cock, sporadic jerks of her hips, but her pace was fast as she chased her orgasm. My fingers clawed into the skin of her hips.

Her head fell back against my shoulder. My hands held her as tightly as possible while I thrust hard and fast up into her. I felt her pussy start spasming, squeezing my cock. Cries of pleasure escaped her lips, going straight to my dick which was on the verge of exploding. Two more hard solid thrusts up into her even tighter pussy had me shooting my cum into her.

Melanie was mine. All mine. I would claim her as much and as often as she would let me. She was going to be my wife, the love of my life. She's my everything. Melanie continued to sit on my lap until she had enough strength to stand up. She turned around and sat with her legs on the outside of mine, but this time facing me, a position that usually held triggers for her. I stared up into her beautiful blue eyes. I was nothing but smiles.

"I love you, Melanie." I brushed my fingers through her hair, and she smiled down at me.

"I love you, too. Where'd that come from?"

"I can't help if I want to please you. You turn me on so much. I'm just happy you didn't call out any colors." Chuckling a little, my hands rubbed along her thighs.

"Because you surprised me, and I didn't have time to think."

"If that's the case, maybe I should do that more often." Hearing her let loose a soft chuckle, her smile became even brighter than her eyes. "I've got some work to finish this morning. Mario sent over some paperwork I need to fill out regarding last night and some events I need to do now that I have the belt."

"Like what?"

"Media, like radio and TV interviews, charity events, or some such shit. He has given me a list of upcoming events in the next week or two. It's like sending the champ to bring business to our fights or keep us in the loop." She simply nodded her head in understanding. "It won't take me long, and then we can binge-watch TV the rest of the day or do whatever you want."

"Sounds wonderful, but may I take your car and drop off

these applications?"

"You seriously want to get a job so soon? We've got a stack of boxes over there that still need unpacking. And after last night with Alex, I think that you should focus on your mental health."

"Corey, it'll take them weeks to even give me a call for an interview or to start working."

"Okay, okay. If you want to work, you can," I said, smiling at her. "Do you know where everything is?" I had to hold back my chuckles as she had this confused look on her face like she was trying to think about it.

"No. Maybe I should consider school?"

"Whatever you want to do, sweetie. Let's finish breakfast so I can get back to work. You can do whatever you want to do."

She leaned down, giving me a soft kiss before she climbed off me. I tugged up my pants and fastened them while I walked around the table to finish my cold pancake platter.

"Our wedding, any ideas of a date?" I subtly asked, poking at the soggy pancake.

"I was thinking summer. Jack will be out of school and can be the ring bearer."

"What about the weekend before July 4th?"

"Wouldn't it be redundant? That's a busy travel weekend." She sighed. Her fork twirled on the plate. "July 20th?"

"Sounds perfect." I said with a smile. "I know a guy whose wife owns this cute little chapel. Do you want to go see it?"

"I would love that." She smiled brightly.

"Maybe tonight I'll take you to dinner to celebrate. But it'll be unfortunate because I won't be able to fuck you senseless over the table." I winked as she blushed. Our conversations continued as she ranted and raved about the wedding. I stood up and helped clear off the table, stepping in front of Melanie. "I love you. If you need anything, you can interrupt me."

"I most definitely will, but Corey," she paused.

My ears perked up. Melanie had something on her mind she wanted to discuss.

"Could I come with you to these media events? I've never been on a news set or to a radio station."

I chuckled in my head, my lips curling into a smile. "I wouldn't want anyone else there with me. You are always welcome to come with me to anything and everything. Where I go, you go. That is, if you want to."

Her face lit up brighter than Florida sunshine. She did this giddy little dance that had me returning her smile. I kissed her forehead before I excused myself to go to the guest room, where I had set up my computer. I powered it up, hoping to do some damage control from last night's occurrence, and filled out all the paperwork for Mario. It was the least I could do since he had a hard job to do in return for me.

Upon finishing the paperwork, I opened a new Word document and stared at the empty page.

What do I say? How do you start a letter like this? Why is this so hard? What parent would want their daughter married to an MMA fighter covered in tattoos and does piercing for a living?

I began to let my fingers take control and pound at the keyboard. When I had signed my name, I leaned back in my chair to give it a full read-over:

'To whom it may concern:

My name is Corey Mathison. I am sure you have no idea who I am, but I am an MMA fighter in Florida. This letter has nothing to do with me. I am engaged to this amazing, beautiful woman named Melanie Jameson. She told me how she ran away from home in high school because she thought she was in love with a guy named Alex. She dearly misses her family, and I hired a private investigator to find her family. We are engaged to be married soon. We haven't made any official decisions besides having the wedding on July 20th, but I think she needs her family present. Don't most girls dream of having their dad walk them down the aisle? If you have a daughter named Melanie, please call me at 555-820-9911.

Thank you.

Corey Mathison'

I pushed the print button and rolled over to the machine to grab the letter when it finished printing. I folded it up and slid it into an envelope. I rolled back over to the computer, clicked to open a new blank document, and began to list what I knew about Melanie. Her full name, birthdate, hair, and eye color. I listed everything and anything that I thought would benefit Mario in trying to locate her parents. I sent that to the printer to accompany the letter I wanted him to deliver to her parents.

Chapter Twenty-Two

Melanie's Point of View-

I've lived with Corey in Florida for two blissful months. My life has seemed so refreshing now that I feel safe. I have my life back, living without fear, and my anxiety has lessened. Alex was transferred to a jail back in Pennsylvania since they said Florida was out of their jurisdiction. Now he's thousands of miles away and still locked up in a gray cell block, wearing an orange jumpsuit for the rest of his life.

Corey had booked our wedding at a local chapel. He said it was a small venue since we did not have a lot of people to invite. We asked a few of his fellow fighters he was close with and his boss, Mario. Kevin and his family flew down from Pennsylvania, along with Corey's parents and siblings. I didn't have anyone to invite since I wasn't a social butterfly like Corey and hadn't spoken with my family in over ten years.

I stood in the women's bathroom at the chapel, staring at my reflection in the mirror and trying to smooth out the wrinkles in my mermaid dress with my hands. I loved this dress because, after the wedding, Anita could help me convert it into a mini dress so we could all go to the buffet for brunch. I dreaded eating because I had been feeling under the weather lately.

I experienced nausea throughout the day, extra sensitive nipples, overall tiredness, and mood swings. Unbeknownst to Corey, I had picked up some pregnancy tests while he was out for work and brought one of the tests with me today so I could take it in privacy without him knowing my suspicions. The test was lying upside down on the blush pink sink counter, so that I couldn't see the pending result. I had to focus on making myself look perfect for my wedding day.

I brushed my hair up into a ponytail before winding it into a tight bun, smoothing out all the bumps that formed, before wrapping the elastic holder around my hair to hold it in place. I used hair spray on any stray hairs, forcing them to lay flat. I grabbed the short veil I had picked out, slid the hair comb into my bun to hold it, and flipped the netting over my face to see what it would look like.

I flipped the veil back to apply a light layer of makeup to my face. After a light coat of mascara on my lashes, I put the tube aside, took a deep breath, then slowly exhaled. I stared at the white stick I had left lying across the sink, knowing that the result would be there when I flipped it over to see. The anticipation made my nausea worsen. My anxiety flared up, and little by little, the trembling in my fingers grew as they grasped the plastic stick.

Life turned into a slow-motion video as I turned the stick over to read the outcome shown on the little screen.

"Pregnant." I read the result aloud quietly enough so no one outside the bathroom door would hear me. Tears began to roll out the corners of my eyes from happiness and disbelief.

I was finally going to live out my dream of being a mother. I may not be living in a cottage with the white picket fence, but I lived with a man I loved and who worshiped me in every way.

A knock sounded, causing me to panic that the person on the other side would see the test in my hand if they opened the door. I scrambled to hide it somewhere quickly, unsure who it could be. I thought I had more time to get ready. Another knock sounded as I quickly tried to adjust my ensemble to be ready if it was time to start the ceremony.

I stopped at the wooden door, letting out a quick breath to steady myself, before I opened the door to see who was on the other side. There stood Corey in his tux, and fuck did he look good. My panties dropped at the sight of him, and if we had the time, I'd have let him fuck me over the sink.

"Corey? What are you doing? You're not supposed to see me before the ceremony. It's bad luck," I said firmly.

"I have a surprise," he said with a bright smile before stepping aside. I let out a startled gasp. Standing behind Corey was my dad. He may have seemed a bit shorter than I remembered, his hair already receding, and there was more gray than brown, but he still looked like the dad of my memories. Tears started leaking out of my eyes again. I was never more thankful for waterproof makeup in my life than I am right now.

"It's nice to see you again, Melanie. It's been too long," my dad said, pulling me into a hug. I cried into his shoulder as he wrapped me in his embrace. "Your mom and siblings and their families are already in the chapel."

"How? How did you find me? When did you get to Florida? I'm so confused."

"Corey found us. He wrote us this beautiful letter about how he hired a private investigator to find us and express his love for you. We just connected last week. We had a long chat, and he told me everything he knew. I'm so sorry we weren't there to protect you from the monster Alex had become, but you take after me in the stubborn department. Corey seems like a fantastic guy. He flew your mom, sister, her husband, their kids, your brother, his partner, and their kids down yesterday. After all, we couldn't miss our baby girl's wedding day."

I was an aunt? Shock and happiness filled me at the news. I couldn't wait to meet my nieces or nephews.

"You look stunning. But Corey seriously needs to learn how to tie a tie, and I never got to teach you. Over brunch, I'll have to show you how because he needs to know so he can teach my grandson one day." Corey had a shocked expression on his face, then laughed it off.

"Dad, may I speak with Corey alone real quick?" I darted a glance at Corey.

"Absolutely. I'll be out here waiting to give you away." He walked outside as Corey stepped into the bathroom with me confused. I pushed the bathroom door shut and locked it to ensure our privacy.

He turned to lean back against the sink, his hands reaching out to grip mine, and pulled me to stand in front of him. My hands landed on his strong chest. His arms automatically wrapped around my body to hold me there.

"You look gorgeous. You picked the best wedding dress. I can't wait to get you out of this tonight to celebrate."

I playfully smacked his chest and blushed a little. "Corey, we are getting married, but we need to be serious for a moment."

"Right, serious. What's up, beautiful? What is so important that we must have a serious talk before we say our vows? You aren't getting cold feet, are you?"

I stood there shaking my head no. I couldn't look him in the eye, and I could tell he was confused about what was happening.

I took a deep breath, and quickly, the words tumbled out. "I'm pregnant."

I broke free from his grip, taking a couple of steps toward the bathroom stalls and wrapping my arms around myself. I waited for him to respond. I didn't know how he was going to respond. Neither of us had planned on me getting pregnant this soon, nor were we trying. What if he wasn't ready? Was I ready?

I was lost in my thoughts, waiting for him to say or do something. Suddenly, Corey tugged me around to face him, and his lips slammed onto mine.

"I'm going to be a dad?!" Excitement was evident in his voice, a wide smile spreading from ear to ear. I nodded, breaking from his grip to retrieve the stick with the positive test result. He stared at the little white plastic stick in his hand. "I'm so happy, beautiful. I've always wanted to be a dad."

"You aren't going to leave me?"

"Why would I do that? I love you more than life itself, and now we've got a baby on the way. Can we get the wedding started? I can't wait any longer to start the rest of our lives together." A smile was permanently cemented on his lips.

"Absolutely." I smiled back at him. His hand gripped mine as he led me out of the bathroom to where my dad stood waiting for me.

"Hey, Donald. Are you ready to give away your daughter?" Corey asked.

"Yes, I am. Let's get this show on the road." My dad was

smiling. Corey kissed my cheek before walking through the double doors into the chapel. Moments later, The Wedding March began to play. My hand gripped my dad's elbow tighter when the doors opened again.

I peered into the room, tears threatening to fall when my eyes landed on my mom. My sister, with her husband and kids, stood beside her, and my brother was next to his husband and their kids. Kevin and Anita were in the row in front of them, dressed in matching black and white outfits. I looked to the groom's side, overflowing with friends from his MMA league and school. The front row held his mom, dad, and brother with his wife and kids. My attention went ahead of me to where Corey stood at the altar with Jack standing beside him, holding the white pillow that held the rings. Jack had on a tux similar to Corey's, and it was very cute. I sighed as I looked at my dad before we took the first step that led me down the aisle to Corey, my future.

Made in the USA
Middletown, DE
02 November 2024

63272874R00166